Lord of Secrets

ERICA RIDLEY

Chapter 1

London, 1817

*L*emonade. The mission was to fetch the baroness a glass of fresh lemonade.

Miss Eleanora Winfield squared her shoulders and prepared to enter the fashionable milieu before her. She could not help but feel like a plain brown minnow diving into a pool of brightly colored fish.

Despite the bright red of her hair, and despite the beautiful gown the baroness had commissioned of pale pink gauze over a rosier silk underdress, Nora did not stand out. Not here in London. At a Society ball. In the home of an earl. In the midst of the Season.

She clutched Lady Roundtree's empty glass and inched her way through the crowd toward the refreshment table.

It was hard to focus on something so mundane

as lemonade whilst surrounded by a world she had
never dreamed of one day entering.

The music from the orchestra danced in her ears
and vibrated through the soles of her brand new slippers. The constant swirl of aristocratic faces and rich
fabrics dazzled her eyes. The onslaught of expensive
perfumes, the barrage of strange faces, the dizziness
of not knowing the right words to say or the right way
to act...

It was all too new, too foreign, *too much*.

The lords and ladies had been born into this elegant madness. They'd had a lifetime to learn its rules
and taboos and nuances.

Nora had had six days.

It was a temporary post, she reminded herself as
she glimpsed the end of the refreshment line. Eight
weeks at most. She could do this. She had to. Her family was counting on her.

Besides, it wasn't as if she was expected to know
how to waltz. Or even supposed to speak to anyone
besides Lady Roundtree.

Nora moved to join the queue. All she had to do
was keep the baroness happy and entertained until
the splints came off her injured leg. The resulting salary could be enough to support her family for the rest
of the year. With luck, she might save their farm.

She took a few steps forward with the rest of the
queue. This was nothing like back home; she already
boasted far more advantages than when she'd started.
The pale pink silk swishing elegantly about her body
had cost more than Nora had believed possible to
spend on a single gown.

Yet Lady Roundtree had referred to the expense
as a *mere trifle*. A half-dozen "serviceable units" of
just-sufficient-enough quality for the baroness not to

be embarrassed to be seen in public with her distant country cousin.

Fortunately for them both, the camouflage was working. For all the attention she garnered, Nora might as well blend into the wallpaper. Even in a crowd of this size, no one had so much as made eye contact with her.

Why would they? The *beau monde* preferred to associate with one another. Not only did their names fill the pages of *Debrett's Peerage*, the aristocracy had a secret language all its own.

Since entering the ballroom, she had spent most of the past hour watching the debutantes flirt coyly with painted fans at dapper gentleman who responded thrillingly to silent messages Nora could not comprehend.

Everything was different here. Rousing instruments the likes of which she'd never heard, spiced biscuits and French tortes she'd never known existed, the strangely cloying sweetness of ratafia coating her tongue for the first time. And the candles! Aristocrats like the baroness and the earl lit more candles in a single chandelier than Nora's family used in an entire month.

"Miss?"

Nora's cheeks heated. It was her turn. She'd been too busy gawking at all the brilliant jewels and fancy fixtures to notice she had reached the front of the line.

"I'm sorry." With a shaking hand, she reached for the ladle in the crystal lemonade bowl.

With an almost comical expression of horror, a footman relinquished her grasp on the baroness's soiled glass and gestured to a waiting pyramid of clean goblets. "Allow me."

Nora's cheeks flamed even hotter. Of course one

would not be expected to serve one's own beverage in a place as elegant as this. There were servants to do absolutely everything, including ladle scoops of lemonade into fresh goblets.

With trembling hands, she accepted the brimming glass. "Thank you."

She was not at all certain if one was meant to thank the servants, but as Nora was now essentially a fellow servant herself, she would err on the side of politeness.

Her head pounded as she stepped away from the refreshment table to a much safer location near the wainscoting. She needed to calm her pounding heart.

"Freeze," she whispered.

In her mind's eye, the ballroom froze in place. Lemonade paused mid-stream, embroidered flounces arrested mid-swish, a droplet of wax from the chandelier above floated high above the dance floor, suspended in time.

This was how she'd draw the scene tonight to send home.

To give her family a sense of the opulence, she'd make the pyramid of crystal goblets and the tower of little cakes rise taller than the footmen serving them. She would draw the lords and ladies right where they were, but add herself among them as though she were having the time of her life.

She wished such a treat were possible.

It was difficult to convey how the music from the orchestra seeped in through her toes and seemed to fill her completely, but she would sketch as many musicians and instruments in the background as she could fit onto the paper. In fact, she'd caption this one—

"Oh!" Wet liquid splashed onto her brand new

gloves as the overfull goblet of lemonade collided with a passing gentleman's elbow.

Drat her daydreaming. Would her cheeks ever cease heating in embarrassment? Lost in another artistic reverie, she must have leaned away from the wainscoting and right into the path of the most handsome man she'd ever seen.

Bright hazel eyes. Dark brown hair. Starched cravat. Silver waistcoat. Elbow dripping with the finest lemonade in London.

"I'm so sorry," Nora gasped, mortified.

"Nonsense. 'Tis nothing." As casually as if lords like him regularly spent their days dodging goblets of all sorts, the gentleman drew a perfectly creased, blindingly white handkerchief from the breast pocket of his tailored dark gray jacket. Rather than apply the square of linen to his own elbow, he handed the handkerchief to Nora with a charming smile. "For your glove."

Her heart skipped. She accepted the pristine cloth not because her soiled glove was in any way more important than the gentleman's wet elbow, but because she was tempted to hide her face behind it until she disappeared into the floor.

"Thank you." She dabbed at her glove with a light hand, careful not to actually touch the damp parts, lest she stain the gentleman's handkerchief. She handed it back as fast as she could. "Here. For your arm."

He smiled as he pressed the linen square to his elbow. "I rather like it. Perhaps I will start a new fashion, and make it all the crack for gentlemen to gad about with wet spots on one's arm."

Nora couldn't return his smile; she was trying too hard to keep her shaking fingers from splashing even more lemonade over them both.

What was she meant to do? He was the first Society gentleman who had ever spoken to her. Now what was she meant to say? Her head filled instantly with all the wrong things.

You are so handsome I cannot think properly did not seem the most prudent tack. Nor did babbling that he might truly be able to start such a trend, given the shocking number of young ladies of his class who dampened their bodices in the retiring room to display their assets more clearly.

She hunched her shoulders self-consciously. Was that the sort of woman men like him preferred?

Heaven help her. She'd crashed into him with a glass of lemonade and all she could think about was whether she should have dampened her bodice before doing so.

"I'm sorry," she stammered, wishing the ground would swallow her whole. "It won't happen again."

"I hope it does," he said cheerfully. "One meets new faces much more efficiently this way, rather than mucking through all the proper channels to wrangle formal introductions. It can be our secret handshake. The next time you wish to speak with me, just dribble a few drops on the other side, and you'll have my undivided attention."

Proper channels.

Formal introduction.

Oh no. She sucked in a breath. He thought she was of his class! "My lord, I am afraid I'm not—"

A sudden swell of music swept through the ballroom.

"Oh, dear." The gentleman glanced over his shoulder and waved at someone through the crowd assembling on the dance floor. "I cannot dally. Indeed, my attentions are promised for the next few sets. I hope your card isn't full by the time we're properly presented."

Her what? She stared at him blankly.

"Alas, there's no more time. I cannot leave my partner waiting." He sent her one last apologetic look as he edged away. "I'll find you as soon as I can beg a true introduction. With luck, you'll still have a spot free."

With that, he disappeared into the throngs flocking toward the orchestra to dance the next musical set.

Nora gazed after him speechlessly.

Her card.

A spot free.

Lady Roundtree had done such a splendid job outfitting Nora like one of her peers that the handsome gentleman had mistaken her for someone who might possess a dance card. With names on it. Perhaps even room for his.

A sudden rush of yearning washed over her. If only it were true. If only it were *possible*. She would have loved nothing more than to dance in a place like this. To dance with someone like... him.

But girls like her didn't have fairy stories.

She was not a secret princess who would win the heart of a prince before the clock struck midnight. Her living conditions had already improved dramatically just by becoming Lady Roundtree's temporary paid companion.

A servant girl, she reminded herself. Who should definitely not be off dousing aristocrats in lemonade or engaging in flirtatious banter about dance cards.

In fact, Nora had better hurry back to Lady

Roundtree's side before the baroness was forced to sack her for taking so long to fetch a simple glass of lemonade.

As out of her element as Nora felt, she could not afford to lose this opportunity. The future of her family farm depended on her bringing home the whole salary, which would only happen if she remained gainfully employed.

The refreshment queue had dispersed now that the next dancing set was underway, so she exchanged the sticky goblet for a fresh one and made her way back to the rear of the ballroom where duennas and matrons filled two rows of Queen Anne chairs.

Nora took her place in the back and handed the lemonade up to Lady Roundtree, who was seated in the front row amongst her friends.

"Oh!" the baroness gasped as she accepted the glass. "I was ever so parched. These salons are positively stifling when one cannot promenade near the open doors. These splints are a dreadful bore, Winfield. I wouldn't wish a broken leg on my worst enemy."

Nora nodded quickly.

The day she'd arrived, the surgeon had been present to check on Lady Roundtree, and Nora had overheard the prognosis.

Due to the size of the swelling, one of the bones almost certainly had a crack, but fortunately nothing had snapped in two. Had there been fractured ends to contend with, Lady Roundtree would be prostrate in her bedchamber with her limb elevated inside a fracture box for the foreseeable future.

The surgeon had advised her to stay off her leg as much as possible. The baroness was to keep the splints firmly in place until the swelling was completely gone and the surgeon pronounced her good as new.

"From this distance, I can scarcely discern what's happening," Lady Roundtree groused to a few of the friends seated near her. "Dorothea, can you see who Wainwright is dancing with? Remind me to tell Carlisle he should move the seats closer to the dance floor."

"If he does, someone might trip over your broken leg," came the stern-faced matron's swift rebuke. That was Lady Pettibone. Nora had heard quite an earful about her.

She leaned back in her chair to stay out of the line of sight. Listening was adventure enough.

Lady Roundtree's favorite pastime was gossiping about her peers. Lady Pettibone was infamous for putting people in their place. Cowering debutantes referred to her as the "old dragon" in hushed whispers, but never to her face.

Nora didn't call her anything but Lady Pettibone. She was the reason Nora had this post.

The truth was, she'd been surprised either of the ladies had remembered she existed. They had not seen each other in years. Lady Roundtree was not only a baroness, but the niece of a duke. Nora had no aristocratic blood at all.

Her mother had been Lady Roundtree's first cousin on the other, non-duke side of the family. Nora's lips curved into a wistful smile. Mama had even had a Season once, thirty years earlier, before unfashionably marrying for love and leaving London forever.

Nora had not had a Season. Now she was too old for one.

Instead, she lived with her brother and paternal grandparents on a very uncomplicated farm in the very pretty countryside where no one referred to anyone else as "old dragon" or "common bit of baggage" or worried about impressing matriarchal patronesses for the privilege of purchasing a voucher that would allow admittance into Almack's hallowed dance floors.

Sometimes there were country dances in the assembly rooms of nearby towns. Nora had even danced. Once in a while, there were picnics in the meadow. Or bathing in the river. Or a lazy afternoon sketching fancy gowns she would never be able to afford. She was content with her lot.

Back home, she knew exactly what to expect and what to do. Here, she couldn't help but feel trapped inside a perfect, floating bubble that could pop at any moment.

If she made the wrong move, said the wrong thing... And it would be so easy to do, wouldn't it? The subtle conventions of the *haut ton* were as baffling to her as ablative Latin declensions. Books were her brother's domain. Nora had never even had a governess.

Not that it would have done much good. Carter had tried his hardest to help, but still the letters rarely stayed put on the page for Nora to manage reading them.

Until meeting the baroness, books had been Nora's greatest fear. The entire paid companion position would disappear in a puff of smoke the moment Lady Roundtree demanded Nora read aloud to her, and discovered she could not.

Fortunately, the baroness's primary literary interests lay in the scandal columns of her daily newspapers and lady's magazines, which she read to herself first thing every morning before breaking her fast.

Now, however, Nora worried she'd been glimpsed making calf's eyes at a handsome lord.

Reaching above one's station was just as unpardonable a sin as being unable to read. Had Lady Roundtree glimpsed Nora's interaction with the elegant gentleman, the baroness would have been just as likely to sack Nora for daring to converse with him as for dumping lemonade on his suit jacket. Her fingers trembled.

Distant cousins or not, Lady Roundtree would have no truck whatsoever with a companion who did not know her place.

Nora lifted her chin. She didn't expect a baroness to be friends with her. Nora just needed to keep her post for the next six to eight weeks. She didn't mind at all if her cousin never thought of her as anything more than the help.

If the baroness even thought of her at all.

To Lady Roundtree, Nora was no more noticeable than the molding around the ceiling. Which meant she was privy to all sorts of scandalous information about personages she'd never meet firsthand.

Some duke had compromised some debutante in a closet. Someone else had been spotted attending a salacious masquerade. Someone else had run off to the Scottish Highlands. Each tale was more riveting than the last. During their afternoon carriage rides in Hyde Park, Lady Roundtree gossiped about every single soul they passed with gleeful attention to detail.

As a break from her habit of designing richly drawn fashion plates, Nora had begun to sketch little cartoons of all the overheard stories for fun. She sent the best ones home to her brother with little, pains-takingly drawn captions. The last one she'd dubbed *The Lord of Pleasure*, after an earl who apparently made matrons and debutantes alike swoon with pal-pitations at the mere glimpse of his golden curls. She grinned at the fanciful notion.

Sketching, whether in her head or on paper, was not only the best way to keep sane as she traversed the upside-down world of the *beau monde*, but also a way to document the humor she spotted in each situation. The foibles, the hypocrisy, the boundless riches, the decadent feasts, the thousand-and-one ways that High Society differed from life back home.

She reminded herself to direct her focus to her patroness.

"Bryony Grenville?" the baroness was saying to the lady on her left. "I vow, were that chit less skilled with a violin, she would not receive invitations to soi-rées like this one."

Nora straightened with interest. The Grenville siblings were a frequent subject of gossip among the baroness and her friends, but they had not put on one of their famous musicales in the week since Nora had arrived in London, so she had yet to put faces to the names.

She leaned forward to whisper to Lady Round-tree. "Which one is Bryony?"

The matron on the baroness's other side sent Nora a look sour enough to curdle milk. "I daresay *you* are in no position to speak ill of your betters."

Nora's face heated with embarrassment. She faced forward again without meeting anyone else's eyes. Curse her tongue. She hadn't spoken ill of Bry-ony Grenville or anyone else. She'd simply asked who the others were gossiping about.

And yet the point held true.

The Grenville siblings and everyone else who had received an invitation to the ball were indeed Nora's betters. She knew it as well as they did. Farm girls like Nora did not belong among them as anything other than a servant.

Nor was she complaining.

It wasn't even difficult work. She'd been granted every comfort and more: delicious meals, new gowns, an entire stack of sketchbooks. In return, all she had to do was keep Lady Roundtree happy... and keep herself quiet. Being as bland as the woodwork was literally the job.

A companion was like a bell pull—silent and unnoticed, except when given a sharp tug.

Help the baroness in and out of her wheeled chair? Yes. Fetch lemonades and pour tea and ring for extra laudanum? Yes. Indulge in gossip or anything even peripherally related to scandalous topics?

Absolutely not.

"I'm sorry," she whispered to Lady Roundtree when the other pinch-faced matron wasn't looking.

"Oh!" the baroness gasped with a glance over her shoulder. "And quite well you should be, Winfield! Humiliating me like that. You are not paid to gossip."

Nora nodded tightly. She would do better. This post was too important.

"But since you asked..." Unable to help herself, the baroness pointed her fan toward the doors leading to the garden. "That's Bryony Grenville walking past the terrace with her brother. She's the chit with the bone-straight hair. Her mother never could get it to hold a curl. Mr. Grenville is the gentleman with the unsightly stain on his elbow."

No.

It couldn't be.

Nora followed the line of the baroness's painted fan straight to the handsome gentleman she'd been speaking with earlier.

It was.

A week's worth of overheard gossip came flooding back as Nora picked through her memory for scraps of information about the handsome lord.

He played the pianoforte at his family's musicales. He was well-acquainted with—and well-liked by—all his peers. He had not yet taken a wife. His first name was Heath. Not that someone like Nora would be first-naming anyone in the *ton*.

Especially not a man like him.

Mr. Grenville was known as a problem-solver. The sort of gentleman fabulously wealthy folks summoned when there was a scandal that needed hiding. He was also heir to a baronetcy. When he inherited the title, he would become Lord Grenville rather than a plain mister. He was *important*.

Definitely not the sort of gentleman one's companion should be baptizing in lemonade.

"Over there are the Blackpool brothers and the Duke of Wellington," the baroness continued, directing the tip of her fan toward various personages in the crowd. "You recognize the earl who just walked in, don't you? That's Lord Wainwright. Or, as some choose to call him, the Lord of Pleasure."

Nora blinked at the uncanny coincidence.

Well, bother. It seemed the caption she'd sent home to her brother wasn't nearly as original as she'd thought. Thank heavens she'd sent that sketch away. She'd hate for anyone to stumble across one of her silly drawings and think she was attempting to spread gossip. Especially since it could cost her post.

"The lord of what, again?" she asked, in case she had heard incorrectly.

"Pleasure," the baroness repeated and tittered behind her fan. "Don't ask me to show you the caricature everyone is talking about. It's not fit for common eyes. My friends must have sent me at least ten copies before noon. So droll, with Wainwright looking positively baffled as swooning henwits drop like flies at the very sight of him."

No.

No, no, no, no, no.

This could not be happening. Goosebumps raced across her flesh, a cold sweat chasing in their wake.

"Lord of Pleasure" *was* Nora's drawing.

A popular earl had a horrid new nickname thanks to a few strokes of her pen.

Chapter 2

*F*or the first time all Season, Heath Grenville found himself intrigued.

As the premier scandal-fixer of the upper classes, little occurred in London without his awareness. As heir to a title, a graduate of both Eton and Oxford, and a gentleman who regularly put his dancing slippers to good use, Heath was long-acquainted with everyone even peripherally related to the *beau monde*.

Today, he had been surprised by a stranger.

The beautiful young lady he'd bumped into near the refreshment table possessed a face no gentleman alive could forget. And yet Heath could not place her. Nor could he understand how it had taken all evening to notice her.

With her soft pink gown and lustrous red curls, she more than stood out from the sea of pastel hopefuls. Wide blue eyes, blushing cheeks, lips a perfect, dusty rose...

"Who are you looking for?" his sister asked.

Heath started and forced his attention back to Bryony.

"Nothing," he said quickly. "No one. Do you want some lemonade?"

"I don't even want this ratafia." Bryony sent her cup a baleful glance. "I wish ladies were the ones who retired for port. Have you picked a bride yet?"

"Not yet." An image of glossy red curls filled his mind.

Heath had not introduced himself because he had been embarrassed he did not already know the young lady's name. The *ton* was so insular that new blood was always a ready source of gossip among its members.

A new crop of debutantes? The patronesses of Almack's would have already decided the girls' fate before they took their first curtsey. Relatives on holiday or old friends from out of town? The happy occasion would have been boasted about for weeks before the visit even transpired.

His heart thudded. He had not overlooked a *wallflower,* had he?

In alarm, he swept his horrified gaze about the perimeter of the dance floor.

As elder brother to three sisters, Heath took wallflowers' enjoyment of public functions very seriously. He had witnessed long ago the mortification that came from staring longingly across a crowded ballroom for six excruciating hours, only to leave with one's empty dance card hanging limply from one's wrist.

After he had dried his sister Camellia's tears, Heath had made it his sworn duty to ensure even the shyest of wallflowers at least bore his name on their dance cards. Not out of pity, but because he assumed every young lady was secretly a force to be reckoned with.

"Have you seen Cam anywhere?" he asked Bryony.

She shook her head. "I think she faked a megrim so she could stay home and practice."

Probably. Their talented sister Camellia might be quiet in a party environment, but she had the biggest singing voice in all of England.

In fact, all the wallflowers Heath had befriended over the years possessed unique personalities well worth getting to know. If the dandies and young bucks couldn't be bothered, more fool them. Heath would not make that mistake.

Except he had, had he not? He'd let the red-tressed goddess go without ascertaining her name or securing a spot on her card. And in doing so, he seemed to have lost the intriguing young lady entirely.

"Why aren't you dancing?" he asked his sister.

"I'm bored with the company," she answered honestly. "There is only so much one can say about the weather and how lovely the cucumber sandwiches are tonight. I keep hoping to stumble across someone interesting."

Heath had done precisely that—and then allowed her to slip away. He clenched his jaw.

His set had been promised, and he would never disrespect a waiting woman by failing to promptly present himself for a waltz. But now that he was free...

He scanned the ballroom. After two hours of nonstop dancing, he had few sets left in which to get to know the young lady. If he could determine where she was. Or who she was. He could kick himself for his oversight.

How was he meant to secure a proper introduction when he didn't even know who to ask?

"Have you seen a woman with red hair and a pink dress?" he asked his sister.

Bryony's eyes laughed at him. "A *beautiful* woman with red hair and a pink dress, I presume?"

He gave her a flat look.

She took pity on him. "A debutante?"

"I don't know," he said honestly. "I don't think so. She seemed older than you are. Perhaps Dahlia's age. Or Camellia's."

"A beautiful *spinster* with red hair and a pink dress?" Bryony asked slyly. "The horror!"

Heath regretted having broached the topic with his sister.

Pretty women didn't just materialize out of thin air. She must be *someone's* daughter or sister or friend. She also had to be connected to someone Heath knew well. Otherwise, how would she have secured an invitation to Lord Carlisle's ball?

Carlisle! Of course. Heath's shoulders relaxed. The earl would know the names of all of his guests. Carlisle and his countess famously wrote every invitation together. Brilliant. The mystery would be solved in no time.

He glanced about the ballroom in search of his hosts. Ah. There they were, swirling in each other's arms in the middle of the dance floor. His lips curved into a smile. He was glad to see them dancing. They deserved the happiness they'd found in each other. Tonight's fête to celebrate their home's recent renovation to its former splendor was merely the cream on the puff pastry.

"I haven't seen your mystery lady," Bryony said, "but I adore watching the Carlisles. Don't they make a beautiful couple?"

They made a *happy* couple, which in Heath's estimation was far better than beauty. They were obviously in love. What more could a man desire?

Not that he would dare voice such romantical thoughts aloud. Especially not in front of his family. Mother's endless pleas for him to quit wasting time with wallflowers and take a proper bride were insufferable enough already.

As if he didn't know the rules! Whomever Heath chose as his future baroness must come from the best family, with the impeccable decorum and breeding, and be completely above reproach in every way. Et cetera. Et cetera.

Of course he would comply with such societal dictates, not just for his title's sake, but for his own. Just as soon as he found the right woman.

Mother might fear her son's tastes too liberal, but the truth was, Heath's wife-hunting standards were even more exacting and rigid.

They had to be. As a gentleman who had dedicated his life to ameliorating other people's disasters, Heath could not risk wedding the wrong woman himself. The idea made him shudder.

"Mother has been preaching at me again," Bryony said. "Be honest. Is my hair's inability to hold a curl the reason I haven't found true love?"

"Maybe," he replied. "Or it could be emblematic of your complete lack of attention to every other concession to fashion. I'm always surprised when a lady's maid gets you to sit still for more than five minutes."

"Why does my fashion have to match anyone else's?" Bryony pointed out reasonably. "All these other girls look just like each other, and it hasn't helped them ensnare *your* heart."

True enough. After more than a decade of such functions, Heath had yet to find the woman he wished to have at his side for the rest of his life.

It wasn't that he sought physical perfection. Or even to increase the baronetcy's social ties by marrying the daughter of an earl or a duke.

Heath cared less about external traits like titles, and more about the caliber of the woman inside. Only someone completely aboveboard—whose heart and ethics he could trust implicitly—would do. Someone who would never embarrass his family with a scandal. All other conditions were secondary.

And in the meantime, he was perfectly happy to dance with wallflowers. Who knew? Perhaps the shyest debutante in the room would be the one to steal his heart.

At the other side of the large chamber, a flash of pink and red caught his eye. He straightened.

There. His mystery woman. Reentering the salon from one of the side passages.

"Found her," he murmured to his sister.

"What are you waiting for?" She jabbed him with her elbow. "*Go.*"

He glanced over his shoulder. The current waltz was still underway. There was no time to arrange a formal introduction. What if the young lady had been summoning her carriage? His jaw tightened. He had to catch her now before she disappeared completely.

Heath sliced through the crowd in pursuit.

"We meet again," he said as soon as he reached her side.

She opened her mouth to speak, then closed it just as suddenly. Her head tilted in bewilderment. Wide blue eyes studied him as if memorizing every aspect of his person. "Did you just run through the crowd?"

"Yes. No." Dear God, what if he looked a fright?
Heath cleared his throat. "Perhaps I strolled a touch
hurriedly."

"I see." Her deep blue eyes stared back at him as
if she did indeed see far more than he had intended.

"Let us start anew. I am Mr. Grenville." Heath
made an extravagant leg. "Would you be so kind as to
let me know your name?"

Rather than curtsey in return, she took a step
back. "You have me confused with someone else, my
lord."

"How can I, when I haven't the slightest inkling
who you are?" he asked reasonably.

At least, he hoped he could still count on reason.
He had never witnessed a debutante fail to curtsey after an introduction. Much less retreat backward, as if
heirs to baronetcies were to be avoided at all costs.

He did not close the gap. His goal had been to
befriend, not frighten her.

"May I know your name?" he asked more gently.

"Eleanora Winfield," she mumbled, the words
almost too soft to hear.

"Miss Winfield." Heath gave an even deeper,
more elegant bow. "It is my delight and honor to make
your acquaintance."

She narrowed her eyes at him suspiciously.

This was not going well at all.

Heath smiled back at her winningly. Perhaps she
was even shyer than any wallflower he'd ever met.
What could he do to put her at ease? He took stock of
what he knew so far.

Her name was Eleanora Winfield. Including
one's first name in an introduction was usually an in-
dication that one was a younger sister. Heath's sister

Camellia was Miss Grenville, the next eldest was Miss
Dahlia Grenville, the youngest Miss Bryony Grenville.
Using first names to differentiate sisters was standard
practice, particularly when all three were present.

Yet he was not at all certain that was why Miss
Winfield had done so. After all, if he had no idea who
she was, how could he possibly confuse her with her
siblings?

And then there was the curtsey. Or lack thereof.

It had been *rude* not to offer at least a perfunc-
tory bend of the knee. Rude as well to completely
ignore his initial request for her name, under the odd
circumstances.

Yet the pretty wallflower was not sneering at him
in disgust or anger, but instead wore a rather adorable
expression of utter confusion. As if she were uncertain
why he would wish to introduce himself to her at all.

There. That was a matter easily resolved. He
would give her a good reason.

"The orchestra has only just begun this set," he
said with his most engaging smile. "If you haven't another name already promised on your card, perhaps
you would do me the honor of taking a turn about the
dance floor with me."

The color drained from her face. "No."

Heath blinked. Perhaps she was very, *very* shy.
Perhaps she believed herself awkward, or possessed
of two left feet. Perhaps he had just gallantly offered
to drag her straight into her greatest nightmare by
forcing her to move rhythmically in front of a crowd.

"No dancing. Are you peckish?" He glanced over
toward the refreshment table to see what was left. "I
would be happy to fetch you some lemonade. Or... a
sponge cake."

She shook her head, blue eyes filling with something akin to panic. "I cannot possibly accept."

"I didn't like them either," he admitted. "Something to do with the squidgy texture. There might still be a lemon square—"

"It's not the sponge cakes." A pink flush crept up her cheeks as her voice dropped to a whisper. "I'm a paid companion."

And now it was Heath's turn not to take an involuntary step back.

A paid companion.

An employee of one of the invited guests.

He hid a grimace. No wonder she hadn't accepted his offer to dance. She might have been sacked for the audacity.

And it would have been his fault for insisting on being too friendly to a stranger.

"My apologies," he said gruffly. "I'm sorry."

"I am not." She peered up at him through her lashes and gave a crooked smile. "I thought my post was the best thing that had ever happened to me. Now I think it was the moment I was mistaken for someone with permission to dance."

Heath returned her smile automatically, but inside his mind whirred. This was a positive development. Perhaps not all was lost. Now that they had met, he and Miss Winfield could at least converse for a short moment, could they not? Even in a ballroom as public as this.

He winced. Well, *technically* a paid staff member of any household was by definition a servant. But just as a lady's maid had far greater status than a chamber maid, and a governess had even greater status than a lady's maid, a companion was even higher than that.

In fact, companions were the very highest of all staff in one's employ. Often the only difference between a companion and her employer was the size of her purse, not the quality of her bloodline. If Miss Winfield's parents had possessed slightly more coin, she might have attended this ball as a guest rather than as a member of the staff.

But she was right: that had not transpired. They could not dance.

Nor would he be fetching her any sponge cakes.

He gave an understanding nod. "It was a true pleasure to have made your acquaintance, Miss Winfield. Even without a dance. I shan't make such a request again."

"I know." Her smile wobbled. "It isn't done."

It *wasn't* done. And yet Heath couldn't help but like her honesty. She had only tried to save him from himself.

He stepped out of her way. "Have a good evening, Miss Winfield."

"You, too." She bit her lip as she glanced back at him one last time. "Mr. Grenville?"

"Yes?"

Her eyes twinkled. "I'm glad I spilled lemonade on your jacket."

"I'm glad I dipped my elbow in your glass," he returned with a smile.

As Heath watched her walk away, he wondered which of the many dowagers and spinsters present had employed Miss Winfield as companion. Was she the poor relation of someone he knew? His eyes tracked her as she made her way toward the rear of the salon.

"There's Grenville," came a voice. "Why don't you ask him?"

Blast. Heath turned to see who had interrupted his bout of shameless sleuthing.

A cluster of dandies swarmed around him like a cloud of gnats.

"Is it true you helped the Duke of Lambley, Grenville?" asked one.

"Of course it's true, you ninny," said another before Heath could reply. "Grenville can do anything."

"Should he, though?" asked a third. "Lambley's name is still shockingly scandalous, I say."

"Then just imagine what we'd be saying about those masquerades if Grenville hadn't worked his magic!" said the first.

They all began talking over each other at once.

"There would likely be a caricature about him posted on every window in London."

"So true! Did you see the one about Wainwright?"

"*Lord of Pleasure?* Who hasn't seen that? Poor sap is spiraling on a mission to 'reshape his image.'"

"Saw that nonsense in the betting book. Went against him, of course."

"There's no chance of the Lord of Pleasure avoiding further infamy!" exclaimed another. "Unless he hires Grenville to fix the matter in his favor... That would be poor sportsmanship, wouldn't it?"

"Poor sportsmanship?" said the first dandy. "Cheating, I say! Paying a scandal-fixer to solve one's problems takes the sport right out of it."

The second dandy whirled toward Heath. "Tell the truth, Grenville. Is Wainwright one of your clients?"

A hushed silence fell as the entire gaggle of dandies waited breathlessly for Heath's reply.

"I never disclose my clients' names, or their business," he admonished, his tone final.

But he couldn't fault them for asking.

Since the ubiquitous sketches first appeared all over London, the anonymous artist had become the sole topic across town. The caricaturist was a cretin. In a scant few days, his irresponsible drawings had caused more uproar than Cruikshank and Gillray combined. Unconscionable.

As a member of the very society being mocked, Heath was morally and personally offended. As a professional dedicated to minimizing scandal for the betterment of all, he was both annoyed and outraged. Worse, after witnessing his sister's charity work cost poor Dahlia a fair portion of her status, Heath was frightened by the possibilities.

If the idle stroke of this man's pen was enough to turn a gentleman like the Earl of Wainwright into the most celebrated rake of the *ton*, what damage might he cause to someone more helpless to defend herself?

Chapter 3

*N*ora had just carried her pencils and sketchbook of fashionable dresses to her adopted corner in one of the baroness's numerous receiving parlors when a footman arrived bearing the morning's correspondence on a silver platter.

"Lady Roundtree is still abed," Nora informed him with a smile.

He ought to know as much, even if he never ventured upstairs. The baroness rarely roused before noon, especially now that she'd taken to adding a few more drops of laudanum to her nightly cup of warm milk.

Nora, on the other hand, had suffered a restless night. Between heart-pounding recollections of the moment when handsome Mr. Grenville had believed her worthy of an invitation to dance, and nightmares of how and why private sketches she'd sent to her family had become gossip fodder for the entire *ton*, sleep had proven elusive.

Perhaps the resulting exhaustion explained why a long moment passed before she realized the footman still stood in the open doorway, silver tray outstretched with stoic patience.

"For *me?*" Heart racing, Nora leapt to her feet and flew across the room.

In the center of the silver tray rested a single folded letter.

The parchment was thin and of obvious poor quality. Its contents had been secured not with a large seal and expensive wax, but with a small teardrop from a cheap, tallow candle. Worn indentations in telltale patterns indicated the paper had been previously employed for some other task, and later repurposed in the form of this letter.

A note from her family. Nora clutched it to her chest in relief.

"Thank you," she whispered to the footman.

He bowed in acknowledgement before disappearing with the now empty tray.

Nora spun in a circle before sudden fear gripped her heart. What if this was not happy tidings from the farm? What if something had happened to Grandmother or Grandfather, and she was too far away to help?

She pulled a footstool as close to the fire as she dared and broke the droplet of wax with trembling hands.

The writing was definitely her brother's hand. His penmanship was the only one she could easily read. Not because his handiwork was more refined than their grandparents', but because Carter made it purposefully less so.

Big, printed letters instead of tightly flowing

script. Large spaces between each word. Nora swallowed. Grandfather would have an apoplexy to see Carter "waste" precious paper so, but whatever was in the message, Carter had wished to ensure Nora capable of reading it.

She tamped down her fears and focused on the first line.

To my brilliant and talented sister,

As she was alone in the receiving parlor, Nora did not bother to hide an amused roll of her eyes. Carter had always begun correspondence to her in this manner. According to her brother, it was to remind Nora of her own worth.

Perhaps that was true. But the familiar greeting also served another—arguably more important—purpose.

It centered her on the task of reading. Reminded her which way the "b" and "d" pointed. And it allowed her to begin each letter with at least one line of easy comprehension—of success—before the arduous, humiliating work of making it through the rest of the words, letter by dancing letter.

Nora straightened her shoulders. She hated feeling so stupid. So helpless. So frustrated with her inability to simply scan the contents to find out if Carter had written with news of her grandparents' health, or perhaps some insight into how the sketches she had mailed to their farm might have ended up in a London printing press a hundred miles from their home in the West Midlands.

She would have to decipher this line by line. Word by word.

You must be the queen of the ball by now.

Wasn't that just like an adoring younger brother? Nora lowered her eyes with a sad smile. She was glad he did not suspect the truth.

She was queen of fetching items from other rooms, of helping the baroness in and out of chairs, of enduring long stretches of being no more noticeable than a speck of dust on the carpet by sketching better versions of her life in the sanctity of her own mind.

Recasting reality so that *she* was the one who received fancy invitations. So that *she* was the popular debutante laughing with her friends. So that *she* was the lady whirling gaily amid a crowded dance floor.

Instead, despite finding herself in the most populous city in England, attending the biggest crushes of the Season, Nora was far lonelier than she had ever been back home on their simple sheep farm. There, she had been an important part of everyday life.

Grandmother's fingers are doing much better.

Nora doubted this. In her six-and-twenty years, she had seen more than enough elderly farmers progress from spry and capable to bent husks of the people they had once been.

Already it took a full hour each morning for Grandmother to uncurl her warped hands. The once slender fingers were now disfigured by painful, swollen knots at each joint. Her reward for long years of dipping candles, chopping vegetables, scrubbing pots, washing linens, churning butter. The list of chores was endless.

As soon as Nora was big enough to wield a

broom, she had helped out as best she could. Her grandparents were her entire world.

When she and Carter had been orphaned, they had taken both children in without hesitation. Never mind that there was never enough money. There was always more than enough love.

Grandfather shouts louder every day, although he denies it.

Her heart gave a homesick pang. Both of her grandparents' hearing had steadily declined over the last several years. Grandmother tried to mask the issue by speaking softer and softer in an attempt to blend with those around her, whereas Grandfather simply increased his volume as if it were not he, but rather everyone else, who had gone deaf.

If only that were the extent of their problems. Just a matter of raising one's voice.

Nora's shoulders slumped. They needed so much more. Grandfather's eyesight and poor hip were even worse than Grandmother's arthritis, rendering him little able to tend the crops anymore. Nora had taken over Grandmother's duties, and Carter had taken over all of Grandfather's, but mere labor wasn't enough.

The farm needed money to stay afloat.

The sheep miss you. So do I.

Nora's vision blurred. She missed him so much. Her brother had been her confidant, her rock, her tutor, her playmate, her best friend for her whole life. In as long as she could remember, they had never once been separated for more than a day.

Until now.

She took a deep breath. Here she was, in a receiving parlor the size of their cottage, perched on a footstool that cost more than their farm earned in a year, accepting the morning post from a literal silver platter that was polished and burnished every single day by a coterie of maids dedicated solely to the task of ensuring every silver surface in the house reflected as brilliantly as a looking-glass.

Carter, on the other hand, was back home doing the work of four people. He was going to make himself sick. But what else could they do?

Guilt twisted Nora's stomach. Keeping up with the farm had been exhausting enough when divided between the two of them. She had no idea how long he could possibly manage alone. It wasn't fair.

Although I do enjoy eating your breakfast portion every morning.

She let out a choking laugh. Of course he would; Carter's stomach was a bottomless hole.

His heart was just as boundless.

He was the real reason Nora was in London. When the summons came from some spoiled, distant cousin, Nora's first impulse had been to disregard it entirely. The farm needed her. So did her brother. Her grandparents. Their encroaching forgetfulness alone required near-constant oversight.

Besides, Nora barely knew this cousin. More importantly, the baroness didn't recall much about her country bumpkin cousin at all, or why on earth would she have invited a farm maid to London?

But it wasn't a social visit. It was employment. Six to eight weeks, just until the splints came off and the baroness regained range of motion.

> *Please do not brag to me of your break-*
> *fasts with the baroness.*

Nora snorted. She had yet to take a meal with Lady Roundtree.

Her shoulders tightened. She hadn't wished to come to London. But Lady Roundtree was prepared to pay handsomely to have Nora attend her. Her years as caretaker to her grandparents and her blood relation to the baroness made Nora the perfect choice.

If only she wasn't needed more at home.

She stared at the wiggling words on the page.

Carter had been the one to point out that this was their chance. With the money she earned, they could purchase more sheep and use *them* for income, rather than rely on backbreaking fieldwork. There would be more free time to spend with the family. The four of them could finally have lives beyond slaving to maintain the farm.

All she had to do was spend a couple easy months as nursemaid to a baroness. How hard could it be?

> *Confession: We have had the strangest*
> *bout of good fortune.*

Nora frowned. Good fortune was inherently... well, *good*. So why did Carter's confession sound so ominous? She worked out the next line.

> *I wished to prove to you how skilled an art-*
> *ist you are,*

She sighed. Carter was always trying to make her

feel better about her difficulties with book learning by
pointing out that pencils could be used for more than
just sums and penmanship. No one in town could
draw half as well as Nora, even when she barely paid
attention. It was a skill most people didn't have, he
claimed.

Sure. That might even be true. But what did it
matter? Nora couldn't sketch a successful harvest into
their larder or collect milk and wool with judicious use
of ink. Art was an idle pastime, not a source of income.
Her hands were better employed elsewhere.

*so I sent away a few samples via a confi-
dential intermediary.*

Nora groaned. The sketches she'd sent home
hadn't gone *astray*. They'd been purposefully di-
verted. By her well-meaning, feather-brained,
supportive-to-a-fault little brother.

*They sent back a pound note for each one
and a request for more drawings.*

Nora blinked and started that line over. Surely
she had misread. She tried again.

*They sent back a five-pound note for each
one*

A five-pound note. FIVE.
For *each one*.
Her breath caught. That meant a single sketch
was worth the same as fifty loaves of bread. That
meant her family now *had* fifty loaves of bread, or the
wisest equivalent purchase. Her brother would have

immediately replenished their larder. Or acquired more sheep.

Her heart pounded.

On an annuity of five hundred per year, a frugal family of four could afford not only themselves, but a servant or two. Could Nora potentially earn the same sum with a hundred satirical sketches? Might their days of poverty soon be behind them?

This was life-changing.

This was madness.

This could not be.

and a request for more drawings.
None of your fashion sketches will do, but
of course I sent what few caricatures I
could find.

Nora's fingers shook with sudden terror as the full ramifications gripped her.

The sketches were raw, unfiltered glimpses into *ton* life. They were quick, rude, irreverent. They poked holes in High Society's glossy veneer solely for the private amusement of the Winfield family. And Carter had *sold* them?

Panic tightened her chest. She had not signed the sketches, but that did not mean she was safe from discovery. Or being sacked from her current position. This reckless act could jeopardize her companion salary as well as any hope for more drawings.

What had Carter done?

No more ball gowns and fancy portraits.
Draw as many caricatures as you can. The
wittier, the better.

They'll pay TRIPLE for famous people.

Triple.

No. Absolutely not.

She'd already seen what could happen when ten thousand people with nothing better to do got their hands on the same silly sketch. Overnight, the Earl of Wainwright had become the "Lord of Pleasure," and not just in the tongue-in-cheek commentary Nora made at home, but to the entire *haut ton*.

Not just the upper classes, she realized at once. Caricatures were just as popular with the have-nots as the haves. Perhaps more so. Not only were such sketches a window into a life peasants could never experience for themselves, the accompanying biting commentary offered *power*. A way to mock one's betters, to laugh right back at the vaulted paragons who had long belittled their "lessers."

Nora bit her lip. She could see the allure: the commercial value her art might have to a printing house, the impact the money earned could have on her family.

She could also see the danger. Carter claimed the confidential intermediary protected their identities, but for how long? Every published drawing risked the very employment opportunity that made the sketches possible. Every new caricature would be another nail in her coffin if anyone should ever learn the true identity of the artist behind the drawings.

If she were found out, she would lose everything. Her post with the baroness. Any hope of earning desperately needed money.

And yet, it was a way to help her family right now.

The *fastest* way to help her family.

She leaned back in her chair. The first salary as companion would not be paid until after the first month.

In the meantime, her already overworked brother was stretched beyond all reason until she could return home to do her part. With even more money, he and both grandparents could hire a maid-of-all-work to take over Nora's duties inside the cottage. With enough earnings, they could all sleep at night without fear of the morrow.

With enough sketches, they could free themselves from poverty.

From your brother with love,
Carter

She lowered the letter to her lap and stared at the crackling fire.

Was it worth the risk? The sole reason she was in London was because Nora and her brother hoped the money she earned as a paid companion would change their fate. To be able to survive without fretting over every ha'penny.

Her grandparents had built their country home with their own sweat and blood. They loved their farm and never wished to leave it. Not that there was anywhere else to go. Their land was all they had.

With enough money to purchase a crucial quantity of sheep, the farm could finally become self-sufficient. Milk, cheese, wool. A maid for the cottage, a young farmhand or two for the sheep. Carter could finally have a life outside of the farm.

Nora could finally have a life.

And her grandparents would never have to lift an arthritic finger again. They could spend the rest of their lives in much-deserved peace. They could be *happy*.

She rubbed her face with her hands.

To caricature or not to caricature, that was the question. One potential outcome was anonymity and financial security. The other potential outcome was total ruination and a return to abject poverty. But was it already too late to walk away?

The price of refusal held nebulous returns.

In the best-case scenario, Nora would somehow remain gainfully employed, never once be asked to read aloud to her mistress or commit any other failures that would prove her unworthy of a role as companion, and she would return home ten weeks from now with eighty pounds in her pocket. A respectable amount that would at least cover the purchase of more sheep.

In the worst-case scenario, Nora's shortcomings as a proper companion would be quickly discovered, her post summarily withdrawn, and herself returned to her family just as destitute as she began.

Neither path held any guarantees. There was no way to see into the future.

Her stomach churned.

Was this how Society gentlemen felt when they wagered the deeds to their unentailed properties on the turn of a card?

She'd sketched *ton* life as a lark. Not to poke fun at anyone or anything specific, but because it was easier than trying to write a letter. She could dash off a far more eloquent sketch in half the time it would take her to scratch out a single, painstaking, illegible, misspelled sentence.

And she loved to draw. She always had. It had never hurt anything. Even this time.

Once she had gotten over her initial horror at *Lord of Pleasure* replacing the Earl of Wainwright's actual name, the baroness's gossipy friends had quickly pointed out that the infamy only added to his rakish allure, rather than harm his reputation in any way.

It made sense, Nora supposed. She hadn't been mocking him, but the vapid ninnies who swooned at his very name.

So what if Nora drew vignettes of real people? Did not more celebrated caricaturists do the very same thing? Indeed, was that not the *job?*

There was no consequential difference between Nora's anonymous sketches and the infamous drawings of men like Gillray and Cruikshank.

Except for the part about her hopes, dreams, reputation, and future being dashed to bits if her secret ever got out.

She turned over her brother's letter to hide the dancing, damning words from view.

A tiny drawing greeted her on the other side.

Three circles with sticks for bodies joined stick-hands on the left. A speech balloon emanating from all three smiling mouths read, *We love you!*

Nora straightened her spine. She couldn't afford to turn down any opportunity to provide for her family.

If a pair of drawings could garner more money than she could earn in a week, was there really any choice but to say yes and draw as many as she could while she was still here?

She'd already been feeling guilty about not being present to do her share of the chores. This was how she could help. Working as both companion and secret caricaturist would essentially be holding two jobs instead of one, and could earn her far more in the same amount of time.

More importantly, she owed it to her grandparents. Not only had they taken her in when there was nowhere else to go, they were Nora's only family. *Carter's* only family.

She couldn't bear the thought of a loved one suffering all over again. Nora was determined to do everything in her power to keep her family safe and fed for as long as possible.

Even if it meant assuming a hidden identity as the most infamous caricaturist in London.

Chapter 4

*S*hrieking from the ground floor wafted all the way upstairs to the guest room.

Nora laid her pencil atop the escritoire and rubbed her temples. It was not Lady Roundtree's shrill tone that was causing her megrim, but rather the challenge of responding properly to her brother's letter.

The dozen lines he had written had cost her half an hour to read. She'd spent twice as long attempting to pen a coherent reply. Her stomach was sick with frustration.

If only writing letters was as easy as drawing sketches! In a matter of minutes, she would have been able to explain the need for heightened secrecy, that he should never again mention the business arrangement in his letters to her, and that he should never, ever breathe her name to the intermediary, lest the printing house learn her identity.

Above all, she needed to ensure Carter would not accidentally make things worse. Nora ground her teeth at the few lines she'd managed to eke out. If words were as easy as sketches, she could have already conveyed her inspired plan to—

"Miss?" A timorous maid hovered at the open doorway. "Milady requests your immediate presence downstairs. There's a... situation."

Nora leapt to her feet. Of course she would go at once; she was here at the baroness's whim. It would be a great irony for her to be sacked for dereliction of duty because she was in her guest chamber, failing to write a stupid letter.

Her fingers trembled against the balustrade of the spiral balcony. What if the "situation" below was that the baroness wished for her new companion to read the morning newspaper aloud? Or the latest gothic novel for her book club?

Nora pushed through the fear and forced her feet to march down the stairs. Dillydallying after a summons would be just as bad a crime as borderline illiteracy. Promptness, on the other hand, was a trait she was delighted to display.

Besides, there might be nothing worrisome afoot. Perhaps Lady Roundtree had decided she no longer trusted maids or footmen, and it would now be Nora's sole and solemn duty to starch handkerchiefs and fetch fresh pots of steaming chocolate. Or to place pearl-studded pins in the baroness's hair.

Heaven help them both.

The intricacies of High Society hair styles were just as foreign to Nora as the contents of *Debrett's Peerage*. Lady Roundtree's private lady's maid was nothing short of a wizard with hair pins and curling tongs. The addition of splints and a wheeled chair did nothing to reduce the baroness's elegance.

As Nora reached the foot of the staircase, a single

sharp bark rent the air. What on—

"Good!" came Lady Roundtree's voice. "That's Winfield now. She'll handle him."

Nora spun to see a cluster of maids and footmen fanning in a half-circle about the baroness's wheeled chair.

"Handle who?" she asked.

A flash of golden brown fur shot from behind the baroness's wheeled chair and disappeared under the hem of a maid's skirt.

The maid unsuccessfully stifled a shriek. "Help! It's—"

The bundle of fur darted out from under her skirt and latched itself to the foreleg of the closest footman, upon which it delivered several frantic thrusts of its fawn-colored hips.

"—it's on my leg," the footman completed the sentence, his face a mask of pained stoicism.

Nora edged closer. "It's a dog?"

Of course it was a dog. A pug, to be exact. The adorable curled tail with its little black stripe, the golden-brown coat, the floppy folded ears, the distinctively wrinkled face with patches of black about the muzzle and eyes. From the diminutive size, the puppy could be no more than a few months old.

The only question was what it was doing inside Lady Roundtree's house. Besides humping the servants' legs. Had it snuck in somehow? Or was—

"This," Lady Roundtree informed her proudly, "is Captain Pugboat."

Nora blinked. "Captain... Pugboat?"

"My new puppy," the baroness added, in case the situation was unclear. "You will henceforth be responsible for his actions and appearance."

"I am henceforth responsible for... Captain Pug-boat," Nora repeated faintly.

"Precisely." The baroness waved a white-gloved hand. "Begin by removing him from John Footman's leg. He smells of wet dog and must be bathed and dried at once."

"She means Captain Pugboat," the closest maid whispered to Nora. "Although by now, all of us smell like wet dog and ought to be bathed."

The tiny pug snorted in delight as he continued to thrust against the footman's foreleg.

Nora hurried forward and plucked the bucking puppy from the man's ankle. Captain Pugboat immediately burrowed against her bodice and gave her bare arms a happy lick. He indeed smelled of puppy and morning rain. Nora could not have fallen more deeply and instantly in love if she'd tried.

The rest of the servants immediately fled before Captain Pugboat could greet them anew.

He was too busy trying to lick the side of Nora's face.

She laughed and turned toward the baroness. "He's adorable."

"That is why I acquired a pet," Lady Roundtree said with a nervous flutter of her hands. "My husband does not share a favorable opinion. He believes the only useful animals to be horses and hunting dogs. You are to ensure Captain Pugboat does not bother him."

Nora nodded.

Avoiding Lord Roundtree would be her easiest task to date. Nora had glimpsed the baron only once in the week since she'd been installed in their house-hold, and doubted his wife saw him much more than that.

To Nora, the idea of practically remaining strangers with one's husband even after years of marriage was baffling. She recognized that the upper classes often wed for reasons far removed from love, but the idea that they wouldn't try to make the best of things once they'd tied the knot had not occurred to her until she'd seen the phenomenon firsthand.

According to Lady Roundtree, her situation was far from unusual. In fact, many aristocratic men kept mistresses whose company they preferred over their own wives. Not that the wives were much different: once they'd produced the requisite heirs, a few even found their own lovers, although careful to be discreet about it.

There was no way Nora could ever withstand a *ton* marriage.

Not that anyone was asking.

A delicious shiver whispered down her spine at the memory of Mr. Grenville enquiring whether there was space on her dance card. She had not been able to quit the moment—or the man—from her mind since. All she could think about was what might have happened if she'd been at the ball as a guest. As an *equal*.

Perhaps he *would* have begged a proper introduction and stood up with her for a dance. Perhaps a cotillion... or perhaps a waltz. A full quarter hour with nothing to do but be whirled about in his arms amongst all the other dancers.

Not that Nora would have eyes for anyone but Mr. Grenville. He had charmed her so effortlessly with mere words. What would the touch of his hand do? His arm, wrapped about her waist? Her breath quickened. A waltz with him would leave her head in the clouds for the rest of her life.

If she were someone other than Nora Winfield,

that was.

She cuddled the new puppy to her chest and turned to the baroness. "Where did Captain Pugboat come from?"

"I ordered him." Lady Roundtree beamed with satisfaction. "Dogs are fine companions. Addington has one, Underhill has one, even that dreadful Epworth has one. Pugs are the present rage, you know."

Nora did not know. But she was glad to have a puppy in the house. She had been in London scarcely more than a week, and each hour had seemed even lonelier than the last. The baroness might regard Nora as an employee like any other, but a dog would be delighted to have her around. Already the day seemed brighter.

"Who gave him his name?" she asked.

"I did," the baroness answered with pride. "Leviston thought I should call him Spot or Goldie. Such uninspired twaddle. I prefer Captain Pugboat to stand out from the crowd."

Perhaps it was Lady Roundtree who stood out from the crowd. Nora smiled. Anyone who would name a pet Captain Pugboat with a straight face had a clear sense of whimsy. Perhaps the baroness wasn't as difficult to please as Nora had feared, but rather a lonely woman in search of companionship, wherever she might find it.

Nora curtsied to her patroness. "I think you chose splendidly. I shall be honored to care for him while I am here."

"I should hope so," the baroness said with a sniff. "You're paid to do whatever I desire."

Nora bit back a sigh. More proof she would forever be seen as an employee, not a cousin. Or even as a thinking, feeling person who loved animals and silly puns and filling her sketchbook with fashionable gowns. Here in London, she would never be worth anything as herself.

She was just as anonymous as her caricatures.

Chapter 5

$\mathcal{U}$ nder normal circumstances, Heath would have enjoyed a balmy afternoon at the Vauxhall pleasure gardens. The Turkish Tent and the House of Mirrors were both charming, and the Rotunda was a particular favorite.

Today, however, he had not paid for admission merely to join the well-heeled throngs taking in the fresh air along the Spring Gardens. He was not even primarily here to act as escort to his mother and sisters. Not only did the women of his family not require a male gaze hovering about, the task was itself impossible. The moment their half-booted feet stepped free of the family coach, all four women immediately dispersed in opposite directions, leaving Heath standing alone amid the sculpted gardens.

Momentarily alone, that was.

This afternoon's purported goal was to take his duty to select a bride more seriously. While this direction was new for Heath, the idea of becoming someone's bride was the obvious intent behind the sea of bright-eyed debutantes throwing themselves into his path, as if sheer proximity would be enough to secure his heart.

Heath's heart, however, had precious little to do with the matter. He had no wish to be swept away by passion. His reputation, his status, his livelihood, his very future depended upon careful selection of the *right* woman.

Wealth did not signify. Looks did not signify. The one thing that mattered was strict adherence to unwaveringly proper comportment at all times.

What the determined debutantes with their rouged lips and artfully dropped handkerchiefs didn't realize was that the very act of brazen flirtation took them quite out of the running. He was the gentleman who quashed gossip and vanquished scandals. He would never align himself with someone likely to become fodder.

Which mayhap explained why Heath was still unwed. Thus far, he had been perfectly content to enjoy his bachelorhood until he met someone who could change his mind. The only woman to interest him had turned out to be a paid companion. But he had sworn never to settle, much less disgrace his family with scandal.

Unbidden, the memory of the pretty, red-haired young lady from the other day sprang to his mind. Miss Eleanora Winfield. She of the flying lemonade and beautiful smile.

Last night, lying alone in his bed, Heath's thoughts had not been filled with images of pale, insipid debutantes, but rather of sparkling blue eyes and shining red curls. The strict societal rules prohibiting him from asking her to dance had unfortunately done nothing to rid him of the desire. If anything, the thought crept into his mind more and more.

No matter how hard he tried to focus on propriety and duty, the strains of the orchestra would whisper from his memory and suddenly Heath would be right back at the refreshment table.

In the make-believe version of events, he would not have been in such a godawful hurry to sweep someone else onto the dance floor that he nearly mowed down the rosy vision in pink and red. In this version, his time would not be promised anywhere at all. He could spend the next half hour—nay, the rest of the night!—getting to know Miss Winfield. Perhaps coax her into his arms for a moonlit waltz...

"Looking for someone special?" came an unsubtle female whisper at his shoulder.

Heath cleared his throat to hide his preoccupation and offered his elbow to his mother. "There you are! I wondered where you'd got off to. Shall we take a turn about the gardens before the sun sets?"

"Not *me*." She folded her arms rather than accept his proffered elbow, and narrowed her eyes. "You promised. Not half an hour ago, you said the very words. 'Yes, Mother, this year I'll take a bride.' All three of your sisters heard you."

Heath bit back a sigh. As soon as the words had tumbled from his mouth, he'd known they were a mistake. But today's carriage ride to the gardens had been claustrophobic with his mother's unremitting despair about her recalcitrant daughters' embarrassingly unwed states, all of whom cast beseeching eyes at Heath, imploring him to distract their mother before one of the younger two took matters into her own hands. The next thing Heath knew—

"I did indeed promise," he agreed firmly, as he

placed his mother's gloved hand in the crook of his elbow. "What I did not imply was that the selection
would take place this very day in the middle of a pleasure garden. Surely a son can spare a brief moment
from intense bride-hunting to promenade a yard or
two with his own mother."

"You've already spared two-and-thirty years,"
Mother rebuked him without hesitation. "If you would
choose from the hundred or so suitable ladies present,
we could finally have done."

Heath clenched his jaw. "I've no wish to 'have
done' by wedding the first young woman I stumble
into."

Although, the other night, stumbling into a
woman had been the highlight of the evening. His far-
too-brief conversations with Miss Winfield had been
well worth the price of a lemonade-soaked elbow. She
hadn't thrown herself at him, flirting outrageously in
the hopes of landing a future title. Miss Winfield had
been open, honest, sweet. A refreshing change of
pace.

"You've no wish to wed *any* eligible young lady."
Mother pursed her lips in pique. "You're as wretched
as your sisters. How did this happen? Camellia is too
quiet, Bryony too loud, Dahlia too headstrong, and
you are too choosy. Go ahead and take your pick of
any of the girls who have been presented to Court.
What difference is there between any of them?"

"Have you considered that perhaps I might *wish*
to be able to distinguish my wife from all the other
women?" he asked dryly. "A novel thought, to be
sure."

"Enough to make me tear my hair out," Mother
agreed with vehemence. "It's absurd. You won't take a
wife because these debutantes are all the same, yet no

gentleman will wed any of your sisters because they're far too different. What am I to do with you?"

"Take a curtsey?" Heath suggested. "You've raised four children who know who they are, and what they want of life. Is that not the sign of a successful parent?"

"A successful mother is one who manages to marry off her brood," she answered with a sniff. "I shall have to console myself with holding you to your word. This Season is the Season you take a bride. You said so this very morning."

"Those are indeed the words I said." Heath regretted them more with every passing moment.

Mother wrinkled her nose. "It cannot take long. If witless seventeen-year-olds can manage to make a match during the course of a single Season, certainly the heir to a baronetcy can do no worse."

Heath slanted her a sharp look. "You are not expecting me to wed a witless seventeen-year-old, are you?"

"As long as she has good bones and is from good blood, what should I care?" Mother's sharp eyes gazed out across the forest of pastel gowns and fluttering fans. "Are you certain today isn't the day?"

"The day for what?" asked a soft voice from behind his other shoulder.

Camellia, the eldest of Heath's three younger sisters. He nearly melted in relief. Of his three siblings, stalwart Camellia was the reliable pillar who could be counted upon never to upset their mother.

"The day your brother selects his future baroness." Mother narrowed her eyes toward the flocks of well-heeled passers-by. "It cannot be difficult. Half these girls would kill for a title."

"Perhaps he would prefer one more interested in

him," Camellia suggested softly.

Mother stared at her in bafflement. "Of course the title is most important. Once any young lady discards all the *unsuitable* suitors from the chaff, she then turns her head to the most eligible of whatever is left."

"First I'm 'chaff,' then I'm 'whatever is left.'" Heath offered his elbow to his sister. "This is quite a motivational speech, Mother."

"Meant to instruct me as much as you, I suspect," Camellia said as she took his arm.

"There is no excuse for you staying on the shelf as if you wish to remain a spinster," Mother chastised her tartly. "Regardless of your own desires, it's rude to your sisters. You know the eldest must be the first to marry. If you do not bring an appropriate gentleman up to scratch in the next few weeks, your father intends to select a husband for you."

Camellia blanched. "Can we please go back to picking apart Heath's life choices?"

"Lovely," he murmured to her beneath his breath. "Selflessly done."

Mother sighed. "Heath knows his duty. When the time comes, he shan't disappoint. Neither will you. It's your sisters I'm most concerned about. Dahlia has all but ruined her reputation with that preposterous boarding school in the middle of a godforsaken rookery, and Bryony... I don't even know where to begin with that child."

"Nobody does," Heath assured her. "Recall that she's last in line. By the time it's her turn to worry about settling down, her wild ways will have softened."

"Now *is* the time to worry. It has been so since the moment each of you had your first Seasons."

Mother's face went alarmingly purple. "Settling down is the entire purpose!"

"I promised to look for a bride," he reminded her in soothing tones. "I meant every word. You're right: a garden as beautiful as this might just be the place to find her. But it will never do to have one's mother squinting sourly in one's direction whilst one attempts to woo a fair maiden. I shall make my rounds in search of perfection, if you promise to try to enjoy the afternoon."

Camellia dropped her hand to link arms with their mother. "Heath's right, you know."

"He's not right," Mother grumbled. "A lady does not squint, sourly or otherwise."

"I meant that we should enjoy the afternoon while the sun still shines. A miracle at this time of year, is it not?" Camellia gave her a gentle tug toward one of the many long, sweeping avenues dividing the formal gardens. "A relaxing stroll can work wonders on one's constitution."

"Very well." Mother frowned. "But I expect a daughter-in-law by the Season's end."

"Look, isn't that Lady Jersey?" Camellia made a covert shooing motion at Heath as she herded their mother toward a wall of Society dames. "I'll wager she'll be delighted to see you."

"A lady never wagers," Mother said sharply, but already her attention was focused on Lady Jersey rather than rebuking her children.

"Thank you," Heath mouthed to his grinning sister, and turned his boots toward the piazzas before his Mother could change her mind.

Perhaps this *would* be the day he met his future bride. Why not? The afternoon was unseasonably balmy, the sun uncommonly bright, the bustling crowd lively and cheerful. What better omen could a wife-hunting gentleman desire?

Unfortunately, Heath did not feel like a wife-hunting gentleman. He felt like an utter fool whose mind had never left the Carlisles' ballroom.

From the very first, he had felt a strange sort of connection with Miss Winfield. Yet he had not hesitated to part company the moment she'd made her circumstances clear.

Heath had regretted that haste every moment since.

Perhaps he should not have been so quick to excuse himself from her company. Just because she was not a potential bride did not mean a gentleman must retreat from an innocent conversation. The moment Miss Winfield had walked away, Heath wished she had not.

What if there *had* been a connection between them? He wasn't thinking of an attachment, of course, but the dozens of wallflowers and other women he'd befriended over the Seasons. He could have spared Miss Winfield another moment or two, at least. Given himself a chance to discover what that spark might have meant. What if they never chanced to meet again?

"How do you do, Mr. Grenville?" came a quiet baritone from the edge of the throngs.

Startled, Heath blinked and broke into a grin. "Parson! How splendid to see you in Town. And you, Mrs. Blaylock. Is that a new bonnet? I must confess you've never looked finer."

"Oh, you." She fanned her cheeks. "You make all the old women feel like it's their first Season."

"Old women?" Heath shook his finger. "I have yet to lay eyes on one. I daresay you danced more sets than I at the Carlisle ball, young lady."

Mrs. Blaylock laughed and shooed him with her painted fan. "Off with you, Mr. Grenville. Go find a proper young lady to flatter. Heaven knows you set all their hearts a-flutter."

"Second only to the Lord of Pleasure," put in a nasally voice with haughty accents from just behind Heath. "If the penny caricatures are to be believed."

With a barely restrained sigh, Heath turned to face Phineas Mapleton, the *ton*'s most dedicated gossip. "The earl's name is Lord Wainwright, not whatever moniker some petty cartoonist decides to label him. I do hope you don't give credence to such rubbish?"

"I may be a stallion among pups, but even I have seen Wainwright's curious effect on women," Mapleton said with a careless flit to his wrist. "I've no need to wait for a Sunday sketch to see debutantes swoon into each other like drunken bowling pins."

With a mumbled excuse, Mrs. Blaylock and the parson slipped back into the crowd.

Heath wished he could do the same. Unfortunately, his reputation depended upon avoiding scandal at all cost. Rumor of a public disagreement with Phineas Mapleton would sweep through the crowd in a trice. Particularly with Mapleton himself helping the gossip along.

"Come now," Heath said, keeping his voice pleasant. "Surely we've better topics of conversation than idle talk. Did you see how they've improved the Rotunda?"

"Actually..." Mapleton lowered his voice with great portent as he cast the least subtle glance over each of his shoulders that Heath had ever witnessed. "I do wish to speak to you about a matter pertaining to gossip. You are the keeper of all of London's secrets, are you not?"

Heath took a half-step backward. "A gross exaggeration, I'm afraid."

"Not at all!" Mapleton leaned in. "You helped Kingsley and Turner, and of course there was the dust-up with Quinton and Whitfield, and then absolutely everyone saw you bow heads together with Wellington one week and Underhill the next. You cannot deny your involvement. Everybody knows who to call upon if a scandal needs to disappear."

Heath narrowed his eyes. "If I *were* to have represented the private interests of any of the individuals you mentioned, it would only have happened under complete confidentiality. I cannot say more."

"Precisely what they want. And what they're willing to pay handsomely for, am I right?" Mapleton's eyes glittered. "What if we could earn double that amount? Triple. Quadruple."

Heath's hackles rose. "There is no 'we' in this topic. Nor is it any of our business how others save or spend their pennies."

"But it *could* be," Mapleton insisted. "And I'm not talking about pennies. There is no limit to what we could earn. All you have to do is suggest that the payments rendered were the first in an... installment plan, if you will. To maintain your silence. If they balk, that's where I come in. While you're off in a visible, public place, I'll—"

"Are you suggesting we embark on *extortion* schemes?" Heath asked in horror. He'd known Mapleton was a shameless gossip, but he hadn't anticipated this level of darkness in his soul. Nor could Heath imagine why on earth the daft man would believe anyone in their right mind would agree to such a heinous plot.

"Not extortion," Mapleton said hurriedly. "Scheduled installment payments. Think about it: you already charge a fee for your services. Your clients pay eagerly and happily. I'm simply proposing the possibility of turning that revenue into a river, rather than an isolated drop."

"You are literally proposing blackmail, Mapleton. *Blackmail.*" Heath seethed at the thought. "My clients' money isn't for me to guard my tongue, but to solve a problem. Not to cause them new ones. The answer is no." Disgust curled his lip. "And if I discover you've continued in this vein for even a moment—"

Mapleton lifted his palms and affected a wounded expression. "At ease, Grenville. I was speaking in jest, of course. Testing your loyalty. After all, I might require your services one day. I wouldn't wish to place my trust in the wrong person."

Heath tightened his jaw. He had no doubt that Mapleton would someday embroil himself in a scandal so deep, he'd have no hope of crawling back out. Heath would not be offering his services. He doubted very much that Mapleton's alleged "test" had been complete fiction. The man was obsessed with gossip, and openly convinced of his superiority over his peers. Yet this was far from someone's first attempt to devise some twisted game to test Heath's integrity.

He always passed, of course. Heath's word was more than his bond—it was his very identity. Honesty and confidentiality weren't incidental occupational skills required by his job. Integrity was something he required of himself, as a gentleman. As a person. He expected no less from his family and friends.

Which was why men like Phineas Mapleton did not count among that number.

"In case it was unclear, I am both professionally

and morally opposed to any uninvited third party exploiting someone else's private pain for their personal profit," Heath said, his voice cold. "Money cannot tempt me. Now you know. And if you'll excuse me, I was on my way to the supper tables."

"Of course, of course. Everyone knows you've made your name by keeping secrets, not spreading them." Mapleton fell back. "I didn't doubt you for a moment. Just having a bit of fun, that's all. Do enjoy your supper."

With that, Mapleton swept an exaggerated bow.

Heath refrained from responding in kind. He simply inclined his head and stalked away from Mapleton before the gossip could come up with any more so-called jests.

He swept his gaze along the long rectangular canal leading from the gardens to the supper tables. Sunlight sparkled in the water, dancing with the reflected blue of the sky and the bright colors of the piazzas. Heath's jauntiness returned. He would not allow his distasteful encounter with Phineas Mapleton to destroy his good mood.

After all, his future bride was waiting to be discovered.

The Italian-styled piazzas overflowed with familiar, smiling faces. Heath traded quips with friends, bowed to matrons and dowagers, and managed to exchange the usual light banter with young ladies he'd danced or conversed with at this ball or that.

Thanks to his mother, however, he could not completely tamp the sudden misgiving that perhaps the most blatant of the flirtatious bunch were more interested in becoming a baroness than being his wife.

Heath's muscles tightened. Now that he, too, was considering each lash-fluttering debutante with an eye for marriage, he could not deny what he had long suspected to be true. These were not the debs he was looking for. His search would not be easy, if indeed a perfect match existed.

From across the crowded piazza, a flash of color caught his eye. The jewel-red ringlets shimmering in the sunlight belonged to none other than Miss Winfield, the delightful young lady he definitely should not still have on his mind.

He stared in helpless fascination as she tucked an errant tendril behind her ear and nodded at someone he could not yet determine.

Heath couldn't help but feel Miss Winfield was rather like a painting.

She wasn't portrait-perfect in a *ton* kind of way, with regal dress and colorless blonde tendrils, as befitted a classic English rose. She was far more interesting. The salmon pink of her gown brought out the bright red of her hair, and vice versa. She wasn't understated. She was stunning.

Nor did Heath believe the color choice was an accident.

Miss Winfield had been wearing pink the last time he saw her. It was her look. Her signature. Although she made every other attempt to blend into the background, the eye-catching pink-and-red combination meant she wasn't afraid to stand out, to try something new, to do things differently.

He watched with interest as a footman rolled a wheeled chair to the bench near Miss Winfield. Of course. Lady Roundtree's broken leg. Miss Winfield had said she was a companion. The baroness must then be her patroness. He wondered how that was going.

Many people claimed they could withstand little

more than afternoon tea in Lady Roundtree's company. Not only was the baroness often excitable and dramatic, she was niece to Lady Pettibone, a formidable society matron referred to as the "old dragon" exclusively in hushed whispers.

Lady Pettibone was the Duke of Courteland's highest-ranking relative, and ruled a great swath of the *ton* with her sharp tongue and iron will. For that reason, many peers feared that idle words spoken around Lady Roundtree could reach Lady Pettibone's ear and ruin their standing forever.

Heath and his siblings had no such concerns. As the elder of the four, his and Camellia's comportment were famously impeccable. The youngest, Bryony, was an unrepentant free spirit who didn't give a button what anyone said about her behind her back, or even in front of her face.

Their middle sister, Dahlia, had once been as faultless as her elder siblings. Now that she'd begun a charity school in a poor neighborhood and actively sought donations from those with deep pockets, the poverty of the orphans she was attempting to save had begun to taint her own reputation.

Like Bryony before her, Dahlia had simply decided not to care. She did not seek to keep her standing, but to raise the fortunes of others.

Heath found her priorities commendable. Their mother despaired of Dahlia's ever finding a match.

Marriage. That was what he was supposed to be thinking about. Conversing with potential brides, not keeping beneath the shade of a sycamore tree in order to watch an intriguing companion coddle an excitable, chair-bound baroness as if she were the next Queen of England.

Yet he could not look away. Rather than treat

Lady Roundtree's sometimes-difficult personality as a bore, or as a job to suffer through with a healthy amount of eye-rolling, Miss Winfield's manner was unflinchingly warm, her expression relentlessly kind.

He tilted his head as she lifted a wicker basket to her lap. Curious. Guests of Lady Roundtree's class were far more likely to purchase their repast here than pack their own picnic. Whatever the reason, Lady Roundtree appeared pleased with the arrangement— a miracle unto itself. Heath smiled. Miss Winfield must be an exemplary companion.

He pointed his feet in her direction.

When he was within a half-dozen yards of her, the lid to the wicker basket popped open and a flurry of fur shot out with the speed of a cannon, aiming straight for Heath.

He froze in surprise, then grinned at the idea that either Miss Winfield or Lady Roundtree—or both—could not conscience an outing in Vauxhall Gardens without allowing their puppy to enjoy the fine weather as well.

Before he could kneel in preparation for greeting the excitedly yipping pug, Miss Winfield fairly flew across the lawn. She scooped up the puppy and popped him back inside the swinging basket before Heath had a chance to so much as rub behind the pug's ears.

A charming blush heated the apples of her cheeks. She lay a hand atop the wicker lid to keep its contents corralled inside. "Mr. Grenville! I just... I'm so sorry he got away from me."

"I'm not," Heath replied honestly. "I wondered if we would chance to meet again, and your puppy has answered the question."

"Oh, he is not mine, much as I love him. He's

Lady Roundtree's dog." Miss Winfield glanced over her shoulder at her patroness.

Heath followed her gaze. He could not imagine Lady Roundtree doting on a pet, but he was pleased to be proven wrong. That was, if one could consider paying an assistant to keep one's pet contained out of sight in a basket "doting."

"Do you come to Vauxhall often?" he asked Miss Winfield, and grimaced.

'Twas precisely the sort of opening gambit rakes poked fun at other gentlemen for using. But if the lady had tired of hearing endless variations of the same question, she gave no sign.

"It's actually my first time," she admitted, eyes bright and sparkling. "I had seen a few prints in Lady Roundtree's collection, but nothing compares to the actual experience."

Heath could not help an odd pleasure at simply being present to witness her first time among the gardens. Her obvious delight was infectious.

He stepped closer. "What do you like best?"

"I cannot decide," she said with a happy laugh. "The grounds are enormous. Everywhere I turn, there's more. The trees, the flowers, the architecture... An artist could paint a thousand color prints and not capture it all."

"Do you like art?" He hoped his voice did not betray his eagerness.

Although he had no talent for producing anything worth viewing, art had always been Heath's secret passion. Until now, no one had truly shared his enthusiasm.

Many people claimed to like art, when what they meant was they enjoyed boasting about having glimpsed a famous sculpture, or that they never

missed an opportunity to purchase a penny caricature. He was suddenly very interested in learning Miss
Winfield's thoughts on the matter.

"I…" Shadows warred in her eyes, as if his innocent question had stirred up memories she would
much rather keep forgotten.

"Forgive me." He wished he had not asked. "I did
not mean to pry."

"Of course you are not prying." Her blush deep-
ened. "I do appreciate beauty. Nature's glory, fanciful
architecture, all these endless rows of perfectly
pruned flowers. Isn't that why we're all here?"

"I wish it were," he said with a wry chuckle. "You
and I may be two of the few who paid our shilling in
order to see the gardens, rather than to gawk at other
people."

Her eyes widened. "Truly?"

"Unfortunately." He raised his brows. "I imagine
the prints you've seen of Vauxhall feature its clientele
more prominently than its gardenias."

Her eyes twinkled. "I daresay you are right. I am
glad I did not rely on prints alone to inform my opinion about the gardens. I would have missed out."

As would Heath. Something wistful curled in his
chest. He often wished someone would come along
and paint London's most picturesque locations without including a flock of onlookers. Then again, who
but dreamers like him would purchase such a thing?
An artist would starve if he failed to include vignettes
of London's elite.

"I am pleased to hear Vauxhall exceeded your expectations," he said with a smile.

Miss Winfield gazed up at him shyly. "Everything in Town has so far. I'm certain pleasure gardens
are only one of the many things I'll miss dreadfully

when I return home."

Heath frowned. "And when is that unhappy day? Do you live so far away as to make a visit to London impossible?"

He realized the impropriety of his questions too late to recall them. If inquiring about her interest in art had been prying, demanding to know her travel schedule and the location of her home was unforgivable.

"The West Midlands," Miss Winfield said without hesitation. "As soon as Lady Roundtree can walk about without my aid, I'll return to my farm." She sighed pensively. "I miss it very much."

Heath stared back at her, nonplussed.

She lived on a farm.

And *missed* it.

He could not have asked for a better reminder of why their lives had never been destined to intersect.

And yet he could not help a small pang of irrational disappointment upon learning that her post was temporary. That she would soon quit London permanently, with no plan to return.

A small yip escaped the wicker basket in Miss Winfield's arms, and her eyes widened.

"Please pardon my haste, Mr. Grenville. I must get back to Lady Roundtree while I've still a post to return to. But it was lovely talking with you." She hesitated. "You seem more..."

Although he leaned forward with interest, he did not learn in what way he was *more* than the others.

Miss Winfield dipped a rushed curtsey and dashed back to her patroness before Heath could so much as bid her goodbye.

When she disappeared from view, he forced himself to stroll in the opposite direction. Toward giggling flocks of proper, eligible debutantes. The young ladies he was meant to be courting.

He rubbed his face in disbelief of his predicament. He was supposed to be hunting for a suitable wife, and thus far the only woman to catch his interest for more than a moment was someone else's paid servant.

Heath squared his shoulders. He would simply have to put Miss Winfield out of his mind for good. It shouldn't be too hard. After all, soon she would be returning to a farm in the West Midlands. By then, he was bound to have found a proper baroness.

Even if she were someone...

Less.

Chapter 6

*T*he musicale.

Heath had almost forgotten.

He placed the elegant parchment summoning him to his mother's salon across from his morning tea and returned his attention to the urgent matter of breaking his fast while his eggs were still hot. Today could require his strength.

Some would opine that the seasonal Grenville musicales afforded the eponymous Grenvilles significantly more social status than their baronetcy. Theirs was a title, yes, and not the lowest possible, but his family could not enter a garden or a ballroom without bumping into half a dozen viscounts or earls or marquises or dukes who outranked a paltry baronetcy.

At the Grenville musicales, all of that changed.

No one outranked shy Camellia's powerful singing voice. No one outclassed Bryony's astonishing skill at the violin.

At least half the audience could trounce Heath's talents at the pianoforte, but the Grenville musicales were not about him. They were his mother's Colosseum. Her daughters were gladiators among pawns, showcasing fearless strength to prove themselves worthy of knighthood.

Rather, *duchesshood*, if Mother had her way.

Heath held no illusions that the current summons, ostensibly to discuss the upcoming musicale, was anything other than a pretense to cover her true objective: marrying off her children. The only mystery was whether today's strategizing summit would center on himself, on one of his sisters, or on all four stubbornly unwed offspring.

He had never been able to resist a mystery.

After dispensing with the rest of his meal, he presented himself in his dressing chambers where his valet awaited him with this morning's freshly starched and pressed neckcloth.

Most gentlemen would not have left their quarters in the first place without a perfectly tied cravat billowing about their necks like a flower in bloom. Although Heath did not usually flaunt Society's customs, he deeply appreciated the one hour each day when he needn't worry about keeping up appearances.

After all, years of dedicated personal research had taught him there was nothing more inviting to marmalade stains than crisp, white folds of starched linen.

As his valet worked his magic, Heath's gaze tracked across the framed paintings he'd chosen for his private chambers. Contentment filled him at the familiar, pleasing sight.

He loved his town house. It didn't contain a single musical instrument, and was all but wallpapered with canvases featuring his favorite works of art. Each evoked a strong emotion, transporting him into the artist's imagination.

It had taken years to amass the perfect collection. He liked to believe his *objets d'art* rivaled any art gallery in London.

Heath straightened. Nothing to get maudlin about. Silly thoughts like these accomplished naught. His role was clearly defined. He had only to walk into it.

The moment his valet pronounced him a pink of the *ton*, Heath quit his cozy, bachelor-sized town house and steered his landau to his parents' much larger home. He would have much preferred to drive his barouche, but neither the damp air nor his freshly styled coiffure would do him well in an open carriage.

When he arrived, he handed the reins to a footman and strode briskly up the manicured walk to the austere entranceway.

Although his parents' town house was devoid of meaningful art, it was home to all of Heath's favorite people.

Camellia, who sang like an angel. Dahlia, who *was* an angel to the orphans she rescued. Bryony, the wild one. Their proud mama.

Their absent father.

Heath's chest tightened as the door swung open to reveal the family butler. Prate's years of "Good morning, sir," and "Good evening, sir," amounted to far more hours of conversation than Heath had ever shared with his sire.

After he and Prate had exchanged their customary pleasantries, Heath made his way to the private "family" parlor. His lips twisted in irony. As far as Heath knew, he was the only male member of the family who had ever entered the room.

He doubted today would be any different.

The old familiar resentment crawled along his skin. "Today" was never a day during which Lord Grenville had time for his son. Or his wife. Or his daughters. Merely being first in line to inherit the title afforded Heath no particular advantage.

He had been trying his entire life to carve a place for himself in the baronet's busy schedule. To be spoken to. To be noticed.

As things stood, the best chance at securing a brief moment of his father's attention would be at Heath's wedding. And even then, only if he secured exactly the right type of bride.

Which was likely the cause for his mother's summons, after his failures to select a wife among several Seasons of debutantes. Finding *a* woman was simple. Finding the right one...

Once again, an image of Miss Winfield fluttered to mind.

Seeing her again had not extinguished the simmering desire for her company that had plagued him ever since their first meeting. Their conversation had proven what they'd both already acknowledged; the distance between them was too wide to cross. There could be no future between them. No romantical future, at least.

And yet that spark, that persistent damnable *spark*, had fueled the undercurrent behind every word, every gesture, every stolen glance. It was as if something crackled between them, something that did not care about station or propriety or duty. An ignited flame that brought both light and warmth to secret yearnings he could never acknowledge.

Although he liked to believe he was not as superficial as others of his class, Heath was well aware that dallying with someone's paid companion in any capacity, from courtship to stolen kisses, was completely out of the question.

Ms. Winfield wasn't just below his station and in a peer's employ. She was an innocent country girl who lived on a bloody sheep farm, which she willingly intended to return to. Heath could no more picture himself in her world than he could imagine her fitting into his.

Yet he could not keep her from infiltrating his every thought.

"There you are!" came a sharp voice from the corridor.

Although his mother did not precisely rush into the family parlor—a well-bred lady never rushed—the heightened rustling of her intricately embroidered gown betrayed her urgency.

Heath bowed. "I am, as always, at your service."

"If that were true, you'd be wed by now. Which you have promised to take care of," she added quickly, as if confirming that portion of her worries would soon resolve itself. She reclined on a chaise longue and gestured for him to take the wingback chair opposite. "I've called you here today to discuss what's to be done with your sister."

The corner of his mouth twitched. "How odd. I distinctly recall your summons mentioned the family musicale."

Mother threw up her hands in despair. "Dahlia refuses to perform in the musicale!"

"She hasn't any musical ability," Heath reminded his mother gently. "Surely you wouldn't wish for your daughter to become the laughingstock of the *ton*."

"She's doing that on her own," Mother insisted

with a sniff. "She could develop a skill as accomplished as her sisters if she devoted half as much time to proper feminine talents as she does to that ridiculous orphanage."

"You know it's not an orphanage. It's a boarding school for indigent girls, and a very lovely cause. Dahlia has the biggest heart of anyone I know."

"And the emptiest dance card." Mother scowled at him. "You must stop encouraging her. I know you've been giving dancing lessons to those urchins. Things are dire. Dahlia's association with that rookery has already begun to affect the quality of her Society invitations. If she keeps treating every ballroom like a golden opportunity to raise funds for some charity—"

"Any aristocratic gathering *is* a golden opportunity to raise funds for a charity," Heath pointed out.

Mother ignored him. "—then she will soon find herself with no invitations at all. Camellia may soon be wed, but I despair of finding anyone to take Dahlia!"

"Camellia has a beau?" Heath leaned forward with interest. If a wallflower as quiet as his sister had ensnared some young buck, he must be a very special gentleman indeed. "I had no idea."

"Of course she hasn't a beau. Do be serious. Your father will select one for her and have done." Mother frowned. "If only it were that easy with Dahlia! Even with the size of her dowry, she is nothing but a—"

"—fine young woman," Heath finished firmly. "There is nothing wrong with Camellia *or* Dahlia, Mother. Have you considered just letting them live their lives?"

She recoiled in repugnance. "I suppose next you'll tell me that there's nothing wrong with Bryony either, and we should all just let her run wild?"

"Bryony is completely and utterly mad," Heath agreed cheerfully. "It's one of her best qualities. One is never bored in her company. Or in any of the others'. I suggest you leave them be for a little while longer. They're still young."

"They may be younger than *you*, but they're far from young." Mother pursed her lips. "Camellia's so high on the shelf that potential suitors don't notice her presence, and Dahlia's so far out to pasture she can't even find her way home."

Heath sighed. "What is it you wish for me to do, Mother?"

"I wish for you to *fix* it!" She glared at him. "Is that not what you do for everyone else under the sun? Don't make a sour face; I'm quite proud of you. There cannot be a nobler hobby than upholding the *beau monde*'s image."

Amusing. His mother knew quite well that his efforts were far more than a mere hobby, but she would never allow a word like *profession* to pass her lips in relation to her own children.

"Mother—"

"No, no. Don't you start." She arched a thin brow. "While your activities are unconventional to say the least, I heartily approve of any and all efforts to make the upper classes outshine themselves. My son is famous for fixing untidy little problems. I could die happy if he would only turn his efforts to fixing his own siblings."

Heath's temples pounded at the return of the same circular discussion.

He had no wish to "fix" his siblings. To change his strong, intelligent sisters into completely different people. He preferred them to pursue the lives they chose for themselves.

Although his mother had never understood such reasoning, women like Heath's sisters were the reason he had become a problem-solver in the first place. Not out of affinity for the veneer of *ton* perfection, but to allow people the opportunity to live the lives they wished without being judged for their choices.

As far as he was concerned, gossip helped no one. He was happy to do his part to make scandals disappear. Quashing his sisters' personalities, however, was going too far.

This argument had gone on long enough.

"I understand your concerns," he said as he rose to his feet. "I know you love your children and wish the best for them. I presume the girls are in Camellia's sitting room?"

"Where else?" his mother replied with a disgruntled sigh.

He hesitated. "While I'm here... Is Father in?"

"Oh, darling..." His mother's eyes filled with something painfully close to pity. "I'm afraid he is too busy with important matters to grant any of us an audience today."

Heath shrugged his tight shoulders. He'd asked about Father because he always asked about Father, not because he'd expected the answer to be any different. Heath's feelings weren't wounded. The baronet's absence didn't even hurt anymore.

There was certainly no reason for the pleading apology in his mother's eyes. It wasn't as if Father had time for her, either.

Perhaps that was why she obsessed about raising perfect children.

"Stay here and relax," he told her gently. "I'll go speak with the girls."

Mother lifted one of the hands from her hips.

"Focus your efforts on Dahlia. I beg you to talk sense into her."

Rather than make any promises, Heath bowed and strode from the room.

A single flight of stairs separated the family parlor from Camellia's sitting room. Heath took the steps in twos, his heart lightening with each leap up the stairs.

The door to the sitting room was open, spilling daylight and warmth from a crackling fire into the corridor. Bryony and Camellia's voices could be heard bickering. Dahlia's voice was missing. Either she was being uncharacteristically silent... or she had heard him coming.

Heath grinned to himself as his muscles tensed in anticipation.

Years earlier, when he had taught Dahlia self-defense, they had quickly developed the habit of ambushing one another to keep their skills sharp.

Although they were no longer adolescents, they had kept up the game. Heath was proud of his fearless sister, and glad he could help keep her safe even when he was not present to watch over her.

No doubt she would wish to prove herself as nimble and capable as ever.

Rather than edge closer and expose himself to a potential attack, he lowered his head and rushed into the room at full speed.

Dahlia was ready. Instead of lying in wait, she somersaulted in front of him the moment he crossed the threshold, catching him at the knees and quickly rolling out of the way as he tumbled forward off-balance.

Rather than land on his face, Heath turned his rapid fall into a somersault and sprang fluidly to his feet before she could attack again.

Dahlia was already standing upright with her fists in the air.

"A tie!" Bryony exclaimed in delight. "How long has it been since you've had a tie?"

"It's not a tie," Dahlia protested. "Heath wasn't ready. He went down!"

"Down into a somersault, which he quickly leapt out of. He didn't *stay* down." Bryony pointed out, to her sister's exasperation.

Camellia's eyes twinkled. "If we're being picky, you were the first to go down. You were flying boots over bonnet before Heath even entered the room."

"My somersault was *tactical*," Dahlia said with high offense. "His was reactionary!"

"Do I have a voice in this discussion?" Heath asked drolly.

"*No*," all three sisters chorused at once.

Laughing, he threw himself onto one of the chaise longues. "Mother would like to know why you three unmarriageable wretches are still spinsters."

"Mother would never say such a thing," Bryony replied primly. "She knows precisely why we're all unmarriageable spinsters."

Camellia threw a pillow at her sister's head. "Speak for yourself. Mother has said that if I fail to bring some sap up to scratch before the end of the Season, Father will select my future husband."

"Poppycock." Dahlia settled herself on the floor next to Heath's chaise. "Father is too busy to wish us well on our birthdays. He'll never take the time to comb through eligible bachelors in search of a perfect match for his daughter."

"Exactly." Bryony's voice was dark. "He'll pack her off with the first wily roué who asks. Cam, you cannot let him do it. You must find a husband first."

Heath suddenly realized he had hoped all his sisters would find love matches. They deserved happiness. One person in the family taking a bride for the baronetcy rather than for love was more than enough. He would do his duty so that his sisters could follow their hearts.

Duty meant choosing a chit based on bloodlines and good stock and impeccable comportment. Selecting from a limited pool of debutantes the way one might deliberate horseflesh at Tattersall's. One didn't expect to *speak* with the horse, to experience some sort of otherworldly *connection* with the horse. One simply did one's best to procure a creature that would not embarrass him in front of his peers.

Just because Heath knew these things did not mean he must like them. If he was shocked to discover he had always taken such strict protocol for granted, he was even more shocked at the tiny part of him that wished exceptions could be made. Not forever; he was heir to a baronetcy that he would one day pass down to his own son, and could not in good faith do anything to tarnish that gift.

No, not forever... but perhaps for a single moment. If he could freeze everyone else in time for a single, reckless hour, he really could ask a woman like Miss Winfield to dance. They would be the only two whirling amongst the frozen dance floor. They would not require an orchestra to find the rhythm to waltz.

For that hour, he would not be Mr. Grenville, first in line to a title, upholder of all that is proper and *good ton*. For that hour, Miss Winfield would not be a sheep maid or a paid companion or off-limits at all. They would simply be a gentleman enjoying a waltz with a pretty woman.

And perhaps a kiss or three, if the lady were amenable. No need for promises, or apologies, or regrets. Just two people without a care or worry, finally allowing the spark between them full rein before the wheels of time came crashing down again to separate them for good.

"Pay close attention, Dahlia." Bryony stabbed a plume in her sister's direction. "As soon as Cam's married, then it'll be your turn."

Dahlia blanched at the realization. "I refuse. There's no time for such nonsense when I've a demanding schedule as headmistress of a school. How can Mother expect me to waltz through every dinner party in Town and still manage an overcrowded, underfunded boarding school?"

"She does not wish for you to do both," Bryony pointed out dryly. "You would make her the happiest of creatures if you would stop caring about other people and focus your talents on flirting with painted fans."

"Mother isn't evil," Heath reminded them all. "She's this way because she loves all of you. In the world we live in, a daughter's duty is to be wed, and a successful mother ensures that happens. She doesn't view you as unworthy. She views herself as a failure."

"To be fair, she also views *us* as failures," Camellia said with a sigh. "I'm likely the worst of the lot. Unlike my hoyden sisters, I'm not 'on the shelf' on purpose."

"I'm not against husbands," Dahlia protested. "If I could find a man who didn't mind that his wife's priority was taking care of—"

"Stop right there," Heath interrupted, miming taking written notes on the conversation. "If I report back to Mother that you are open to the idea of marriage, that will settle her nerves considerably."

"What about you?" Camellia asked. "Are you truly going to find a bride this Season?"

"I promised Mother I would," he replied. For better or for worse.

"One couldn't ask for a firmer 'yes.'" Bryony shook her head. "Heath has never broken his word in his life."

"True." Dahlia tossed him a saucy grin over her shoulder. "That's how I tricked him into giving me self-defense lessons all those years ago."

"You didn't trick me," he protested. "You said you wanted to know how to defend yourself if you encountered a situation that required it, and I found that a quite reasonable request."

She leaned her head against his arm. "And I thank you, dear brother. You're my favorite for a reason."

Camellia's mouth dropped open in mock offense. "No favorites allowed!"

She and Bryony showered him and Dahlia with every pillow cushion within arm's reach.

Heath let the pillows fall where they may. He couldn't have been more content.

He'd often wished that instead of the stodgy portrait Mother had commissioned of the four siblings when they were young, that they'd opted for an irreverent moment-in-time painting instead.

Days like today. Camellia and Bryony showering the room with bright satin cushions. Heath, sprawled on an elegant chaise. Dahlia, her prim coiffure resting against his shoulder while the telltale cuffs of boys' breeches poked out from beneath the hem of her day dress.

A niggle of doubt cracked his happiness. He *had* taught Dahlia to defend herself because he never wanted any woman to feel helpless. And those *were* his castoff trousers that allowed her to tumble across the floor without fear of indecent exposure.

Dear Lord. Why would Mother believe he was in any way the right person to talk "sense" into Dahlia? Heath was the one to blame for her turning out strong and capable and stubborn.

For all intents and purposes, he'd been the only male figure present for most of his siblings' lives. What if he'd conveyed the wrong message?

He sat up abruptly. "Listen, all of you."

Three pairs of eyes turned to him expectantly.

Camellia did not require his impending words of wisdom. She had never once gone against Society's expectations or their parents' wishes. Bryony and Dahlia, however...

He took a deep breath. As their elder brother, it was important to do and say the right thing.

"I love all of you. I love who you are, I love how you are, and I cannot wait to see what you'll become."

Bryony narrowed one eye. "But?"

"But I'm just me," he said simply. "One man. Your big brother. And much as I wish I could control how you're treated by the rest of Society, I cannot change their views, or their rules, or their expectations. In this room, you can be whoever and however you want. But for the rest of the world, what others *think* about who and how you are carries more weight than how and who you *actually* are. Do you understand?"

Bryony scoffed. "No."

"I understand." Dahlia leaned away from him and crossed her arms. "But I disagree. It isn't the rest

of the world that cares more about appearances than
souls. It's the peerage. Do you think the girls at my
school gave a fig when I lost my subscription to Almack's?"

"Your girls might not know what Almack's is,"
Camellia said, her voice soft. "But it's naïve to say they
don't care about what others think. Why else would
they be in a boarding school?"

"To prevent their fathers from beating them? If
indeed they are 'lucky' enough to have one?" Dahlia's
face darkened with anger. "To finally end night after
night of shame and agony when some drunken toff
catches them in the street and decides to—"

"You're both right," Bryony interrupted quickly.
"Almost everyone is driven more by how others per-
ceive them than by their own passions. But we can
choose to be the same or to be different. I, for one,
choose not to give a button what anyone thinks."

Heath groaned. This conversation had taken a
sharp detour. "What I'm trying to say is—"

"They know what you're trying to say," Camellia
said gently. "You've made a career of helping Society
keep up appearances. People *pay* you to stop them
from becoming other people's gossip fodder. The impact of one's reputation is an indisputable, obvious
fact."

It was his turn to narrow his eyes. "...but?"

"But it's not the whole story. I happen to agree
with you. Bryony does not. And Dahlia..." Camellia
gazed sympathetically at their sister. "Dahlia knows
you're right, and has chosen to follow her heart anyway."

"What Cam means," Bryony began with a toss of
her head, "is that we received your message. Just
don't expect us to change a thing. We are not your

paying customers."

No, they were not. Heath gazed at his sisters. They had become his responsibilities the moment of their births. Nor would he have it any other way.

When Camellia had been too shy to attract dance partners, Heath had made it fashionable to ensure no wallflower's dance card went empty. When Dahlia had opened her boarding school, Heath had personally assuaged the concerns of Society matrons suddenly unsure about extending their invitations to all members of the Grenville clan.

His sisters had always been Heath's top priority clients.

They just never realized it.

"While you're here..." Camellia rustled some papers atop her writing desk in an obvious attempt to change the subject. "Can we discuss the score for the next musicale?"

Dahlia lay back, resting her head against the plush carpet. "What's to discuss? The songs haven't changed since Mother created the first arrangement. You all sound perfectly lovely each time, and everyone returns home deservedly astonished by your talent."

"By Camellia's and Bryony's talent," Heath corrected. "Mother is far more accomplished at the pianoforte than I am."

Bryony glanced over at him in alarm. "You cannot let her replace you. It would no longer be the Grenville sibling musicale!"

"I'm not going anywhere," he assured her. "My semi-competent fingers are yours for as long as they can be of middling service."

Dahlia turned toward him. "You don't have to, you know. I don't go on stage, and lightning hasn't struck me yet."

"Yet," Heath teased back.

He didn't participate in the musicales because he loved the pianoforte, but because he loved his family. Camellia's voice was unparalleled; her passion for singing was present in every note. He was awestruck of her.

Bryony might not feel passionate toward the violin, but she found the exercise amusing. Watching his sister have fun with four strings and a bow was just as much fun for Heath as it was for her. That Bryony had been a child prodigy with the violin and had only grown more skillful as she matured made sharing the stage with her an honor, not a duty.

He was just as proud of "unmusical" Dahlia, who never missed a performance and still managed to find the time to manage a growing boarding school that required round-the-clock administration. Family came first to Dahlia, which now meant the Grenville clan *and* two dozen indigent dependents who looked up to her like a mother.

Of the four, Heath was the only one not following his true passion. Not that he was meant to have any passions. From the moment of his conception, he had been destined to inherit the baronetcy one day. That was to be his sole and defining duty: become as competent and successful a baronet as his father.

Perhaps it was foolish of him to dream of making a name for himself in his own right. No one else expected him to be anything more than heir to his father's title. That was enough for his mother. Enough for Society. So why wasn't it enough for Heath?

More importantly, why should his sisters feel any different? He rubbed his pounding temples. Shouldn't he and his mother "let" Dahlia ruin her standing if that was what she chose to do? Were life-long passions not worth the risk?

A footman entered the sitting room with the morning post.

Dahlia and Bryony pounced upon the pile of folded missives as if awaiting a personal note from the Prince Regent himself. Camellia never glanced up from her sheets of music.

"Eighty pounds." Dahlia rifled through her post with a happy sigh. "Not as much as I'd hoped, but any donation is better than no donation."

Camellia nodded approvingly. "Excellent work. The post will come again this afternoon. Bry, how did you do with your correspondence?"

"My investment report still hasn't arrived," Bryony answered with obvious disappointment. She slid Heath a frustrated look.

"Something I can help with?" he inquired in a low voice.

Bryony sighed and shook her head. "It'll come eventually."

Because most men balked at the idea of doing business with a female, Heath had helped his sister invest anonymously. It had begun on a dare. Bryony had thought it would be great fun to purchase shares in projects owned by men who would never open their books to a woman.

To Heath's surprise and Bryony's delight, she had been brilliant at it. She quickly got out of the three percents and into the riskier but far more lucrative business of funding private ventures.

Because of his fame as a secret-keeper, her marks never bothered to ask where the money came from. They already knew Heath would never betray a confidence, and besides, the business owners and project managers needed the money too much to concern themselves with minor details.

Bryony had tried to pull out of all her investments some months ago in order to divert her capital gains toward her sister's school. When Dahlia had refused to siphon money from her sister's dream to fund her own, Bryony had gone through Heath to make as many small, anonymous donations as she could.

The majority of her earnings, however, were contractually tied up in fixed-timeline investments. The letter she was waiting on was likely a quarterly report detailing the progress-to-date of one of her speculative ventures. Bryony's gift with numbers enabled her to draw accurate conclusions from such reports that even the financiers who wrote them had been unable to anticipate.

His mouth twitched. If she'd been born a different gender, she'd own half of London by now. She was probably still on that path anyway, one pseudonymous investment at a time.

And if Heath had been born a second son, or a third, or a fourth, there would be little chance of him inheriting the title. He could not wish away the baronetcy, but nor could he shake his longing for a freedom he could never have. To make decisions for himself, rather than duty.

What would he do with freedom such as that? Would he give into his desire to sweep Miss Winfield into his arms? Lower his mouth to hers and plunder—

"What are you smiling at so wolfishly?" Camellia asked.

He glanced over at her with a guilty start, then realized her words were not directed at him, but to Bryony.

"Gossip columns." Bryony held up a sketch with

a caption beneath. "Have you seen today's carica-ture?"

"Ugh, I despise them." Camellia pulled a face. "Why do you insist on having them delivered?"

Bryony grinned back. "To see if I'm in them."

Heath's heart stopped. Bryony's flippant words might be in jest, but he wasn't so certain the idea was far-fetched.

Having a beloved family member appear in some mocking caricature was his worst nightmare. Not just as the problem-solver famed for quieting *ton* scan-dals, but as elder brother to three unwed sisters. How was he supposed to protect them from the damage a printing press could do?

He reached out a palm. "Give it to me."

Bryony handed it over without comment and turned her attention to the rest of her mail.

Good God. Heath could not look away from the ghastly caricature. That this rubbish was sketched with a deft hand did not signify. Every visage was in-stantly recognizable. Not just the poor saps being mocked in the foreground. All the faces. The footman in the background was just as familiar as the salon in the sketch.

His breath caught. This wasn't some outsider's biting commentary on the perceived iniquities of aris-tocratic life. This was *Lady Carlisle's ballroom*. A real place. A real moment in time. Real quotes emanating from jauntily drawn mouths.

Worse, Heath didn't just recognize the room. He recognized the exact soirée. He had *been* there. And if London's newest critic had been there as well...

Heath crumpled the drawing into a tight ball. Small wonder these savage works of "art" were un-signed. The mystery caricaturist was a member of their class. Shamelessly betraying his peers for a penny. Too cowardly to spew his poison to their faces.

Heath tossed the crumpled sketch into the fire and watched it burn.

When Lady Caroline Lamb had written *Glenarvon* last year as a thinly veiled attempt to exact romantical revenge after being jilted by Lord Byron, the viscountess had lost far more than permission to attend Almack's. She had been ostracized from Society completely.

The caricaturist deserved no less harsh a fate.

Chapter 7

*N*ora perched self-consciously on a pristine carriage squab and wondered if she would ever become accustomed to parading about Hyde Park in Lady Roundtree's landau.

Even with one leg jutting stiffly forward, the baroness looked as confident and elegant as ever. An exquisitely crafted gown hid the splints well out of view, and a smart blue hat towering with fresh flowers and a false parakeet drew one's eye toward Lady Roundtree's regal visage.

Not that anyone would be distracted by Nora's presence. She sat backward in the landau, her spine to the plush wall separating the groom from the passengers. Her lace-trimmed bonnet was the finest headpiece Nora had ever owned, even if it lacked both flora and fauna.

Her awkward posture was also due to her twin responsibilities of keeping Captain Pugboat inside his wicker basket, while also ensuring passers-by did not fail to notice his adorably wrinkled presence.

Every afternoon was exactly the same.

Or at least, it had been until she found herself spending every free moment drawing sketches of herself and Mr. Grenville in situations that could never happen. Standing up with her to dance at a ball. Skating with her across the frozen Thames. Presented to his friends and family as a diamond of the first water, rather than a mouse that belonged in the shadows...

Even when she was far from her sketchbooks, she could not quit the wistful images from her mind. What would it be like to feel her hand in his? Better yet, to taste his lips on hers? To parade down the busy streets in an open carriage as if he was proud to have her by his side? To—

"Captain Pugboat needs to be petted!" Lady Roundtree ordered with a sudden start.

Nora lifted the wicker lid at once. "Shall I lift him to your lap?"

"And let his dirty fur stain my skirt?" The baroness stared at her, aghast. "You are to do what I cannot."

"Of course," Nora murmured.

She slid her hand into the basket and gave Captain Pugboat a good rub behind the ears.

"Not too much," Lady Roundtree snapped. "A pet mustn't be spoiled."

Nora nodded and slid her hand from the basket.

She had quickly learned how much the baroness loved to "promenade" in an open carriage in order to see and be seen. Even prior to breaking her leg, Lady Roundtree had taken her late afternoon walks from atop a high carriage to make certain she was glimpsed by everyone of import. Nora was half-convinced that the primary reason the baroness had hired her as companion was to resume her daily gossip fests in

Hyde Park.

After the injury, Lady Roundtree had only become more popular. It seemed every fashionable
person in London made a point of pausing beside the
landau to wish her well, even if they had conveyed exactly the same sentiment just the day before, and the
day before that.

Between well-wishers, the baroness kept up a
low running commentary on the lives and loves of everyone within sight. Currently, the carriage was
strategically paused halfway around the circle so lords
and ladies on foot, on horseback, or in carriages could
more easily stop to enquire about Lady Roundtree's
health.

"That was Major Blackpool," the baroness whispered. "He used to be the most dashing rake in Town
until he lost his leg at Waterloo. I'm sure you noticed
the horrid clapping sound it makes when he moves."

Nora blinked. She had not noticed any strange
sounds, or anything odd about the major's limbs at all.
He sat astride one of the finest stallions Nora had seen
in her life.

"I thought he seemed nice," she said.

Lady Roundtree sighed at the major's retreating
back. "He still cuts a fine figure, wouldn't you say?
How he ended up with a vicar's daughter, of all creatures..."

A vicar's daughter might seem scandalous to a
baroness, but such a situation was still far above
Nora's station. She knew gentlemen of the *ton* were
outside her reach. Of course she did. But she could not
help but fantasize about one particular gentleman. No
man in London cut as fine a figure as Mr. Grenville.
His tousled brown hair, his warm hazel eyes, the way
he looked at her as if he'd forgotten the rest of the

world existed...

If an Army major could not wed a vicar's daughter without scandal, no wonder a future baronet could
have nothing to do with a farmer's granddaughter.
Mr. Grenville did not make the rules. He was forced
to follow them just like Nora.

Yet more and more each day, an ache in her chest
made her wish there *were* no rules. That she could
dance with anyone who wished to invite her, kiss anyone her heart begged for her to kiss.

No... not *anyone*. Who she longed for was Mr.
Grenville.

Even though she knew it could never be.

"Oh, here comes Lady St. John!" the baroness
squealed. "Amelia's a viscountess now, when we'd all
been so certain she'd never settle for less than a
duchy. Still the biggest busybody this side of the
Thames."

Nora jerked her gaze toward a striking couple
smiling and waving from a mind-bogglingly extravagant carriage. Between the couple's obvious wealth
and the equally obvious lovestruck glances they exchanged between conversations, Nora doubted the
viscountess had "settled" one whit.

Nora was unable to hide the wistful note in her
voice. "She looks happy."

"She's related to a duke," the baroness replied.
"Of course she's happy."

"I meant they seem like a well-matched couple,"
Nora clarified. "A love match."

Lady Roundtree was no longer listening. "Make
certain she sees my puppy. She'll be beside herself
with jealousy, and with a memory like hers, she won't
be able to forget it. Captain Pugboat's sweet face will
haunt her for days. Don't be surprised if everyone you

see suddenly starts bringing pugs with them to Society events."

Nora did her best to ensure she stayed in the background and Captain Pugboat in the foreground as the endless parade of dandies, debutantes, and aristocrats streamed past the landau to pay their respects to her patroness. Her visitors were quite the colorful lot.

Lady Roundtree wasn't always ill-tempered, Nora decided as she watched the conversations unfold. Perhaps she simply liked to hear herself speak.

Although she was fairly certain Lady Roundtree held no ill will toward any of her contemporaries, Nora could have filled dozens of sketchbooks with biting caricatures based solely on the baroness's pithy "hasn't a shilling to her name" or "cuckolded him with his own brother" gossip between each visit. Or the shockingly candid comments the well-wishers themselves made, as if a companion's presence was no more consequential than a lamp post.

Indeed, Nora yearned to have her sketchbook handy. But not for drawing caricatures.

When the idea of leaving for Hyde Park had occurred to the baroness, Lady Roundtree had noticed that Nora was in the middle of drawing the scene outside the sitting room window, and had graciously suggested that Nora bring her book and pencil with her. How she wished she could!

She longed to faithfully capture the beautiful clothes, the towering bonnets, the prancing horses, the ducal carriages. At night before bed, she did her best to illustrate all the finery she'd witnessed over the course of the day, and hated that many of the small details were lost forever.

But she could not risk other members of the *ton*

taking note of any particular artistic tendency. At present, High Society did not tend to notice Nora at all, and while their complete disinterest did little for one's personal esteem, her relentless invisibility was the gift that allowed her to earn desperately needed funds for her grandparents' struggling farm.

If that meant a month or two of awkwardness and discomfort for Nora, then so be it. Family was worth any sacrifice.

Besides, it was no hardship to be draped in warm, fashionable gowns, served sumptuous meals with multiple courses, to be seated on a comfortable carriage cushion with an adorable pug wagging his curly puppy tail. She was *blessed*.

Nora slipped her gloved hand into Captain Pugboat's wicker basket. She couldn't snuggle his soft, wrinkly face against her cheek with the baroness right in front of her—Lady Roundtree frowned on such unseemly behavior—but surely no one could object to her giving the very good puppy a quick rub behind his floppy, coal-colored ears.

When he rewarded her with an instant tail wag so emphatic that he nearly lost his balance, Nora forced herself not to laugh out loud. He was adorable. When the weeks were up and it was time to move back home, what she would miss most was not the exposure to finery, but silly moments like these with her best and only London friend, the delightful Captain Pugboat.

"It's Dorothea!" Lady Roundtree's spine snapped even straighter and she motioned for Nora to do the same. "Sit up, sit up! You mustn't hunch over the basket. Straighten your shoulders. She's almost here!"

Nora wiped the smile off her face and snapped

up straight.

An even fancier open carriage approached.

It had been less than a fortnight, but she had quickly learned that "Dorothea" was Lady Pettibone, ruler of the *ton*. That the society matron and Lady Roundtree were related did not afford the baroness any exemptions to the consequences of her displeasure. One cross word from universally feared Lady Pettibone, and the life of even one as lofty as a baroness would be ruined.

Nora dutifully affected what Lady Roundtree referred to as "solemn but subservient" composure, as befitted a paid employee. She tried not to allow the subtle reminders of how expendable she was wear her down.

That Nora was also the baroness's cousin had merely landed her this opportunity. Only by never disappointing her patroness could Nora hope to maintain her post.

She could not help but note the irony as the baroness affected a similarly false posture and expression. A wry smile curved Nora's lips. At their core, she supposed they weren't so different after all. Everyone's position in Society depended upon the whim of someone else.

"What's this I hear about adopting some animal?" Lady Pettibone barked in lieu of a greeting.

Her companion, a blindingly bejeweled lady, gasped and clutched a hand to her powder-pale throat. "Never say there's a filthy *cur* in that carriage. How did such base animals suddenly become all the rage?"

"He's not filthy," Nora protested without thinking. "Captain Pugboat is bathed twice daily."

The fine lady's nose wrinkled as if Nora, and not

Captain Pugboat, were the filthy cur. "And who, pray tell, is *this* unfortunate creature?"

Nora clamped her teeth together. The back of her neck flamed with heat at the question.

Whoever this stranger was, she'd somehow known at a glance that Nora was no young lady in Town for her come-out, but rather some poor servant playing at dress-up.

Her cheeks burned. These were the richest clothes she'd ever worn. But though they might make her feel a princess, her betters still knew her for a pauper. Small wonder most of them ignored her.

Lady Roundtree waved a gloved hand in Nora's direction. "Winfield is my companion."

"Oh, thank heavens." The bejeweled lady gave a delicate shiver. "I dreaded to think how any debutante intended to find a match with hair that... *red*. The pink gown makes the garish hue clash all the more."

Nora sucked in a deep breath. She didn't know whether to laugh or cry. The Society lady hadn't mistaken her for a servant, after all. She'd simply recoiled at Nora's repulsive appearance. Apparently her wild red mane was so monstrously offensive, no fine gentleman could ever possibly condescend to withstand the presence of such an eyesore.

Thank God Nora would soon be going home, where hardworking, country-born men had better things to do than rate women's worth based on the color of their hair.

"Petty insults do not behoove a future countess," Lady Pettibone informed her companion coldly.

The fine lady's porcelain face blushed just as red as the rubies encrusted in her gown.

Or as red as Nora's hair.

"And you." Lady Pettibone turned her sharp gaze

toward Nora. "We have discussed proper comportment. Your first position will be your last if you fail the simple task of minding your silence unless spoken to."

Nora gulped and nodded. She held this post because Lady Pettibone herself had ordered the baroness to acquire a companion. Nora could not afford to lose it by jumping to the defense of a small, innocent, extremely clean puppy.

Probably cleaner than the heavily powdered future countess sweating to death under the weight of so much satin and jewels.

"And I would beg *you*," Lady Roundtree replied with obvious nervousness, "not to publicly reprimand my employees."

"Then do so yourself." Lady Pettibone swung her imperious gaze toward Nora. "Well? Let's see it, then. Or is the mutt confined in that basket because it has rabies?"

Nora startled into action, flipping both wicker lids wide and tilting the basket toward Lady Pettibone's carriage.

With a rebel yip, Captain Pugboat immediately leapt into the air, front paws reaching toward the ornate carriage, nails first.

Lady Pettibone's eyes widened in surprise.

Lady Roundtree buried her face in her hands.

The bejeweled countess let out a bloodcurdling scream as if the hounds of hell had been unleashed upon them all.

Nora released the basket and snatched the flying puppy from the air before his little paws could reach the forbidden coach.

Saved.

She clutched Captain Pugboat to her chest in victory.

The tumbling wicker basket made contact with Lady Roundtree's broken leg.

The baroness's resulting shriek of agony drowned out every other sound in the entire park.

Nora yanked the basket away, trapped Captain Pugboat inside, and knelt in abject horror on the carriage floor beside Lady Roundtree's trembling, broken limb.

Lady Pettibone motioned to her driver. "I'll leave you to your reprimanding."

The coach shot away as if fleeing a losing battle-field.

"I'm so sorry," Nora babbled, unable to wait until directly addressed before apologizing profusely to her wounded patroness. "What can I do to help?"

"Nothing." Lady Roundtree's elegant shoulders slumped back against her satin squab in clear relief. "Sit, sit. You didn't harm me. I just wanted them to go away."

Nora blinked in confusion. "You wanted Lady Pettibone to go away?"

"Both of them." The baroness fluttered her eyes skyward. "You cannot imagine how tiresome it is to be constantly judged by those who outrank you."

"That... must be dreadful for you," Nora managed to choke out as she forced her still-shaking hands to relax.

"You have no idea." Lady Roundtree lowered her voice. "Did you know they call her the 'old dragon?'"

Nora did know.

Her patroness had informed her of this and every other aristocrat's nickname countless times, along with allegedly verbatim stories about how each reputation had come to be earned. The baroness's en-thusiastically repeated tales were the source material for almost all of Nora's caricatures.

"Oh?" she said aloud, as if the moniker was surprising news.

If her patroness did not recall her many mindless confessions to a companion, Nora saw no need to draw attention to the matter.

"Even my husband says she's a tyrant." Lady Roundtree pursed her lips. "And my husband..."

Would know, Nora finished silently. The baron did not possess a warm nature.

It was fortunate that Nora had been employed to provide the baroness much-needed companionship, for Lord Roundtree certainly could not be bothered to do so.

Attending to his vast wealth not only made him richer, but the baron also became ever more distant and irritable with his wife. This served to increase the baroness's propensity to fly into a panic or spend unbroken hours prattling to Nora about aristocratic peccadillos in an obvious attempt to fill the silent, cavernous rooms of her home with something besides loneliness.

Nora didn't mind that accepting this temporary post had reduced her already-lowly status from poor relation to paid servant. Although she had never longed to define herself by some tenuous family connection to Someone Important, she was glad she could provide comfort to her cousin. Even if they never saw each other again after Lady Roundtree's broken leg finally healed.

With this post, the baroness had given Nora an advantage that would serve her the rest of her life. Not a letter of recommendation to future employers. Not just the money sent home to her grandparents. But the surprising realization that greenhorn, country-born Nora wasn't missing anything after all. This life was not for her.

The same pinch-nosed countess would have made the same belittling comments if Nora had been the baroness's daughter rather than her distant cousin.

Horse hooves clopped up to the carriage, followed by a concerned male voice. "I'm sorry it took so long to reach you. I thought I heard a scream. Is something amiss?"

Mr. Grenville.

Already his low, rich voice was imprinted on her soul.

Nora gazed up at him, speechless.

He was even handsomer than the last time she'd seen him. Chestnut hair, adorable tousled. Snowy white cravat against a dark blue waistcoat and dove gray jacket. He was Prince Charming astride a royal steed.

And he wasn't here for her.

His hazel eyes were focused on the baroness.

"No, nothing at all." Lady Roundtree flapped a hand in apology for her earlier shriek. "Lady Pettibone's companion is simply excitable. We didn't mean to bother anyone."

"A lady as charming and elegant as yourself could never be a bother," Mr. Grenville said with a wink. He turned his easy smile toward Nora. "You look lovely as well, Miss Winfield. Seeing the two of you has already made this afternoon's promenade worthwhile."

Lady Roundtree giggled girlishly. "Stuff and nonsense. Every promenade must be a treat for you. Once you inherit the baronetcy, you'll have little time for such idleness."

Something dark flashed across Mr. Grenville's hazel eyes and just as quickly vanished.

Nora's heart thumped. What had he been thinking just then?

"I am certain I can break the mold," Mr. Grenville protested with good humor. "Look about at all the titled gentlemen present. The dukes and earls outrank us, and they appear to have a surfeit of time to devote to their pleasures, do they not?"

Perhaps that was *why*, Nora thought but did not say aloud. Bigger titles tended to correspond with bigger fortunes—vast estates and troves of gold passed down from generation to generation. They must have dozens of barristers, bankers, and paid managers to attend to every detail.

Because baronetcies were the least powerful of all the ranks, perhaps their owners were required to devote disproportionately more time to maintaining both wealth and appearances, lest their title become societally and financially worthless. It would be awful.

Nora doubted such an opinion on the matter would be particularly welcome. She also felt a pang of empathy at the possibility that she was right. Mr. Grenville was so cheerful. So *nice*. The thought of him losing his happy demeanor because he'd chained himself indoors to mind his account balances...

Well, she supposed she knew a thing or two about doing whatever it took to keep one's family afloat. That kinship made her like him all the more.

"Good afternoon, Mr. Grenville!" cooed a quartet of waving young ladies as their grand carriage drew close.

Nora's spine slumped. Liking him did not signify. She would never be one of those girls.

Mr. Grenville greeted the young ladies by name,

with a smile and a friendly compliment for each. When they inquired whether he would be present at this ball or that, he vowed his name would not be absent from their dance cards.

What would it be like to be one of them? To hear him say such words to her, and to know that they were true?

If Nora were a debutante and there was the slightest chance Mr. Grenville would stand up with her to dance, she would be first in line at every ball. She'd curl her hair for hours if need be, embroider flowers and beads onto the finest crepe she could afford.

Once she was there amongst the musicians and the chandeliers and the magic, Nora would not hang back with the wallflowers and risk there being no room to add her name to his list. She would be first to smile at him, to speak with him, to inform him he was in luck because there was still a spot for his name on her dance card.

And then, once she was in his arms...

A few of the debutantes shot suspicious glances over Mr. Grenville's shoulder at Nora, as if desperate to know her identity, but unwilling to break protocol by asking their questions outright. Who was this freckled stranger in a pale pink muslin day dress stealing Mr. Grenville's precious time away from debutantes who deserved him?

Nora looked away. Their jealousy was misplaced. Yet a small part of her was pleased she had the power to engender it, no matter how briefly.

She straightened her shoulders and did her best to project a confidence she did not feel. They didn't *know* she was no one. All their worried eyes could observe was handsome Mr. Grenville tarrying at a landau containing a Society matron and an unknown young woman near their age.

Perhaps they were even beginning to wonder whether distressingly red hair had become all the crack overnight, and their perfect blonde ringlets horribly out of fashion.

A giggle escaped Nora's throat as she imagined painting such a scene. The soft watercolor of the debutantes' pastel dresses, the strong, red brush strokes of her hair flailing in the wind, the charming prince smitten at first sight.

Mr. Grenville swung a quizzical gaze in her direction. "Have I missed something humorous?"

"I was just imagining red hair as something fashionable," she stammered.

His eyes heated as he gazed intently at her person.

"Fashions come and go," he said softly. "But lustrous hair as glorious as yours will be beautiful forever. Why else would great masters such as Titian become obsessed with painting goddesses with flowing locks the same color as yours?"

"I..." Nora's throat dried as she gazed back at him wordlessly.

She had expected him to laugh off the idea, perhaps tease her good-naturedly about her unfortunate coloring. Instead, Mr. Grenville had compared her to a goddess. Someone important men could become obsessed with. Someone worthy of being *remembered*.

Her heart skipped. She had never received a better compliment.

"Don't start again with your Italian painters," Lady Roundtree said with a flutter of her gloved fingers. "I swear you'd be just as happy to spend a sunny afternoon cooped up in a museum as out here in Hyde

Park."

"Both are filled with beauty," Mr. Grenville agreed. But his gaze did not leave Nora.

She tried to tamp down her runaway pulse. It refused to slow.

He was simply being kind, was he not? From the moment they'd first met, she'd quickly deduced that kindness was Mr. Grenville's signature characteristic. He was kind to ladies young and old, to rakes and dandies, to maids and footmen, to completely out-of-her-element country greenhorns like Nora. He meant nothing flirtatious by it. She should not read more into a simple comment than the politeness he had intended.

And yet, Mr. Grenville had accomplished a seemingly impossible feat.

He *saw* her.

Not as an unimportant servant, or a poor relation, or a romantic rival, but as a *person*.

A woman with Titian hair.

"Thank you," she whispered.

"For having the same exquisite taste as a Renaissance master artist?" he asked with wide-eyed innocence, clearly misconstruing her words on purpose. "'Tis I who should be thanking you. Should you wish for me to continue my observations on your divine tresses one day, simply send a note to—"

"Grenville!" called out a well-dressed, raspy-voiced man in obvious desperation. "I must speak to you. That matter we discussed? The newest development must be handled at once. May we converse privately?"

"Of course. Do try to calm yourself. I will work it out." Mr. Grenville turned back to Lady Roundtree's carriage and managed to sweep Nora and the baroness a half bow from atop his horse. "A thousand apologies to the loveliest ladies in Hyde Park. If you'll forgive my hastened departure, I promise to make it up to you in the future."

Lady Roundtree wagged a finger. "Duty must come first. Go rescue the earl before he has an apoplexy and falls off his horse."

Nora nodded quickly. "Please help your friend."

"Until we meet again." Mr. Grenville lifted his reins and galloped down the path after the panicked earl.

Nora forced herself not to stare after him. The ill-timed interruption had been a boon. She had been so enraptured by Mr. Grenville's meaningless compliment that she'd forgot for a moment the power—and the danger—he represented.

He uncovered people's darkest secrets.

She needed to keep hers at all costs.

A flirtation with him, no matter how brief or innocent, could only invite disaster. Mr. Grenville was not her beau or even her friend. He was a member of the *ton*. Fully capable of destroying her reputation, her position, and her best chance at improving her grandparents' lives if he ever found out the truth.

With luck, they would not meet again.

Chapter 8

*a*s Heath handed off the reins to his landau in front of the Roundtree residence, he could not help but wonder if today's unusual summons was at all related to the Hyde Park encounter with the baroness and her lovely companion earlier in the week.

Try as he might, Heath had been unable to cease thinking about Miss Winfield. How much simpler it would be to put paid to this obsession if he could simply spend more time in her company!

Had the two of them been traversing Hyde Park from the relative privacy of an open carriage, he and Miss Winfield could have conversed without witnesses eagerly spying upon every word. A nice long conversation would instantly clear up the question of whether their personalities actually suited, or if the intense longing to pull her into his arms and kiss her was nothing more than meaningless chemistry.

Heath tried to push such thoughts from his head

as he loped up the stone steps. So what if the chemistry between them was electric? He was not going to kiss her. So what if their personalities suited? He was not going to court her. No matter how many sparks sizzled between them, she would remain in her place and he in his.

Although, the summons here today made him wonder what else might be going on.

Because Heath and the Roundtrees resided on the same social plane, he frequently came across the baroness at various Society events. However, this occasion marked the first time he had received an invitation to their home. He frowned in concern. As much as he enjoyed helping others, Heath was fond of the baroness and hoped he had not been summoned to prevent some personal tragedy from becoming a public scandal.

Before he could rap the brass knocker, a stately butler swung open the large door and ushered Heath inside.

Upon presenting his card, Heath was quickly escorted to a sunny salon in the front of the town house, where Lady Roundtree reclined upon a stuffed chaise. A modest blanket covered any fear of exposed stockings due to her splinted leg resting gently on a truly mountainous pile of cushions.

Heath swept a deep bow. "Lady Roundtree."

"Thank you so much for your prompt attention, Mr. Grenville." She waved a fretful hand toward the chair opposite. "I hope you are not offended by my lack of curtsey."

"I shall only be offended if you fail to accompany me in a lively *Boulanger* the very moment your surgeon pronounces you healed," he teased, knowing full well the baroness preferred to oversee country dances from the sides, in order to note every detail.

The baroness harrumphed, her eyes twinkling. "We shall see if Lord Roundtree allows me to dance with a pup a decade younger than myself."

"A pup!" Heath clutched his hands to his chest in mock agony. "Now you *have* offended me, and grievously. Have I been summoned to this beautiful salon only to bear witness to grave assaults against my character?"

"Quite the opposite." The humor disappeared from Lady Roundtree's countenance. "I'd like to discuss details of someone else's comportment with you."

At the implication, a cold knot formed in Heath's stomach. "Miss Winfield?"

"What?" Lady Roundtree stared at him in bafflement before she burst out laughing. "No, my companion pleases everyone but Lady Pettibone, and that is only because the 'old dragon' is impossible to please."

Heath did not join in the laughter. He had never run afoul of Lady Pettibone, nor was he wont to find witticism in cruel nicknames. Yet the emotion in his chest was not outrage on the absent Society dame's behalf, but rather an intense relief that Miss Winfield was not involved in any scandal.

By the sound of Lady Roundtree's description, her companion was just as unlikely to find herself in an imbroglio as Heath himself. That spoke highly of her character. Despite their class differences being impossible to overcome, sharing a strong sense of personal ethics only made him like Miss Winfield more.

And doubt very much that anything good would come of his summons here today.

His shoulders tensed.

"I hope you did not invite me here to pry for secrets about my clients," he said stiffly.

"Pry?" Lady Roundtree flapped her hand excitably. "A baroness would never do such a thing!"

Balderdash. The baroness was infamous for engaging in precisely that sort of behavior, and they both knew it. Yet Heath believed her when she claimed pumping him for information was not her aim.

Lady Roundtree was a known gossip, although not a malignant one like that rotter Phineas Mapleton. The baroness did not use her knowledge in an attempt to ruin others, but she did like to know every possible scrap of gossip. And this wouldn't be the first time someone had tried and failed to wheedle a secret or two from him.

"How can I be of service?" he asked cautiously.

She pointed at a stack of letters on a silver tray. "I presume you've heard of the new caricaturist?"

He could not prevent his lip from curling in distaste. "Who has not?"

"Indeed." Lady Roundtree sniffed. "I, for one, do not allow such filth into my home. This sanctuary is free of gossip at all times."

Heath slid a doubtful look in the direction of the silver tray, with its towering pile of caricatures and scandal columns.

Lady Roundtree colored when she saw the direction of his gaze. "All those go straight into the fire before anyone but myself has a chance to see them."

The tension in Heath's muscles eased when he realized this would include her companion. Miss Winfield was unlikely to have seen such rubbish firsthand. He was strangely pleased by the idea that being on the outskirts of Society meant Miss Winfield could remain unspoiled by it. Pure.

"What do you know about the artist?" he asked Lady Roundtree without changing expression.

She hesitated before responding. "He is not your client, is he?"

"I should think not!" Heath reared back at the insult.

If anything, he found each caricature more reprehensible than the last. The anonymous coward mocked and taunted the very society he should be striving to uphold, not to break down. Each stroke of ink caused more gossip in a single day than all the scandal sheets put together.

"These caricatures are a scourge," he said with feeling. "This alleged 'artist' should be dethroned. I hope you do not count yourself among his fans, Lady Roundtree."

"A fan?" She leaned closer. "Exposing *ton* foibles is uncouth and wrong. I wish to be the one to unmask the blackguard. I shall be famous!"

He cleared his throat before responding. "You want..."

"To employ *you*, of course. Secretly." Lady Roundtree frowned. "That's what you do, isn't it? Keep secrets for people? If I pay you to discover the identity of this villain, you won't tell anyone how I discovered the man's identity?"

Heath narrowed his eyes.

He was indeed a secret-keeper, and if he accepted a client, complete and utter confidentiality was immediately understood. But thus far, all his effort had gone toward keeping scandals in the dark, not bringing even bigger ones to light.

Yet truly, what claim to privacy held a smug coward who sold other people's private humiliations for profit? Putting a stop to it was the only ethical course of action.

Fewer scandals disrupting Society would create a better environment for everyone.

Lady Roundtree's voice took on a wheedling tone. "I suddenly realize that unmasking this cretin will reduce the amount of gossip about everyone else overnight, thus imperiling your livelihood. Perhaps you condone—"

"I'll take the case," he said abruptly. "My 'livelihood' does not depend on encouraging gossip. I've chosen the path of scandal-fixer out of a passion for helping those in need, not out of some desire to pad my purse. I don't need the money. My clients need *me*."

"Now I've offended you," the baroness said fretfully. "Let us dispense with the formalities and move past all this ugliness. You've said you will take the case. I suppose your services operate on retainer, like a barrister. Let's make it official. Will five hundred be enough to start? Six? Seven?"

Heath blinked.

While he had genuinely meant every word about not pursuing his career out of any need for money, the outrageous sums the wealthy baroness tossed out without a second thought would be enough to sustain a non-aristocratic bachelor for a year.

Or provide a reprieve to his sister's financially beleaguered school.

"Seven will be a lovely start," he agreed, and withdrew a slip of paper from his breast pocket. "An anonymous deposit to this account will do splendidly."

She held a quizzing glass above the parchment. "The St. Giles School for Girls... Why, that's your sister's charity! Never say you donate *all* your earnings to an orphanage?"

"If I answered that question, then you would be keeping secrets for *me*," he replied with a tight smile. "Please don't worry about the state of the Grenville baronetcy. My father has no wish for my assistance to increase the family coffers."

"Your father is a brilliant man," Lady Roundtree agreed. She held up a finger as if to scold him. "I haven't glimpsed a single hair of the baronet for years. I hope you rowdy lot allow the poor man out of his study once in a while."

He didn't have the heart to tell her she likely interacted with the baronet just as much as his own family did.

Which was to say, never.

"I shall pass along your concerns," Heath replied.

"You, on the other hand..." Lady Roundtree smiled benevolently. "You are everywhere in Society. A gathering without Heath Grenville is like tea without biscuits. You do your family proud."

While Heath doubted his father had any particular knowledge of his whereabouts, much less pride in the matter, he couldn't help but be flattered by the sweet observation.

Being important because he was *Heath* had been his dream for as long as he could remember. He couldn't help his position within his family, couldn't help being born to riches, couldn't help someday inheriting the title. What he *could* help was other people.

And he was not ashamed to admit he preferred making a name for himself for that reason, rather than lounging indolently by whilst awaiting a title some ancestor had earned generations before.

"Shall I send you weekly updates on my progress?" he inquired.

Lady Roundtree wrinkled her nose. "Oh, do come by and let me know in person. I don't get out as much with these cursed splints on my leg, and sitting about the house can be so lonely."

Heath frowned in surprise. "I don't doubt that a broken leg offers nothing to recommend it, but surely you of all people are not lonely. You've countless friends, not to mention a companion who—"

Who lived under this very roof.

Who would be present every time Heath dropped by to update his client on their case.

Who might walk into this room at any moment.

Who Heath had daydreamed several times about kissing.

Who was not only a servant, but also now a *client's* servant, and therefore utterly and completely forbidden.

Chapter 9

*N*ora did her best to hold perfectly still so the hot tongs would not burn her scalp.

She still wasn't used to having a lady's maid at her disposal. Much less the thrice-daily wardrobe changes Lady Roundtree vowed were the bare minimum any self-respecting lady and her wide-eyed companion must adhere to.

The baroness would be shocked indeed to learn Nora found submitting to the process more than mildly embarrassing.

"Look to the left," ordered Pepys, the lady's maid responsible for making Nora presentable three times per day.

Nora obediently turned to the left.

It was either that or have her hair singed from her skull with a yank of the tongs.

Not that Pepys was cruel; she was a veritable artist with pins, tongs, and a roaring fire. The young woman claimed she could make anyone's hair match the fashion plate of their choosing, even someone like

Nora herself. Thus far, Pepys had worked positive magic.

As had Lady Roundtree's modiste. The day dress Nora wore of dusky pink figured muslin over a pale pink underdress was not only the finest gown Nora had ever worn, but also specifically tailored for her frame. The puffed sleeves were the perfect fit, the rose-colored ribbon encircling beneath her bosom at precisely the right height.

Whenever she glimpsed herself in a looking-glass, she no longer saw Nora from a farm in the West Midlands, or even Nora, poor relation and temporary employee. The stranger staring back at her was Miss Eleanora Winfield, a proper and well-groomed woman who looked like she could be mistaken as a young lady who belonged in the midst of the London Season.

"Now down," Pepys ordered.

Nora tilted her head toward the sketchbook in her lap, where she had been drawing imaginary gowns to wear to an equally imaginary ball. As much as she loved these dress-up sessions, she never forgot that the result was an illusion. So she drew a universe where it was not. Ballrooms where she belonged. Fashionable friends she would never have. Mr. Grenville's arms, reaching out to pull her close.

Her day would not be so exciting. If anything, she was surprised Lady Roundtree had gone this long without summoning Nora to her side. It would not do to anger the baroness.

"Are we nearly ready?" she asked Pepys, anticipating the maid's trademark, long-suffering sigh.

She was not disappointed.

"By now you should know that one cannot rush perfection," Pepys chastised her. "Lady Roundtree will thank you for ensuring your appearance fits her station. Think of the baroness."

Nora *was* thinking of the baroness. Fancy coiffures befitted Lady Roundtree's station, not Nora's. She couldn't see the logic in hiring someone to be a companion, and then essentially paying that person to spend hours each day primping in a guest chamber well out of sight of the person the companion was meant to be accompanying.

Even Captain Pugboat was here with Nora, rather than with his owner. He yipped softly in his sleep, wriggling in a patch of sunlight beside a spotless bay window.

She grinned despite herself. It was so nice to have a pet, even temporarily. At home, they could not afford to keep non-producing animals from a monetary standpoint, and also due to her aging grandparents' waning eyesight. The last thing Nora needed was for one of them to trip over a puppy, endangering both themselves and the pet.

The sketches she sent home of the myriad dogs she glimpsed would simply have to be enough.

"So lifelike!" Pepys exclaimed as Nora's fingers added Captain Pugboat as her accompaniment to the imaginary ball. "Where did you learn to do that?"

"I taught myself," Nora admitted. This was what she preferred to draw—realistic portraits and hyper-detailed fashions, not boring, simplistic caricatures. "From the time I was small, I've loved art. We rarely have money for paints, but I can always manage to scrounge up a bit of pencil lead. Eventually I figured out how to draw and shade and create various styles. It was just a way to entertain myself."

And now it was a means to an end. Not drawings like these, in which she could hold artistic pride, but the exaggerated cartoons she sent home to her brother to help fund the farm. The companion salary wasn't accruing fast enough, nor did it provide as much relief for her grandparents as the caricatures.

Nora's eyes shifted. She felt like a hypocrite sending a pittance home to her grateful family when even the towel she dried her face on each morning was more luxurious than anything her family could possibly afford. But what else could she do that she hadn't already tried?

"No long faces," Pepys said. "I'm nearly done."

"I wasn't scowling because of you." Nora stopped drawing. "I was just thinking about how different life will be when I go back home."

"Couldn't you find some other lady in need of a companion?" Pepys asked.

Nora grimaced. Was that what she wanted? A life of public servitude and secret sketches, far from her family? She ignored the loneliness in her belly. Perhaps it didn't matter what she wanted. All that mattered was her family.

"You don't think Lady Roundtree would let me stay on a bit after her splints come off?"

"The baron would never allow it," Pepys answered without hesitation. "Those splints are the only reason she has any company at all. I wouldn't be surprised if she broke her leg on purpose, just for a little attention."

Nora shuddered at the thought.

"Stop that," Pepys scolded. "I'll have to redo the last curl."

"You cannot mean it." Nora couldn't believe how sorry she'd come to feel for a woman who seemingly had everything. "Why marry her and then never wish to see her again?"

"He's the baron," Pepys said simply. "He has more important matters to attend to than a wife. All titled men do. That's what *ton* marriages are like."

Mr. Grenville's face flashed across Nora's mind. For the first time, she thought of him not as a charming and genuine Society gentleman, but as a future baronet. Would he be just as cold and distant as Lord Roundtree someday? With nary a moment or a care to spare for his wife?

She suspected it would break her heart to marry a man she loved, only for him to never again have time for her. And if she discovered that her love was one-sided, that he consciously *chose* not to fit her into a purposefully busy schedule... Her heart clenched at the thought. It would be as though she had not wedded a husband, but rather shackled herself to a daydream. A wish that would never come true.

And if the reason he did not have time for her was because his attentions were more eagerly spent at the club or in the practiced arms of a mistress...

"Henwit," she muttered under her breath.

What did it matter what kind of husband Mr. Grenville would be like? It wasn't as if Nora was in any danger of marrying anyone, least of all him. By the end of the Season, she wouldn't even be in London.

"There." Pepys handed Nora a mirror so she could view the maid's efforts in the vanity looking-glass. "What do you think?"

Nora stared at the elegant stranger reflected back at her.

All this finery, the elaborate hairstyles, the sweeping gowns, the luxurious bed, the imposing armoire, the lady's maid whose sole responsibility was to make Nora look like she belonged... She couldn't help but feel like she was living someone else's life.

"Beautiful," she said in awe.

She paged through her sketchbook. These detailed drawings had taken far more effort than the caricatures. Mixed in with endless pages of designs for ball gowns and daywear for fashionable ladies were an equal number of sketches of events that had never happened. Nora as the queen of a ball. Mr. Grenville inviting her to dance. A stolen kiss beneath the light of—

Nora snapped the book closed. It was one thing to sketch fanciful situations as if High Society were a fairy story. For girls like her, it certainly was. But she would do well not to confuse dreams with real life. Drawings did not come true.

"Truly?" Pepys stepped back to admire her handiwork. "You are pleased?"

"You've outdone yourself. Thank you." Nora set the sketchbook atop the vanity and woke Captain Pugboat from his nap. "Come along, snuggle pug. We're on companion duty."

She hurried down the stairs with the puppy bounding delightedly beside her, his interrupted nap completely forgotten with the promise of new adventure. Or at least a brief jaunt from one floor to another.

As they drew closer to Lady Roundtree's favorite salon, muffled voices wafted through the semi-open door.

Nora hesitated just out of sight.

If the baroness was entertaining, was Nora meant to enter as usual, or to keep a discreet distance?

She wished someone would explain the rules. High Society life was so different than the environment back home, where the only title in town was that of "vicar."

Her fingers clenched. Even if someone had penned a tome entitled *How to be a Proper Companion to one's Wealthy Distant Cousin who is also a Baroness*, she wouldn't have been able to read it anyway. The bouncing letters of the title alone would be too difficult to parse. Nora was just going to have to figure things out as she went along, like always.

She took a step forward just as a low, rich laugh reached her ears. Her heart warmed. Might Lord Roundtree finally have carved out a moment for his wife?

"She didn't!" Lady Roundtree exclaimed. "You Grenvilles are a force of nature!"

Grenvilles.

Mr. Grenville.

He was here. Why on earth was he here?

Obviously not for Nora. He had come to visit with Lady Roundtree. A peer. An equal. 'Twas nonsensical to feel disappointed. Nora hadn't come to London to receive callers, but to serve the baroness.

Yet she could not help wistfully imagining how she would sketch the scene tonight in the privacy of her guest chamber. Herself reposed in a salon, Mr. Grenville her gentleman caller, a duenna in the corner so that he should not forget himself in passion. She grinned at the fanciful idea.

"Come along Captain Pugboat," she murmured to the puppy circling excitedly about her feet. "Let us provide some companionship. At least you and I will be a united front."

Captain Pugboat immediately darted off toward the rear of the town house, leaving Nora alone in the corridor.

"Traitor," she muttered.

"Winfield, is that you?" Lady Roundtree called.

"Come join us."

Nora gritted her teeth.

On the one hand, it should be an honor to be invited to join a baroness and future baronet. On the other, remaining "Winfield" rather than "Miss Winfield"—or the far less likely "my cousin Nora"—in front of Mr. Grenville served to not-so-subtly remind her that she was being invited in as an employee, not an equal.

The implicit warning was wholly unnecessary. Nora was unlikely to forget where she stood, or why she was there.

When she stepped into the room, Mr. Grenville sprang to his feet, as if preparing to bow, or perhaps ensure she took her seat first.

Lady Roundtree motioned for Nora to join them. "This is Winfield, my companion. You may recall her presence in my carriage the other day in Hyde Park?"

"I have not forgotten." Mr. Grenville did not bow, but nor did he immediately retake his seat. "How do you do, Miss Winfield?"

"Very well, thank you." Nora dipped a curtsey and perched on the edge of the closest chair.

He retook his seat and held up a book that had been laid on a side table. "How about you? Have you read the latest?"

"Not yet," Nora stammered. Heat climbed up the back of her neck.

Not yet, not ever.

She didn't need to know the title or the author to realize the enjoyment of literature was yet another privilege they were never going to have in common.

Her palms began to sweat. Why had he mentioned the book? They weren't going to ask her to read from it, were they?

Panic assailed her. She could not squelch a rush of fear that after successfully avoiding being required to read aloud thus far, she was going to have to do so in front of Mr. Grenville, and thereby lose her companion post and his respect all in one fell swoop. Her heart pounded.

Mr. Grenville set the leather volume back onto the side table and turned to Lady Roundtree. "How does your book club determine which title to read next?"

Nora swayed, lightheaded with relief that it had been an idle question and not the harbinger of doom.

"We take turns, although perhaps we shouldn't, what with some people's shocking taste." Lady Roundtree affected a shiver.

Nora's eyes bounced between them as the baroness recounted an exhaustive list of past titles chosen, and why each was inferior to her own suggestions. Nora frowned in confusion. She had no idea what had brought Mr. Grenville to this town house today, but she did not imagine he'd come calling in order to better understand the intricacies of Society ladies' book club selections.

There was so much she didn't know. Were visits like these a normal occurrence? Were Mr. Grenville and Lady Roundtree friends? The gaps in her knowledge seemed to widen by the day.

"I suppose you would have fixed it in a trice," the baroness was saying. "You being the most famous professional problem-solver in all of London."

"I am the only professional problem-solver in all of London," Mr. Grenville said with a self-deprecating smile. "And I doubt your book club requires outside assistance. Women who are wise enough to read tend to be smart enough to solve their own problems."

"Oh, you flatterer." Lady Roundtree laughed in delight.

Nora did not.

She knew Mr. Grenville had meant no offense. Had, indeed, meant to compliment female-kind's capabilities. He would be disgusted to learn that she could barely sound out the short, simple letters she received from home.

Her stomach twisted. Of all people, she had no wish for him to look at her with disgust. Not when his opinion had begun to carry more weight than ever. She wanted him to *like* her. If only a fraction as much as she was coming to feel for him.

"Enough about book clubs." Lady Roundtree motioned to the tea table. "Why don't we—"

Captain Pugboat darted into the room and slid on the freshly waxed floor.

Just as the puppy was about to slide directly into the well-stocked tea table, Nora leapt from her chair and scooped him into her arms before he could cause irreversible damage.

"And who is this fine fellow?" Mr. Grenville asked, eyes twinkling.

Nora smiled back shyly. "This is Captain Pugboat."

"Captain.... Pugboat?" Mr. Grenville repeated doubtfully.

"Like a tugboat. But a pug, because he's a dog," Lady Roundtree explained. "A pug dog."

"Yes, I grasped the connection." He raised his brows in amusement. "Captain Pugboat seems like a very good boy."

"Of course he is. Winfield, show Mr. Grenville how he... How he..." Lady Roundtree covered her mouth with a gloved hand to hide an enormous yawn.

Nora sent a sharp glance to the tea table. Of course. Ever since she'd broken her leg, the barrenness had taken to adding a drop of laudanum to every cup of tea. It was not at all unusual for the baroness to fall asleep in the middle of conversations with Nora, but she doubted Lady Roundtree wished to do so in front of Mr. Grenville.

"Winfield?" the baroness began.

Nora was already halfway to the bell pull.

In moments, the same footmen who always carried the baroness upstairs to her bedchamber materialized in the salon with her wheeled chair at the ready.

"Tell him about Captain Pugboat," the baroness ordered as she was bundled into her chair. "Do forgive me, Mr. Grenville. I'm afraid my broken leg has got the better of me."

Mr. Grenville bowed to the retreating baroness. "May you recover quickly."

In the space of a breath, Nora was now alone in an empty salon with Mr. Grenville.

Of course there was no cause for a duenna, Nora realized with a start. As she was essentially a servant, it would never cross Lady Roundtree's mind to arrange a chaperone for her paid companion. It would be like hiring a lady's maid for her lady's maid.

Mr. Grenville had not retaken his seat, but nor had he fled from the parlor in horror at the sudden downward shift in his conversation partner. Indeed, he was gazing at her and the puppy with what appeared to be genuine interest.

"Do you ever let a face that cute out of your sight?" he inquired.

"Rarely," Nora admitted. "Although he *is* Lady Roundtree's pet. I merely care for him whilst she is unable."

Captain Pugboat wiggled up Nora's bodice in an attempt to lick her cheek, as if wishing to prove that Nora belonged to him rather than the other way around.

"I love pets," Mr. Grenville confessed. "I haven't one at the moment. Perhaps that is an oversight I should rectify. Do you favor any certain breeds?"

Nora shook her head. Captain Pugboat was the closest she'd ever come to having a pet of her own. She wished she had esoteric dog wisdom to impart that would make her seem just as clever as the cultured women who participated in book clubs.

"You look particularly lovely today." His gaze was intense and warm.

She shook her head. "You said that last time."

"It's been true every time," he said softly.

A flush crept up her cheeks. "I cannot take credit. The talent belongs to Lady Roundtree's talented lady's maid."

"You must take some of the credit." Mr. Grenville lifted his brows. "My mother has impressed upon me the tragedy that no lady's maid on earth is capable of curling my youngest sister's hair."

The corner of Nora's mouth twitched. "How many do you have?"

"Three, every one of them mad as a hatter. I love them all dearly." He grinned. "I'm afraid I am the only male. How about you? Brothers or sisters?"

"One. Carter has been both my brother and my best friend for as long as I can remember."

"Then you understand." Mr. Grenville nodded, as if confirming a suspicion. "That's how I feel about my sisters. There's nothing I wouldn't do for them. Although they don't make it easy," he added with an indulgent shake of his head.

"Siblings never do," Nora agreed with a tentative smile.

"I imagine you're quite proud of your brother," said Mr. Grenville.

She looked at him in surprise. "I am. But why should you think so?"

"Because I'm certain he's proud of you." Mr. Grenville's hazel eyes locked on hers. "Captain Pugboat seems like a marvelous judge of character."

"He likes belly rubs," she confessed. "He would leave with you right now if I allowed you to pet him."

He stepped forward. "May I?"

"Absolutely not." She pretended to keep Captain Pugboat out of Mr. Grenville's grasp. "I saw him first."

He lifted his brows. "Didn't Lady Roundtree see him first?"

"I saw him fifteenth," Nora amended. "But it's too late. He's ours."

"It's never too late," Mr. Grenville said as he rubbed behind Captain Pugboat's ears. "And I promise to never steal your beau."

Nora grinned back at him.

If she weren't herself and he weren't himself, she could easily fall in love with a man like him. He seemed wonderful. And exactly the wrong person to be exchanging a single word with.

He was not only a charming, attractive man, but also the only person outside of this household to give her the time of day. Once she left London, they were unlikely to see each other again. So why not enjoy the moment?

Captain Pugboat wiggled in her arms.

"Shh," she hushed him. "Be a good little snuggle pug."

The puppy ignored her and kept wiggling.

She glanced over at Mr. Grenville in embarrassment. "I fear it is past time for his afternoon walk."

Mr. Grenville sent a startled glance toward the open parlor door as if he only now realized how long they had been conversing alone. "I did not mean to disturb anyone's schedule. I shall leave you in peace."

Nora wished she could tell him to disturb her schedule anytime he wished. Instead, she dipped a curtsey.

Captain Pugboat immediately sprang from her arms and streaked straight to Mr. Grenville.

"Come back," Nora hissed urgently. "Captain Pugboat! Snuggle pug!"

It was too late.

Captain Pugboat had latched tight onto Mr. Grenville's leg, and began to pump his little pug hips against the side of Mr. Grenville's champagne-shined Hessians.

"Snuggle pug?" Mr. Grenville stared down at the wrinkly pug humping his leg. "That's... not snuggling."

Nora was unsure whether she was about to die of mortification or laughter.

"Perhaps it's a type of snuggling," she offered when Captain Pugboat showed no signs of stopping.

"Odd manner," Mr. Grenville said, his eyes twinkling. "I thought your snuggle pug was despoiling my ankle."

Nora tilted her head. "You do have shapely ankles."

He waved a stern finger at her. "Even shapely ankles should not live in fear of being caught in a pug-of-war."

"Pug of war!" She clapped her hands approvingly. "Excellent play on words. You, sir, are ready for your very own puglet."

Mr. Grenville glanced down. "I believe that's what he's trying to make right now."

"No, no. It shan't do. Not at the first tea." Nora dashed forward and yanked the flailing puppy from Mr. Grenville's defiled ankle. "Next time, try to play harder to get. You promised not to steal my beau."

"Please assure me this wasn't the trick Lady Roundtree wanted you to show me," he said drolly.

Nora burst into laughter. "Captain Pugboat has many tricks. His repertoire would amaze and astound you."

"Then I shall expect to be further amazed at every visit."

"Do you visit often?" she asked, unsure whether her voice trembled from hope or nervousness.

"I do now." The expression in Mr. Grenville's hazel eyes was unfathomable. "Until next time, Miss Winfield."

Without further explanation, he swept a bow worthy of a royal court and left her standing alone in an empty parlor with a yipping pug in her arms and a thousand questions in her heart.

Chapter 10

*A*re you certain my cravat isn't crooked?"
Heath asked his youngest sister.

"Why are you so worried of a sudden?"
Bryony arched an eyebrow. "Will Beau Brummel be in
the audience tonight, commissioning caricatures of
Society gentlemen with crooked cravats?"

Brummel had long since fled to France, and
Heath didn't give one whit what any caricaturist
thought of him. But when his valet had begun to ready
him for tonight's musical performance, Heath could
not help but wonder if Miss Winfield would be in the
audience.

Of course not. At least, probably not. She was
Lady Roundtree's companion, and Lady Roundtree
had a broken leg. The salon was far too crowded for
safety.

Then again, the injury did not seem to stop them
from attending any number of other Society functions. Soirées, tea gardens, carriage rides in the park.

The Grenville musicales were among the most

celebrated ton events of the Season, and if anyone were to risk the elbow-to-elbow packed ballroom with a broken limb, that person would be Lady Roundtree.

Accompanied by Miss Winfield.

His heart gave a strange twist. He *hoped* she was out there. Hoped she was under the family roof, in the same spacious chamber as his mother and father and siblings. Of course it was not the same thing as inviting her to meet his family. Heath and his sisters would be on stage, and as for their parents... No. Tonight he would be fortunate to merely catch a glimpse of her amongst such a large crowd.

Yet the thought of her in the audience, watching him, seeing his family, listening to their music, filled him with simultaneous joy and nervousness. His instrument was positioned at the rear of the dais for a reason. He was competent at the pianoforte, but no prodigy. His sisters were the ones who would truly impress.

He could not help but hope Miss Winfield loved hearing them as much as he did. Her opinion oughtn't to matter so much but, well, there it was. Heath would not be performing tonight just for his friends and family. He would also be performing for her. Surrounding the both of them with music.

Bryony frowned up at him. "Are you well? There's a flush to your cheeks."

"It's nothing," he said quickly.

He must remember that. There was nothing between Miss Winfield and him, and it had to stay that way.

And yet, the beat of his heart remained erratic. He needed tonight to be perfect just in case.

"Is my hair mussed?" he asked Bryony.

His sister burst out laughing. "It's supposed to be

mussed. Unkempt curls flopping every which way is the current rage. Peek through the curtains at the audience if you don't believe me."

Heath grinned back at her. "I meant, is my hair mussed enough? Should I let a badger run through it a few times before we start the show?"

She harrumphed. "You'll do."

A sudden wave of applause rustled through the audience on the other side of the curtain.

"Almost time," his sister called over her shoulder as she flounced off to fetch her violin.

Heath shook his head. He wasn't even certain Bryony bothered to practice her violin, and yet she still took everyone's breath away any time she placed her bow to the strings.

He turned to check on his other sister, and frowned.

Of all of them, Camellia was in a league above any other. Her soaring soprano was that of an angel, capable of making the hardest heart weep or sing for joy.

And for some reason, tonight her countenance was pasty and wan.

He hurried to her side. "What is it? Never say you are nervous. We've sung the same set for nearly a decade."

She looked up at him with a strange intensity shimmering in her eyes. "Aren't you tired of it?"

Heath blinked. Tired of a musical set he hadn't chosen, nor was particularly talented at reproducing? He'd been born tired of it.

That wasn't why he was here. He toiled at the pianoforte at the rear of the stage because someone had to in order to let his sisters shine.

All this time, he believed he was doing this for

them. Particularly for Camellia, who rarely opened her mouth in public for any other reason than to sing. To think that he had been wrong all these years...

"I thought you loved it," he stammered. "Performing, I mean."

"I do," she blurted, her face still alarmingly pale. "It's the one thing that brings me joy."

A wave of relief washed over him. He hadn't been wrong. But she'd had him worried.

Camellia was more than just the "good girl" of the clan. He would not have put it past her to sing at family musicales until she was eighty years old, merely because her mother asked it of her, and Camellia would never disappoint.

Something was amiss.

"If these musicales bring you so much joy, why do you look like you're about to crawl out of your skin?" he asked, careful to keep his tone light.

"These musicals don't bring me joy," Camellia said quietly. "Singing does."

He stared at her in confusion. "But that's what you do at the musicale. Bryony plays her violin, I bang a bit at the pianoforte, and you take center stage and sing."

"That's not what I want," Camellia whispered.

Blast. Performing before a crowded salon filled with everyone she'd ever known might be too much to ask of his shy wallflower of a sister.

He touched her cheek. "What do you want?"

Camellia blinked at him as if no one had ever asked before.

Heath swallowed his guilt, as he realized it might even be true. As the good girl, Camellia did what Society expected. She did whatever their mother expected. She behaved exactly as Heath expected. It had never occurred to him that any of it had been against her will.

"Tell me what you need," he said again.

"Not this stage, and not these songs." Her eyes were feverish, her jaw determined. "I don't want to perform at my parents' home anymore. I wish to be an opera singer."

Heath's world tipped on its axis. "A what?"

"An opera singer," she repeated louder. "I want to try songs that challenge me, to sing lyrics of love and loss, jealousy and joy. I want to perform on the greatest stages in England."

Heath stared at her in shock. Surely she was exaggerating. "Cam, if anyone hears you say that, your reputation will be ruined forever."

"I don't want them to hear me say it—I want them to hear me sing. *Real* songs." Camellia took a deep breath. "Tonight."

"Tonight?" Heath repeated hoarsely. "What do you mean, tonight?"

She gave him a considering look. "We've practiced other songs."

"We've always practiced other songs," he stammered. "We never intended to perform them publicly."

She shook her head. "You might not have, but I always did. This is my chance."

"Your chance to ruin yourself. I may suppress scandals for a living, Cam, but there is a limit to what I can do. You becoming an opera singer would be out of my hands."

Her gaze darkened. "My life should be in no one's hands but my own."

"Perhaps tonight you could sing one of the less salacious songs," Heath suggested quickly. He could not allow his sister to ruin her life. If their mother already despaired of her daughters one day finding good matches, publicly pursuing a career on the stage would ensure it never happened. "Do you understand what you're saying?"

"Do *you* hear what *I'm* saying?" Camellia's eyes took on a glassy sheen. "I want to be an opera singer. I'm tired of living a lie. I want to show London what I can really do. I'd hoped you might support me."

Her simple words slammed into his gut.

Of course he wished to support his sister. He had dedicated himself to supporting her since the moment she'd been born. He thought he *had* been supporting her.

He couldn't believe that he was just now learning his closest sister and bosom friend had long dreamed of pursuing a career on stage.

Heath was ashamed to realize the omission was undoubtedly because she anticipated him reacting in favor of mitigating any potential scandal such dreams could cause her, rather than maximizing the potential to realize those dreams. His stomach turned.

Should he let Camellia ruin her life, if that was what she wished to do? She was her own woman. And yet he was her big brother.

He had always been driven by a compulsion to do what was right. Never had he felt so conflicted. He wanted to give Camellia the freedom to live any life she picked, but he also wanted to protect her at all costs.

Letting his sister be hurt was the hardest thing she had ever asked him to do.

Another round of applause rumbled through the audience, and a footman swept the narrow curtain to welcome them on stage.

"It's time." Camellia hesitated. "Are you going to play the same set Mother arranged for us since we were children?"

Heath swallowed. Camellia was no longer a child. He was going to have to encourage her to follow her dream, even if doing so would ruin her life. The choice was hers.

"What do you want me to play?" he asked simply, despite the ice in his belly.

She lifted her chin. "The sequence we practiced the other day. We'll start with what they're expecting, then segue into the one they're doing this month at the Theatre Royal."

His stomach dropped. "Not... *Don Juan?*"

Camellia nodded. "The very one."

Of course it was. If one's goal was to destroy one's reputation, half measures would not do. That particular opera featured the most scandalous lyrics to sweep through London in years. But tonight was not about Heath. It was about supporting his talented sister. About fighting for one's dreams, no matter what the cost.

He turned to whisper the change of plans to Bryony, then stopped short when he saw the gentle expression on her face. Of course the minx already knew. Camellia's sisters were her best friends. Heath was the one they hadn't been certain would support such a radical decision.

In truth, he could not love the inevitability of her loss of reputation, loss of marriageability, loss of standing. But he did love his sister. For her, he would do anything.

Resolute, he followed Camellia out on stage.

Heath wanted to interrupt her, to protect her, to stop her from doing this reckless, irreversible thing.

He wanted to save her from the pointing fingers, the mocking laughter, the disparaging remarks, the empty dance card... If indeed she would still be invited anywhere.

Their sister Dahlia had lost almost all ties to Society, just for opening a school in the wrong neighborhood.

Willfully following a career path that was often synonymous with prostitution would be a thousand times worse. Society believed that any woman who was paid to perform on stage would be willing to accept money to perform any other act a man desired.

That was not Camellia. But it wouldn't matter; her comfortable Society life would be over.

But with a voice like hers, the best stages in London would just be the beginning. She was more than talented enough to take England by storm. She could become the most celebrated opera singer in all of Europe.

Starting this very night. With the support and unconditional love of her big brother, one of the first to unlock her cage and allow her to fly.

Heath put his fingers to the keys and began playing the accompaniment to the evening of his sister's downfall...

Or the beginning of the greatest adventure of her life.

Chapter 11

*N*ora sat at the outer edge of a sea of dames and dandies, crushed side-to-side and elbow-to-elbow in breathless anticipation of the spectacle about to unfold before them.

"I cannot believe I'm here," she whispered to Lady Roundtree.

The baroness lifted her fan so no one would see her gossiping with a paid companion. "Of course you cannot. No one forgets their first Grenville musicale."

Nora didn't bother to correct her misassumption.

'Twasn't just that she was about to witness a performance by the famed Grenville siblings, a feat which by all appearances was an honor and a privilege to everyone fortunate enough to receive an invitation.

It wasn't the *musicale* part of "Grenville musicale" that held her spellbound to her seat.

It was *Grenville*.

Nora was inside Heath Grenville's childhood home. A town house that had belonged to his family for two generations, according to Lady Roundtree.

Mr. Grenville's parents were under this very roof. Possibly inside the same overcrowded salon right this moment.

Even though she knew Mr. Grenville had his own bachelor gentleman's town house elsewhere in Mayfair, Nora could not help but feel that she was peering inside an intimate part of his life.

The entrance hall had been stunning. Spotless checkered floor despite the crush of visitors, intricate plasterwork decorating the high ceiling, a gorgeous staircase curving up to the next level.

The current salon was no less grand. Towering sash windows draped with elegant jade curtains, striped silk wall hangings in a paler tone to match, furniture and moldings and cartouches that Nora could only describe as beautiful and extremely expensive.

Toward the rear of the otherwise empty dais sat a gorgeous, lacquered pianoforte the likes of which she had never seen. Although she hadn't a single musical bone in her body, she itched to run her fingertips over the smooth keys, the delicate curves of the carved cypress housing.

"How many songs will they play?" she whispered to Lady Roundtree. "Is it always different?"

The baroness glanced over her shoulder to ensure they weren't being watched before leaning over the arm of her wheeled chair to whisper back. "Twelve. It's been the same set for years, and as you can see, the fashionable set will never tire of it. *We* know quality."

Nora belatedly recalled herself. She was not the fashionable set, and the baroness was not her personal guide to Grenville musicales. If she could not keep her curiosity in check, she would not be attending another.

"I'm sorry," she whispered. "I didn't mean to be impertinent."

Lady Roundtree hesitated, then opened a painted fan to hide her words from any onlookers. "You are correct to realize that any person in another's employ should remain silent unless first addressed. However, as my companion, whenever we are in a situation where we are unlikely to be seen or overheard... I give you permission to speak freely."

Nora blinked. "You what?"

"*Use your fan*," Lady Roundtree hissed.

Nora unfurled her fan and positioned it just like the baroness. "You give me permission to speak freely?"

"Not *here*, Winfield," Lady Roundtree clarified. "At home, whenever we won't be disturbed."

Nora's teeth clacked together as she immediately closed her mouth, but inside her mind was whirling. The baroness quite understandably would not wish to publicly fraternize with an employee, but the explicit request to be herself whilst ensconced in the privacy of the Roundtree town house...

On the one hand, it felt like yet another double life. But on the other hand, it felt like *freedom*. Freedom to be herself, if only for a few hours each day.

Before she could ruminate more on this surprising turn of events, a footman swept aside the heavy velvet curtain and the first of three dark-haired Grenville siblings stepped out on the stage.

"Miss Camellia Grenville," the baroness whispered behind her fan. "The only one of her sisters not destined to shame her family. The one with the violin is Miss Bryony Grenville. Once again, she didn't bother to curl her hair for the occasion."

Nora was no longer listening. Her pulse had skipped the moment Mr. Grenville emerged from the shadows, and she had not so much as blinked since. How was it possible that he grew more handsome every time she saw him?

His gleaming black boots looked spotless and shiny even from across the room. His formal knee breeches and the dark superfine of his evening coat contrasted brilliantly with the snowy white of an intricately tied neckcloth against a gold silk waistcoat. His dark, perfectly tousled hair looked soft and inviting, but his strong jaw was set at an angle to invite no disruption.

Nora could not tear her gaze from him. How he strode across the dais, how he was far from dwarfed by the enormous pianoforte, how he commanded every stuttering breath she took just from being in the same room. And when he began to play—

"That's the first arrangement," Lady Roundtree whispered from behind her fan. "I told you; there will be no surprises tonight. Wait until you hear Miss Grenville sing."

When the youngest sister lifted her violin to her shoulder, Nora could feel the vibrations of the music beneath her seat, along the arms of her chair, inside her very bones.

But when the eldest opened her mouth to sing, the entire world fell away. Never had Nora heard a voice so pure, so rich and textured. If choirs of angels filled the heavens, they must sound exactly like Camellia Grenville. Each note transported the rapt audience out of their bodies and into the soaring melody itself.

And still Nora's eyes were not on the incredible

soprano or the impressive violinist, but on the devastatingly handsome gentleman whose fine fingers flew across the keys of the pianoforte, yet his eyes appeared lost somewhere far away.

The song ended and another began, even more haunting and arresting than the first.

Lady Roundtree and the rest of the breathless crowd were in raptures.

Nora's forehead creased. The anguished concentration on Mr. Grenville's face hinted he was building up to something far more powerful than a mere crescendo. As if this familiar arrangement he could no doubt play in his sleep was tonight a beast to be vanquished, a battle to be won.

When the song ended without incident, her lungs let out a breath she hadn't realized she'd been holding.

"Is it always like this?" murmured a male voice in the row behind her.

Nora's shoulders relaxed. Apparently she was not the only interloper amongst this crowd of well-heeled regulars. The gentleman must have been just as swept away as she was.

"Always," a low voice responded to him. "Although tonight is even better than—"

All whispers stopped as Mr. Grenville began the next melody, leaving the entirety of the audience frozen in place like a life-sized glass menagerie.

In alarm, Nora turned wide eyes toward Lady Roundtree just as the gentleman behind her whispered, "What is it? What's happening?"

"It's...a new song," came another man's disbelieving voice. "It's *never* a new song."

Camellia Grenville stepped up to the edge of the dais to face her peers.

"Tonight, I am going to sing an aria currently being performed at the Theatre Royal in Covent Garden." She took a deep breath and smiled at the crowd. "With luck, the next time I perform, it will be on that stage."

A collective gasp ran through the audience.

Before anyone could begin to process the shocking announcement, she opened her mouth and began to sing.

Nora stared in awe and disbelief. Miss Grenville had been born to vast advantages that someone like Nora could not begin to imagine, and yet was willingly tossing it all away to pursue a dream she might never achieve.

More startlingly, her elder brother wasn't just allowing it to happen. He steadfastly played an operatic accompaniment despite the pallor in his cheeks, despite the horrified murmurs in the crowd, despite the obvious anguish on his face. Her heart flipped.

This was a man who loved his family just as much as Nora loved hers.

When the song ended, scattered applause sounded from a few brave souls whilst the rest of the crowd erupted into cacophony, each outraged opinion vying to be heard over the din.

Others simply stood up and walked out of the room in disgust.

"*Don Juan: A Grand Opera in Two Acts*," Lady Roundtree whispered behind her fan. "She shouldn't even *know* about such things, much less sing them."

But she didn't motion for her footmen to wheel her from the room. A significant percentage of the audience appeared just as glued to their seats as Nora was, on tenterhooks to see what would happen next.

Poor Mr. Grenville. And his sister! Nora's heart

twisted for the entire family. It had taken a lot of courage for the siblings to be complicit in such a display, and even more bravery for Camellia to destroy her easy path in favor of a difficult one she felt passion for.

An elegant lady with a silver-streaked chestnut chignon leapt up from the first row and whirled toward the crowd in an obvious panic. "Everybody go home! The musicale is over. Out! Out!"

"Lady Grenville," the baroness whispered behind her fan. "Normally, such crass shrieking would be the talk of the Town by morning, but I rather suspect no one will recall a word she says tonight because they're all too focused on Camellia. Mark my words, that chit will be the next face you see in the caricatures."

Nora's sympathy twisted into self-loathing. She had not been thinking about the caricatures. She had not been thinking about the repairs needed on the farm or her grandparents' fragile health or the boatload of money she could earn for her desperate family by turning the Grenville family's pain into a city-wide mockery.

But could she afford not to?

Chapter 12

*M*ore ribbons!" demanded Lady Roundtree from the closest chaise. "He's not
pretty enough yet."

"Hold still, pup." Nora settled Captain Pugboat
on her lap—as much as one could settle a wriggling
puppy anywhere—and reached for the pile of yellow
ribbons. "If I tie any more to his collar, he'll look like
a wrinkle-faced lion."

"He'll look like a prince," the baroness corrected
with a sniff. "Have you not seen my great-grandfa-
ther's likeness in the Hall of Portraits?"

Nora wasn't certain any resemblance between
the baroness's ancestor and her plump, tail-wagging
Pugmalion could be remotely construed as a compliment to either individual.

As she dutifully added more bright yellow bows
to his leather collar, her fervent hope was that Mr.
Grenville would not sweep into the salon and catch
sight of her lunging about the carpet in an attempt to
turn a pug into a lion.

When the last of the ribbons had been added to Captain Pugboat's mane, Nora lifted her brows toward her patroness. "Now is he properly leonine?"

"He is a lion *king*." Lady Roundtree patted the empty footstool before her. "Now set him here."

With a dubious glance down at the yipping, wriggly puppy, Nora swung the pudgy lion king up from her lap and placed him in the center of the footstool.

Captain Pugboat immediately flipped onto his back in an attempt to gnaw the ring of yellow bows tickling his wrinkled chin.

"Make him sit still," Lady Roundtree ordered.

Nora wished it were so easy. "He's a dog."

"A dog who will ruin the portrait if you can't make him behave," Lady Roundtree insisted.

"I draw from my imagination," Nora said for what felt like the hundredth time. "I can sketch him bouncing on his tail or playing a flute, if that's what you want. He doesn't have to really do it."

In fact, the longer they dilly-dallied, the more likely someone would come to call and catch Nora in the act.

A puppy top-heavy with curling yellow ribbon could easily be explained as one of Lady Roundtree's many eccentricities. Nora's skill with pencils, on the other hand... Even though she sketched and shaded her realistic portraits in a style completely unlike the ink cartoons, it would still be best if no one outside this household learned of her proclivity.

Especially not someone like Mr. Grenville.

"He's not listening!" The baroness's voice rose higher with each word. "I need Captain Pugboat on this footstool. The portrait must come out perfectly."

Nora flipped the puppy onto his stomach and held him in position for several seconds. "Stay."

The moment she let go, Captain Pugboat immediately rolled paws-up.

She returned him back upright and repeated the process, holding him in place for an extra few beats. "*Stay.*"

He licked the tip of her nose.

"Don't let him do that," Lady Roundtree shrieked. "It isn't seemly!"

"He's a dog," Nora repeated with deliberate patience. Carefully, she lifted her hands from his soft, wrinkled sides. "Please stay. I'll give you all the teacakes when we're done."

Captain Pugboat gave his curled tail several enthusiastic swishes, then closed his eyes.

"Is he looking in the right direction?" Lady Roundtree fretted. "He'll ruin the portrait if he isn't bright-eyed and leonine."

Nora placed her sketchbook on her knees. "Do you want me to draw a dog or a lion?"

"I want you to draw *my* dog," the baroness explained. "Like a lion."

"Of course," Nora murmured beneath her breath, and picked up her pencil.

She would draw as fast as she could. Not just to reduce the chance of discovery, but also because her mind was still reeling from last week's musicale.

Every moment had been thrilling.

Although the audience could not decide whether the soprano or the violinist was more gifted, Nora's gaze had been locked on Heath Grenville at the pianoforte in back. She'd felt Mr. Grenville's presence before he walked out on the dais. Even during his sister's jaw-dropping announcement, Nora had been unable to tear her eyes from him.

Mr. Grenville had been the only one in the room

who didn't look shocked. He had known the announcement was coming, that a scandal this big would be unveiled.

Her publisher considered it a perfect caricature opportunity. Had already offered to triple her price. Yet Nora could not bring herself to draw the moment of Camellia Grenville's ruination, no matter how much money she was offered.

Lady Roundtree's head jerked up from the pillows. "Would this be easier with watercolors?"

"It would not be easier with watercolors," Nora replied distractedly.

Not for her, at least. Paints of any sort had been far too dear in her family, and she'd rarely had an opportunity to practice.

Drawing, on the other hand... She'd had plenty of practice. And for the first time, what had begun as a lonely habit was now granting her the ability to provide for the family that had always provided for her. Nora had sworn to help them in any way she could. Yet here she was, sketching a leonine puppy for free rather than a caricature whose earnings could restock the empty larder.

Was it selfish of her not to draw the Grenvilles' pain? Her family was suffering, too. Grandmother and Grandfather weren't fighting to save their reputations, but to have enough to eat.

While Nora was here in this comfortable home refusing to dash off a simple cartoon, her little brother was home toiling as *un*paid companion, as maid-of-all-work, as farmhand, as footman, as scullery maid, as caretaker.

That was the family she owed her loyalty to. The Winfields, not the Grenvilles. So why was her stomach tied up in knots?

Lady Roundtree popped her head back up from the pillows. "I can purchase watercolors. I know where to find the best ones."

"It would be a *watercolor* if I were painting with watercolors," Nora explained patiently. "This is a drawing. I sketch drawings with pencil. Please relax, Lady Roundtree. Everything is fine."

Except it wasn't, was it? Her heart beat for one person, yet she had an obligation to another.

Foolish to be torn to pieces over such a thing. It didn't matter how fervently her heart beat for Mr. Grenville. He would not want her even if he knew how she felt. Why would he?

Despite growing up only a few hours' distance from London, she was exactly the green country girl his peers all thought she was. She just happened to be able to draw.

What else was someone like Nora to do with a pencil? Correspondence was out of the question for someone who could not make letters stand still on the page. Nor could she be governess in some nursery. Nannies were expected to know how to read. Essays, literature, primers. Even scullery maids would be expected to follow a simple shopping list for market days.

For someone like Mr. Grenville, a public attachment to Nora would be far worse than a public scandal. She would be a disappointment. An ugly, shameful embarrassment, even in private.

Baronesses were expected to be able to do so much more than *read*. They were expected to be absolutely perfect.

Lady Roundtree lifted her head again. "Do you have enough pencils? I can purchase more, you know. I know where to find the finest in all of London."

"You've purchased more fine pencils than I could use in a lifetime," Nora assured her. "Please don't worry about the sketch. I have everything I need."

Clearly unconvinced, Lady Roundtree lowered her head back down to the pillows.

The beautiful, wood-cased pencils and soft, cubed rubbers the baroness had purchased for Nora were a far cry from the bits of graphite encased in paper that Carter had somehow procured when they were children. Before the management of the farm had fallen completely on their shoulders.

Even the simple luxury of having nothing to do today but draw was so foreign as to make Nora feel as though she were constantly shirking some important task.

Drawing Lady Roundtree and her puppy was no chore—it was a dizzying pleasure. Nora would never tire of being afforded the privilege of losing herself in her art.

Lady Roundtree gasped and lifted her head. "Do you have enough foolscap?"

The corner of Nora's mouth twitched. "One page should be enough for one drawing."

"You have only one sheet left?" the baroness shrieked in alarm.

"There is plenty of paper," Nora assured her. "I have a half-dozen untouched sketchpads. Please don't worry."

The baroness's fretting over the state of Nora's art supplies could not help but warm her heart.

Over the past few weeks, she had come to realize Lady Roundtree wasn't the judgmental Society matron she presented herself to be, so much as a fussy old lady who loved hearing herself complain.

The baroness even nattered to Captain Pugboat

when she thought no one could overhear. Her criticisms were not personal, or even meant to rebuke anyone. Hers was just the voice of a lonely woman who yearned to be heard.

Lady Roundtree turned her head toward Nora. "What if it doesn't come out right?"

"I promise I'm drawing Captain Pugboat as an astonishingly leonine puppy," Nora managed to say with a straight face.

"Not him!" The baroness's lip trembled. "Me."

Nora hesitated. "Are you meant to be leonine as well? Or in a costume of sorts?"

"Of course not. I'm a baroness. A lady accepts nothing less than the unvarnished truth." She immediately returned her head to her pillow as if the interruption had never occurred.

Frowning, Nora stared at her for a long moment before picking the pencil back up and continuing the baroness's sketch.

How she loved to do *real* drawings, rather than caricatures. The level of attention required for a truly realistic portrait was so much more intense... and so much more rewarding than the silly cartoons she dashed off in a matter of minutes. The hardest part of those was managing to add a legible caption.

The last caricature Nora had drawn had been a few days ago, when Lady Roundtree's husband had returned home drunk as a wheelbarrow and a thousand pounds poorer. Nora could not imagine possessing such a fortune, much less losing it over a bottle of port at some gaming hell.

When she'd learned the gambling den in question was an infamous gentlemen's club known as the Cloven Hoof, her imagination had caught fire. Particularly when the baroness claimed that all any proper lady knew of the club's enigmatic owner was that he was tall, dark, and dangerous.

Nora had immediately sketched a rear portrait of a dapper gentleman with impeccable style and cloven hooves overlooking a packed gambling house.

The caption beneath had read, "The road to me is paved with gold intentions..."

Nora smiled to herself. Very well, she *did* occasionally enjoy the caricatures as well. They might not be her passion, like drawing gowns and fashion plates, but they were a welcome release in their own way.

Most of the time.

Her smile faded as she thought again about the musicale. What would she do if her publisher forced her to create a cartoon mocking the Grenville scandal?

She could not bring herself to hurt Mr. Grenville or his family. But if she were faced with a choice between saving face for them, or saving the family farm back home... it wouldn't be a choice at all. She needed to earn as much as possible while she was still in London to do so. Once she went back home, there would be no time for sketches of any sort. Far too much work awaited her on the farm.

Lady Roundtree lifted her head. "About what I said..."

"I vow to sketch you with the unvarnished truth a proper lady requires," Nora promised.

"Not completely unvarnished," the baroness said hesitantly. "But maybe... pretty? I don't mind if you include Captain Pugboat's wrinkles, but in the interest of time, I'll find it acceptable if you fail to capture all of mine."

Nora paused. "Pretty, and unwrinkled?"

Lady Roundtree's eyes shimmered. "Is it impossible?"

"Pretty and unwrinkled is what I always see when I look at you," Nora assured her, her smile gentle. "But I shall ensure such details are not lost to the viewer."

When Lady Roundtree reclined against her pillows anew, Nora took extra care to depict the baroness as a younger, more carefree version of herself. As carefree as Nora wished she herself was.

How she longed for the baroness to view her as more than a servant! Nora saw so much more in Lady Roundtree than a patroness. More, even, than just distant cousins. Nora saw her as a person with hopes and dreams. She was beautiful just as she was, wrinkles and warts and all.

She wished the baroness could see past "Winfield" the employee to the real Nora.

But of course that could never happen. In reality, even if they truly could become "friends" within private quarters, outside these doors their differing statuses created too wide a chasm to bridge. Barons and baronesses would never see someone like Nora as an equal.

She focused on her sketch. The baroness and Nora could be friends and cousins only inside her active imagination.

"It's just... I'm doing this for Lord Roundtree," the baroness said without lifting her head from the pillows. "A gift. So he can see me even when he's too busy to come out of his study."

Nora's pencil stilled. "A fine gift for the lord of the house."

"He doesn't approve of pets," Lady Roundtree added in a small voice. "But I thought... maybe just on paper..."

Nora's throat grew tight.

"I'll make it perfect," she promised, her voice firm. "It will be the best sketch I have ever drawn."

This was how she could be helpful. How she could prove herself as so much more than some uninterested chit suffering through her employer's endless stories because she was paid to be there.

If Nora lived in London with her grandparents, she would voluntarily spend time with Lady Roundtree. And draw her as many pretty, wrinkle-free pictures as she wished.

"There." With a final flourish, Nora handed her the drawing.

Lady Roundtree burst into tears.

Horrified, Nora reached for the offending sketch. "Wait, I can fix it!"

"It's perfect," Lady Roundtree whispered, clutching it to her chest. "Thank you."

Nora wished it weren't unseemly for a paid companion to give her patroness a warm hug. She had a feeling Lady Roundtree could use one just as much as Nora.

A knock sounded at the front door.

Nora scrambled to hide her pencils. "Perhaps Mr. Grenville has come to call."

Lady Roundtree shook her head. "No, he just gave me a status update."

Nora frowned. A status update about what? Something to do with the baron? Was he visiting mistresses as well as the Cloven Hoof?

A footman appeared at the door. "Lady Agnes Febland is here."

"Show her in, of course."

Nora leaped to her feet to be prepared to curtsey. When she recognized the bejeweled guest as the lady in Hyde Park who had hated both Lady Roundtree's dog and the color of Nora's hair, little urge to curtsey remained.

"There you are," Lady Febland said to the baroness, ignoring Nora's curtsey altogether. "I've just come from the monthly book club gathering and, as one might notice, *you* were not present."

Lady Roundtree placed her new sketch on the side table out of her visitor's view. "I decided to stay home today."

"How boring. It is so good I came." Lady Febland seated herself across from the baroness and raised her brows toward Nora. "I'm sure the help has a chore she could be applying herself to somewhere else."

Nora paused in the act of retaking her own seat, her cheeks aflame.

"Miss Winfield stays," Lady Roundtree said firmly. "Did anything of note occur during today's meeting?"

Miss Winfield stays.

Nora eased into a high-backed armchair with far more confidence than she'd felt a moment earlier. Not only had Lady Roundtree undercut the countess's obvious desire to rid the parlor of pesky companions, the baroness had done so by referring to Nora as *Miss* Winfield. Not just "Winfield."

Miss. As if Nora was just as much a welcome guest as any bejeweled countess.

Lady Febland wrinkled her nose as if the rebuke smelled like spoilt milk. "In any case, we scarcely spoke about the book. Have you seen the Cloven Hoof caricature?"

"'The road to me is paved with gold intentions,'" Lady Roundtree quoted without hesitation. "Not that I approve."

"They call him 'Saint Max.'" Lady Febland's thin

lips curved in a knowing smile. "Because he is anything but."

A frisson of panic slid down Nora's spine. Who had referred to the club's owner as Saint Max? *She* certainly hadn't. The drawing hadn't even shown his face, because Nora had no inkling as to what the man might look like. She had been taking such care to avoid another "Lord of Pleasure" situation!

Lady Roundtree reached for her cup of tea. "I don't even know the man."

"I've heard he's worth getting to know," Lady Febland said with a wicked smile. "If one doesn't mind being relegated to the shadows. Thanks to that caricature, he's all anyone can talk about. Even the men are in a tizzy to declare themselves patrons of Saint Max."

Maxwell Gideon was a vice merchant, Nora reminded herself firmly when her stomach began to churn. The man ran a gaming hell designed to take people's money. By the sound of it, his club was more popular than ever. Nora had inadvertently done him a grand favor.

But she had nothing to do with his ironic new nickname.

"My husband frequented all the best establishments long before there were caricatures," Lady Roundtree said. "I'm surprised his face was not among the gamblers pictured."

"I didn't recognize a single one," Lady Febland agreed, then lowered her voice. "You don't suppose the artist is trying to show that the club is primarily frequented by *commoners*?"

Nora heroically refrained from groaning aloud.

The artist's sole intention had been to help feed her family, without inventing new gossip for the sketch's subject, nor implicating anyone else in the process. The faces in the background had been invented whole cloth on purpose.

Even the caption was no earth-shattering revelation. The gaming hell was literally named the Cloven Hoof. The pun had been *right there* all along. Nora had simply been the first to think of it.

"I don't think one should obsess about such silly things." Lady Roundtree lifted her tea. "We have given this anonymous caricaturist far too much power."

Nora stared at the wealthy titled women chatting over a gold-embossed tea set that was worth more than her family's farm.

Power? The word tasted foreign on her tongue. From the moment she had arrived in London, she could not have felt more powerless. And yet Lady Roundtree was right: Nora's drawings indeed held power. They allowed her a say in a world in which she was otherwise silenced.

"I, for one, cannot wait to see what he makes of the Grenville scandal," Lady Febland continued. "I was shocked by the complete lack of caricatures after the eldest became an opera singer, of all wretched things, but I know he cannot disappoint me again. The upcoming wedding is simply too delicious an opportunity."

Lady Roundtree put down her cup. "I believe Camellia Grenville made a good match."

"Oh, she certainly did. What one cannot stomach is our own Lord of Pleasure, not just gadding about as if she made a perfectly acceptable countess, but openly gawking at her during performances as though the Grenville chit were a siren who had bewitched his very soul."

Nora's spine straightened. She did not know Camellia Grenville or her betrothed, but she was
nonetheless indignant on their behalf. How could being in love with one's talented wife possibly be
construed as something to be embarrassed about?

The only thing shameful about it was his peers'
gleeful delight in mocking the happy couple for
achieving what the others had not.

Love.

"I hope the next caricature is of her getting the
comeuppance she deserves for strutting about on
stage like a common actress," Lady Febland said. "Or
of Lord Wainwright returning to his 'Lord of Pleasure'
ways in a dark theater box while she warbles below."

Nora stared at the countess in horror.

Those were *ghastly* ideas, mean-spirited and
cruel for no reason other than to deprive someone else
of their happiness. To make women like the countess
feel even more superior to those around her.

Nora's mind immediately filled with a much better scenario. She would give gossips like Lady Febland
the opposite of what they wanted to see.

Instead of ridiculing Camellia Grenville or Lord
Wainwright, Nora's caricature would mock Society's
ridiculous taboo against a perfectly happy husband in
love with his marvelously talented wife.

Caption: "Bad *ton*! Not done!"

"I'm afraid I cannot stay." Lady Febland rose. "If
I'm to pick out a tiara for tonight's ball, I simply must
come to a decision between sapphires and emeralds."

Nora scrambled to her feet. She had never been
happier to dip a farewell curtsey in her life.

Once the countess was gone, Lady Roundtree
poured herself more tea. "Agnes is far from the only
person entertained by others' sudden falls from grace.

The 'Lord of Pleasure' sketch was a dangerous precedent, if you ask me."

Nora swallowed hard.

Lady Roundtree would have no way of knowing that the artist had also been shocked by the overnight infamy of her sketch, and had sworn to never again invent tongue-in-cheek nicknames for the sake of captioning a caricature. From that moment, Nora only sent home drawings featuring the same information printed in any number of scandal columns within the popular newspapers.

But that wasn't enough. If her plume had power, it should be wielded for good works. To defend the innocent and point out hypocrisy.

More importantly, her family was counting on that money.

Carter had intended to buy more sheep with what she'd earned so far, but between refilling the larder, patching a neglected roof, and hiring a surgeon to finally address their grandparents' various ailments, not a penny had remained.

Without the extra income from Nora's cartoons, there was no hope of lifting the farm from poverty. The caricatures were their only way out.

Chapter 13

*D*ays later, Nora had just finished playing an after-luncheon round of Casino with Lady Roundtree when a footman came to announce that Mr. Grenville had come to call and had been shown into the front parlor.

Her stomach immediately filled with both dread and excitement. All she could think about was how much she truly liked him, and how furious he would be if he ever found out who she really was.

"Show him to the front parlor," Lady Roundtree ordered. "We'll be there presently."

Nora looked up from the cards she had been straightening. "We?"

Lady Roundtree frowned. "You are my companion, are you not?"

Nora gulped. That was indeed one of the things that she was. She was also in deep trouble.

For the past week she'd found herself sketching fantasies of Mr. Grenville when she should be doing other things. Drawing impossible dreams. Him, as her

suitor. Her, attending his sister's well-publicized wedding. She and Mr. Grenville, locked in an embrace.

Nonsense, all of it. Nora knew better. Her days
here were numbered.

No good could come of any relationship between
them, no matter how platonic and benign. Yet the
more fervently she resolved to keep her distance, the
more irresistible the idea of him became.

Was he not perfect in almost every way? Clever
and kind, handsome and happy, popular and powerful. It was that last point where things got sticky. Even
without the shameful secret she must keep from him
at all costs, his title elevated him well out of her grasp.

And yet, her sketchbooks overflowed with moments they would never share.

"Perhaps I should stay here," she suggested.
"Didn't you say he was working on something for you?
I'm sure you don't want anyone to overhear."

"Come, come," Lady Roundtree said in bafflement. "A servant can put away the playing cards. You
are meant to be accompanying me."

Nora rose on unsteady limbs. Yesterday, she had
become "Miss Winfield." Today, she was *not a servant*.

Mayhap it was not quite the same thing as "cousins" but it was an acknowledgement so much greater
than Nora had ever hoped for.

Even if such praise was only in private, it meant
more to Nora than brand new boots and pretty gowns.
For a baroness like Lady Roundtree, money was
meaningless. Until recently, Nora had been meaningless, too.

Today, she mattered more than before.

After ringing for footmen to help the baroness
with her wheeled chair, Nora nervously smoothed the

soft pink percale of her day dress.

Mr. Grenville was waiting on the other side of the townhouse. He might think of Nora as Lady Roundtree's servant, but he had never failed to address her as Miss Winfield. As if she deserved the same courtesies as any other young lady of his class.

How she wished it were true. That she were of his class, that she were *like* all the other young ladies.

Instead, she was a simple country girl with a complicated double life. A secret that would erase the warmth from Mr. Grenville's hazel eyes forever.

As she followed Lady Roundtree and the footmen from the room, Nora glanced at the Ormulu clock upon the mantel. Her reputation, such as it was, only mattered for the next month or two. Yet she must guard it carefully in order to maximize this opportunity for her family. Time was limited. She could not risk exposing the truth—or her heart—to Mr. Grenville. Yet the pull was impossible to deny.

When they entered the front parlor, he was standing at the bay window looking out, bathed in sunshine. Her heart sang at the sight. Tousled brown hair, crisp white cravat, well-made coat, form-fitting buckskins, gleaming black boots.

Nora could spend the rest of her life drawing gentlemen's fashion plates based on nothing more than memories of how perfectly Mr. Grenville filled his tailored clothes. He was exquisite.

At the sound of their wheeled approach, Mr. Grenville spun to greet them. A delighted smile spread across his face when he realized the baroness was not alone.

"Lady Roundtree, beautiful as ever." He swept a formal bow, then turned to Nora. "Miss Winfield, stunning as always."

She opened her mouth to ask if this was how he greeted all the young ladies.

But before she could utter a word, he added with a warm smile, "I cannot decide if you are a rose or a ruby. Pink truly does suit you, you know."

Nora's teeth snapped shut as a blush crawled up her cheeks. She doubted he compared anyone else to a ruby. Perhaps his compliments had never been empty after all.

Perhaps he really did find her beautiful.

"Thank you." She found herself babbling like a featherwit. "I'm not sure which I'd rather be. Roses have thorns and jewels are sharp and cold—"

"I meant nothing of the sort," Mr. Grenville's gaze was heated. "I meant as precious and beautiful as a ruby, as soft and delicate as the petal of a—"

"That's enough. We can't have Winfield's head getting too big." Lady Roundtree instructed the footman as to which settee she wished to recline upon. "Any new gossip about the caricaturist?"

Mr. Grenville forced his gaze from Nora with obvious effort. "Not yet, but it shan't take long. The despicable villain will be unmasked in no time."

Nora choked at the word "despicable." So much for her brief experience with romantic banter. Already she missed the warmth of his gaze. She far preferred Mr. Grenville to think of her as precious and soft than a villain to be reviled.

"Are the drawings so terrible?" she asked timidly.

Lady Roundtree sighed. "You haven't seen them for a reason, child. I would never pass around such filthy gossip."

Nora refrained from mentioning that almost all of the drawings were moments she had heard about secondhand from the baroness's lips.

Mr. Grenville turned to face her, his tone earnest, but his eyes hard. "All people have a basic right to privacy. No one should broadcast their neighbor's faults or profit from exploiting others' peccadillos."

Nora did not think it would help her case to point out that not only did her captions fail to reveal anything High Society didn't already know, they also did not in any way alter her subjects' pre-existing reputations.

She simply bowed her head in silence and took the chair beside the baroness. They waited for the footmen to arrange the settee for transfer. Nora sent a nervous glance toward the door.

Mr. Grenville was positively the worst person for her to be anywhere near if she intended to keep her secret. Yet she could not flee; Lady Roundtree had insisted on her companion's company.

Nora straightened her shoulders and affected a blank stare. She would simply have to act perfectly normal. Subservient. Disinterested. Unremarkable.

As the footmen prepared to move the baroness from her chair to the settee, Mr. Grenville stepped forward and held up a hand to halt them.

"Before you install yourself in this parlor on my account, I have news to share." His eyes shone. "The Dulwich Picture Gallery is open to the public at last. Would you care to accompany me, madam? You cannot stay cooped up all day. There is a special exhibition on display."

Nora tried not to feel slighted that only the baroness was invited. One did not invite one's peers' servants on outings. She knew that.

But from the first moment she'd heard about the Dulwich Picture Gallery, she had been consumed with the desire to attend.

There were no special exhibitions back home. No gallant gentleman to escort her. No money to pay for tickets.

She would simply have to hope that, just like on every other occasion, the baroness returned eager to share with Nora every single moment of what had transpired.

Nora fervently hoped the baroness had a picture-perfect memory.

"And your companion, of course," Mr. Grenville added before Lady Roundtree could respond. "I am certain you would not wish to be without her."

"A picture gallery," the baroness said, as if tasting the idea. "Miss Winfield positively adores pictures. Why, just the other day we dressed Captain Pugboat as a lion and—"

"Thank you," Nora said quickly, interrupting her patroness in as polite a manner as she could devise. This was not the ideal audience for extolling one's talent with a sketchbook, even if the drawing styles were completely different from the caricatures. "I would be honored to accompany the two of you to such a prestigious event."

"Well, of course you'd be honored. You're from the country." Amused, Lady Roundtree turned to Mr. Grenville. "Miss Winfield has probably never been to a gallery in her life."

Nora smiled tightly.

If her patroness painted her as a country bumpkin to Mr. Grenville, well, it was only for the best. Better a lord like him think of her as the outsider she was.

"Shall we take my coach, or do you prefer your own?" he asked the baroness.

"We must take yours," the baroness replied at once. "I want everyone to see me in the company of one of London's most eligible bachelors."

"One of the many? You wound me, madam." Mr. Grenville clutched his heart as if grievously injured. "Very well, my coach it shall be."

As a footman pushed the baroness's wheeled chair toward the front door, Mr. Grenville fell into step beside Nora.

She tried not to trip over her own feet out of sheer proximity. She was neither a rose nor a ruby, but a complete zany.

His eyes twinkled. "If I had likened you to a strawberry, tart and sweet, would you still have been able to find fault with my analogy?"

Her cheeks heated.

Tart and sweet, precious and beautiful, soft and delicate. There was no possible way a handsome *ton* gentleman could ever truly be interested in her as anything more than a momentary diversion. Yet she could not help her traitorous heart from wanting to believe.

"What if I said strawberries give me a rash?" she asked, deliberately more tart than sweet.

"Then I would be in awe of your commitment to theme," he said without missing a beat. "Rose-colored hair, rose-colored gown, rose-colored rash..."

She giggled despite herself. Of course he would have the perfect answer.

But she could not allow herself to thaw. Not when his motives were so unclear. Was he suspicious of her and trying to win her confidence? Or could the heir to an aristocratic title truly be a man this marvelous?

Nora's pulse pounded. She wanted to believe in

him so much that having it all be a game would be devastating.

But if he was sincere... he was even more danger-ous.

When they stepped out the front door, her eyes were dazzled first by the sun and then by Mr. Gren-ville's carriage.

"What a dashing coach-and-four," Lady Round-tree exclaimed. "I like it even better than your landau."

Nora could not believe she was about to be helped inside such a grand vehicle. Mr. Grenville had not yet inherited his baronetcy, but from the look of it he might as well be a fairy prince.

When Lady Roundtree and Nora were both ar-ranged in the forward-facing seat, Mr. Grenville climbed inside to join them.

In order to allow the most room for the baron-ess's splinted leg, he did not seat himself across from her, but rather opposite Nora. Their knees did not touch, but the tips of his boots flanked the tips of hers.

Nora was suddenly conscious of every inch of her body. She shivered. Two pairs of boots nestled against each other should not feel so shockingly intimate.

She would have to get used to the sensation.

For as long as she remained Lady Roundtree's companion, the baroness would require extra space to protect her broken leg. And because the baroness traveled in the same circles as Mr. Grenville, they had already been bumping into each other at every turn. Now that he was paying personal calls, unexpected moments of forced proximity could become all the more common.

Nora's heart raced. The idea both thrilled and terrified her.

Slowly she became aware of Mr. Grenville drumming his fingers on the edge of the squab as if tapping out the keys to a chord. No, not drumming his fingers—*pianoforte-ing* them.

A smile curved her lips. She wanted to point out the chords, to tell him she had witnessed his family's musicale and found all three of them devastatingly talented.

But from the sound of Lady Roundtree's friends, the aftermath had been far from positive. The last thing Nora wanted was to call attention to the matter and make him feel uncomfortable.

"Have you been to a gallery before?" Mr. Grenville asked quietly.

"No," she admitted. "But I'm very much looking forward to it."

He frowned. "I thought you said you liked art."

She nodded. "I do."

"Where have you seen any?" He leaned forward with interest.

"I'm from the country, not the moon." Nora gave him a crooked smile. "Other people have paintings, and the church back home is full of pictures and stained glass. Since I've come to London, scarcely a day goes by without some exposure to the arts. The places we visit are well-decorated, and Lady Roundtree's home boasts a hall of portraits."

"Four-and-twenty portraits, to be exact," the baroness put in proudly. "And a few tasteful sculptures strategically placed in locations throughout the town house."

Mr. Grenville leaned back, a satisfied smile curving his lips. "You're going to love the gallery."

"Of course I will," said Lady Roundtree.

Mr. Grenville wasn't looking at her.

Nora's cheeks heated involuntarily. She prayed she would not spend the next hour with her face flushed scarlet.

When they arrived at the gallery, a row of carriages just as fancy as the one they were in stretched down the street.

Panic inched along Nora's spine. She would not be viewing works of art with Lady Roundtree and Mr. Grenville. She would be swept along in a current surrounded by much better, much bigger, much prettier fish.

Mr. Grenville and the footmen helped the baroness into her wheeled chair.

Nora stepped from the carriage and tried to project an air of serenity.

Before she knew it, she would be back home where everyone not only knew her name but came to her for advice, and invited her whole family to their functions. Invisibility in London was hardly a curse; a few months from now, she wouldn't see any of these high-in-the-instep aristocrats ever again.

She slid her gaze to Mr. Grenville. No. She would *not* miss him, she told herself firmly. How could she miss something she'd never truly had?

As they made their way into the gallery, Lady Roundtree and Mr. Grenville were bombarded on all sides by well-wishers.

The baroness lamented her splint to anyone who would listen, and Mr. Grenville charmed the rest with little compliments or inquiries about their hobbies and loved ones.

The worst were the debutantes. He couldn't go three feet without one of them fairly swooning into his path with flirtatious comments and a flutter of her eyelashes.

That was the sort of young lady he would choose. Moneyed, beautiful, secure in her superiority over the rest.

The debutantes fell over themselves to tell Mr. Grenville they had read about the picture gallery in this lady's magazine or that newspaper. They knew a thousand little details that Nora would find fascinating if she weren't so jealous over her inability to have read such articles for herself.

How she wished she could have done so! Instead of blushing her way through the carriage ride, she could have regaled Mr. Grenville with topical insights and trivia relevant to their outing.

Instead, she had said nothing because girls like her had nothing to say.

She looked away. All the money in England wouldn't make her the intellectual equal of any of these vapid coquettes with the French modistes and personal Latin tutors, because Nora's brain didn't work the same way. It never would.

"Did you know that a Swiss painter was one of the first collectors behind this gallery?" one of the debutantes asked Mr. Grenville.

"Of course he knows," said another. "Didn't you hear him mention that a dealer of French art had worked in tandem with another collector?"

"Your details are so fascinating," another said, batting her eyes at him. "I positively adore history when it's you that tells it."

Nora tried not to gag.

If Mr. Grenville was bothered by the constant stream of pretty young things vying for his attention, he did not show it. Nor did he express any exasperation at the surprising number of fine ladies and fancy gentlemen sidling up to whisper in his ear about a problem they hoped he could solve, careful not to let anyone overhear.

No one except Nora, because Nora was no one.

She clenched her teeth, annoyed with the universe. Enough. She had got the message the day she arrived. Stark status differences splashed in her face every hour of every day. Just because she had an active imagination did not mean she confused reality with what could someday happen.

The other women were foreground.

She was background.

"This way," Mr. Grenville murmured, leading Lady Roundtree and her footmen away from the crowd. "These salons seem less crowded."

Was he ever right. Not only was the next salon far less crowded than the others, there were even a few artists with easels, making sketches or doing watercolor reproduction of the art on display.

Nora's mouth fell open. How she wished she were one of them! Her heart twisted with longing. The richest spectators in the gallery were not those with the most extravagant gowns, but those who had brought a sketchbook and a bit of graphite to take advantage of the location.

Not for the first time, she wished her brother had never sent her caricatures to a printing house. If she had not been launched along that path, she could be here sketching with the others.

Her stomach twisted. She had cheated herself out of her favorite pastime. Now that the caricatures were famous, she didn't dare sketch in public lest a witness put two and two together. She might assume she was too invisible for someone to make such a leap of logic, but it was not a risk she was in any position to take.

Still, Nora's fingers itched for a drawing pencil.

"You two go ahead," Lady Roundtree waved her hand in Mr. Grenville's direction. "I see some old friends that I absolutely must catch up with before I lose them in this crowd."

Nora hurried toward her. "Don't you want me to come with you?"

"And make it even harder to push our way through?" Lady Roundtree gestured toward her broken leg. "It's hard enough to navigate about with this bother. Having to worry about you two will only make it worse."

Before Nora could object further, the baroness turned away and motioned for her footman to push her in the opposite direction.

Nora stared at the retreating baroness, marveling that it was less worrisome to leave her unmarried cousin alone with a gentleman than to have her paid companion accompany her.

But she and Mr. Grenville weren't alone, were they? Nor was Nora here as a cousin, but as a servant. Perhaps these class differences afforded her a freedom she hadn't fully realized. Had Nora come to visit as a cousin, she might not have been permitted to stroll the gallery unattended with a gentleman caller.

Eager to see the art, she allowed Mr. Grenville to lead her deeper into the winding salons.

Some of the visitors around them marched through the gallery, glancing at each picture over their shoulders as if determined to race through every room within a prescribed amount of time.

To her delight, Mr. Grenville's method mirrored her own preferences. He led her directly in front of the first picture and did not budge until they had both had the opportunity to fully observe it.

Nora ignored the little plaques with the dancing letters beneath each work of art, focusing instead on the artistry involved. The choices in perspective, in color, in light.

As they walked, the works she liked least fascinated her as much as the works she liked best due to the attention to detail on the parts of both the artists and the gallery's curator. Someone had *chosen* these works of art. Chosen the order, the grouping into salons. Likely even chosen which works would be shown and which would not.

She could not help but wonder which pictures had not made the cut, and why. Her head was already overflowing with new techniques to try the moment she got back home.

Not *home*, she reminded herself with a frown. When she returned to Lady Roundtree's town house, she could devote herself to art. When she returned *home*, she would have to leave that nonsense behind. Nora's grandparents would need her. Her brother would need her. The farm would need her. There would be little time for experimenting with light or color or perspective.

"I would have switched the last two," Mr. Grenville murmured as they reached the end of a corridor. "And the third and fifth."

Nora glanced at him with interest.

He had been so full of well-read commentary about the styles of art and the probable techniques used that it was hard to believe he was not an artist himself. This was the first time he had spoken critically of the order in which the art had been shown.

"Why?" she asked.

He cast his gaze at the other works in the room. "They sorted them chronologically. Displaying these works by the date painted was a mistake. They're all the same mountain at different times of the year. They should be grouped by season and time of day to truly appreciate the changing nature of time, as the artist intended."

In surprise, Nora swept her gaze about the salon anew.

She did not know where this mountain range might be located, but Mr. Grenville was right: it was the same mountain in different seasons, at different times, from different angles. Grouping them as if they represented a single year rather than the artist's obvious many years of study would have given a far more accurate portrait of the changing nature of seasons.

"You are brilliant." She stared at him in wonder. "They should have hired you to curate the exhibition."

Although he did not respond aloud, Mr. Grenville appeared uncommonly pleased by her observation.

In the next salon, he squinted at each of the plaques and read them aloud, along with his best guess about why the artist had chosen this title for that picture.

Nora was as fascinated with Mr. Grenville as the art around them. Every tiny insight into him made him all the more marvelous. Since coming to London, this afternoon was by far her favorite moment.

"What about that one?" he asked, gesturing toward a picture on Nora's other side.

"The perspective?" She stepped closer to the work he'd indicated.

"No, the title. Is it in the same series as this one?"

He smiled at her expectantly, patiently awaiting her answer.

Nora froze in sudden terror.

She could read some things. She *could*.

If the letters were big enough and the words were familiar and there wasn't a witty and intelligent man she was desperately trying to impress standing a few feet from her.

Her fingers shook. She needed to concentrate without looking like she was concentrating.

She could lean forward a little bit perhaps, but not too much. He knew she wasn't blind. If she could pick out differences in the colors of certain leaves in previous works, obviously she could perform the simple task of reading the picture's title aloud.

Obviously.

Her palms grew clammy, and she wrapped her fingers into tight balls to hide the cold sweat. She could do this. One of the letters was a D, or possibly a B. She would figure it out just as soon as they stopped dancing.

But the more she stared at each letter, the more they seemed to shiver and move. Now she wasn't sure that the wiggling letter was a D or a B at all. She wasn't sure about any of the letters.

The harder she tried, the worse it was going to get. She was going to stand here mute, unable to perform a child's task, proving once and for all just how unworthy she was of the attention of a gentleman like Mr. Grenville, and of being in this gallery at all.

"What does it say?" he asked again, his brows creasing enquiringly.

Her stomach twisted. The letters weren't any clearer. She was never going to be able to read the plaque. The back of her throat pricked with heat.

"I don't know," she whispered, her voice tiny and raw.

Mr. Grenville stepped next to her, glanced from

her miserable face to the printed sign, and burst into a belly laugh.

Nora wanted to die.

"Of course you cannot read it," he said with a shake of his head. "I should never assume that anyone but myself had parents who subjected them to German tutors as well as French ones. It says, 'Snow at dawn.' Look at how he refracted the horizon in the frozen water. How do you think he did that?"

Nora stared back at him wordlessly, unable to theorize as to the artist's technique because she was still shaking in her borrowed boots.

Mr. Grenville had already forgotten her awkwardness while reading the plaque, but Nora would never forget. His kindness made her feel even stupider than usual; she hadn't realized the words weren't in English. She fought the urge to run from the room and bury her flaming cheeks in her hands.

It wasn't the first time Nora had been the least clever person in the room.

The local vicar had organized lessons for male school-aged children back home. Her grandparents had been thrilled about the opportunity and promised her she would learn just as much as Carter, even if she couldn't attend personally.

But when her younger brother came home and attempted to explain the day's lessons to her, Nora hadn't been bright enough to follow along. Within a matter of weeks, her baby brother had quickly outpaced her in anything involving reading.

She had longed to fit in, pretended to control the dancing letters and numbers in a desperate attempt not to be different. Not to be *lesser*.

All these years later, she was still doing the same thing: pretending she was just like all the other girls.

Acting like she could read the titles of portraits. Pretending she belonged.

This was just more proof to the contrary.

She followed Mr. Grenville from one picture to the next, marveling at his complete and easy confidence. Of course he spoke Latin and German and French. Of course he could do sums and enjoyed literature and could recount relevant stories from history or fiction to accompany each painting. This was his element.

"You know everything about art," she said in wonder when he surprised her yet again.

He gave her a crooked smile. "I know very little, but I know what I like. How about you? Do you see much here that you like?"

Nora swallowed, certain her face appeared as lovesick as she feared.

"Very much," she managed. Her pulse raced just from his nearness. Every moment with him was better than the last.

He proffered his elbow. "Shall we try the next salon?"

Nora stared at his outstretched arm.

She knew she should not take it. This was a glimpse into the sort of life she might've had if she had been born into a different time, to a different family, in a different place. She was not his equal. She was a very out-of-her-depth young woman who very soon would be going back home where she belonged.

Perhaps that was why she took his arm and held on tight.

Obviously this could not go anywhere. It meant nothing. Friendship, flirtation, harmless fun. He was a future baronet. She was an illiterate peasant girl dressed up like a debutante.

This wasn't real life. They both knew the path would soon diverge when she went back home.

What harm could there be in living in the moment, when this moment was all they would ever have?

Chapter 14

*H*eath had been looking forward to visiting the Dulwich Picture Gallery ever since it opened, and was enjoying himself far more than he had anticipated.

He had expected to fall in love with the art. What he hadn't expected... was Miss Winfield.

She looked as though he'd brought her to heaven itself. "The play of light and shadow in these paintings is absolutely breathtaking. This technique they're using..."

"It's called 'chiaroscuro,'" he said gruffly, embarrassed that he had learned every possible detail except how to actually produce it. He'd believed enjoying others' art would have to be enough.

He now realized that *sharing* it was even more magical.

"I cannot tear my eyes away," she whispered, clearly awestruck.

It was true. When they had walked past Lady Jersey and the other patronesses of Almack's, Miss

Winfield had not so much as blinked. Likely she had not been in Town long enough to recognize the most important members of Society.

It was one of the many things Heath liked best about Miss Winfield: her lack of knowledge about social hierarchy, gossip, and scandals made her seem fresh and untarnished by superficial nonsense.

She was present in the moment in a way that few other gallery-goers even attempted. Miss Winfield wasn't darting looks beneath her lashes to see who strolled with whom, or who had worn which gown, or had arrived in which carriage. She was staring at each work of art with much the same expression Heath imagined on his own visage.

"This may be my favorite place in the city," he murmured.

"This may be my favorite place in England," she countered with a startled laugh. "Thank you for bringing me here."

In truth, he could not have asked for a better partner. Miss Winfield was the perfect companion to bring to this gallery. To any gallery.

He was pleased by how much she loved art. Flattered by how carefully she listened to his opinions. Delighted that not only wasn't she bored by critical analysis of each painting, but discussed them with even more enthusiasm than his mother discussed shopping for new bonnets.

"My pleasure," he responded, and meant it.

If he were honest, he had called upon the Roundtree residence today not to speak to his client, but in hopes of seeing Miss Winfield. He had been so disappointed on the occasions when he had dropped by to give the baroness his weekly update and her companion had not been present.

Today, inspiration had struck. During a private conference in Lady Roundtree's parlor, he could not reasonably request Miss Winfield's presence, but he could invite both ladies to join him somewhere else. The Dulwich Picture Gallery opening to the public at long last was a happy coincidence that gave him an easy excuse for an outing.

He slid a glance toward Miss Winfield. As it turned out, there was no one else he would rather have by his side.

"I cannot wait to explore the next collection," he said.

The paintings within had been collected for the King of Poland, who had been forced to abdicate the throne before he could enjoy them.

When they entered the room, Miss Winfield clasped her hands to her chest as though her heart had started pounding just like Heath's.

"Have you ever seen anything so lovely?" she breathed.

She was a vision. Her shimmering red curls, her rose-pink gown, her captivating blue eyes sparkling with interest and excitement.

He couldn't stop sneaking stolen, enchanted glances at her. It was as if the works of art began with Miss Winfield herself, before they had even stepped inside the gallery.

"Very few things are this lovely," he agreed gruffly.

She turned in a slow circle to take in the vastness of the salon. "If I had a collection like this, I would stare at it every day."

Heath's opinion exactly. His favorite daydream. The closest he'd come to realizing it were the works on the walls of his private chambers, a collection glimpsed by few individuals. He was startled to realize that Miss Winfield was perhaps the one person who would appreciate it as much as Heath.

With her, he would not have to hide his true self.

"I'm glad you are pleased with today's excursion," he murmured.

"Pleased?" Her eyes shone with joy. "There is nowhere I would rather be."

And no one Heath would rather be with.

A wise man would not allow this infatuation to continue. She was a farm maiden. Someone's employee. Far below his station. The rules had been impressed upon him since birth. Yet he could not help but notice that he was not the only one Miss Winfield had charmed.

Lady Roundtree had once been vociferously against the idea of a paid companion. According to gossips like Phineas Mapleton, it was because the baroness was barren and did not wish to be pitied by her peers for being forced to pay some commoner to spend time with her, rather than birth a proper family of her own.

Heath had no idea whether there was any truth to the rumor, nor did he believe anyone was in a position to judge. He liked the baroness and had gone out of his way to squelch such mean-spirited gossip. Eventually, a new subject of interest had emerged.

Although Heath wouldn't wish a broken limb on anyone, no one had been more pleased than he to hear that Lady Roundtree had acquired a companion after all.

And now that he'd met Miss Winfield for himself...

She turned to him with a happy smile. "One could not ask for a more perfect day."

Heath straightened his spine as Lady Pettibone strode up behind Miss Winfield.

"Where is my hardheaded niece?" She jabbed the tip of her parasol against the floor. "Did you roll her into the Thames?"

Miss Winfield did not cower at the harsh tone or insulting language. Instead, her eyes softened. "Please stop worrying. Lady Roundtree is a perfect doll. I am honored to be her companion."

Lady Pettibone harrumphed. "I suppose that's why you've run off with Heath Grenville."

Miss Winfield's cheeks flushed pink. "I fear it is the baroness who has run off. She saw some friends she wished to converse with, and did not need me underfoot."

"Mabel despises galleries." Lady Pettibone leaned on the handle of her parasol with a scowl. "Her 'friends' are probably characters in whatever lurid book club novel she's off reading in some dark corner."

"Do you think she is unhappy?" Miss Winfield blanched. "I must find her at once."

Lady Pettibone scoffed at the idea. "Mabel is never happier than when her nose is in a book. If she brought you here, it must be because she thought you would enjoy it."

"Oh, she didn't bring me here." Miss Winfield beamed up at Heath. "Mr. Grenville invited us."

Now he'd done it. Heath's cravat suddenly felt uncomfortably tight.

"It was rather spur of the moment," he murmured. "I happened to be visiting, and..."

"I see." Lady Pettibone's sharp, narrowed eyes indicated she likely saw far more than Heath had intended. "Do not forget yourself."

She turned and strode away before he or Miss Winfield could say another word.

Heath pretended not to have understood the message.

Miss Winfield glanced up at him with worry. "Should I have curtsied? We skipped the how-do-you-do's, and I wasn't certain which was the right moment. Lady Pettibone must be mortally offended."

He could have laughed. "That's the nicest I've ever seen her treat anyone. I think she loves you. Lady Roundtree is her favorite niece, and you are clearly very good for her."

"Good for her?" Miss Winfield's eyes widened. "My post as her companion has been incredibly good for me."

"See? That's what makes you different. Instead of looking for ways to tear each other down, you look for ways to help each other out." His lips quirked. "Although as I recall, you were not particularly quick to help *me* out when your dog violated my virgin boot with his lusty passion."

"Lady Roundtree's dog," Miss Winfield reminded him with a sparkle in her eyes. "If you wish to break your betrothal to Captain Pugboat, you'll have to take it up with her."

Heath grinned back at her. He wouldn't undo their private joke for the world.

There was no sense hiding the truth. Despite a lifelong obsession with maintaining reputations, particularly his own, he seemed unable to resist pursuing a highly inadvisable friendship with a paid companion. But *friendship* was as far as it could go.

Heath knew firsthand how quick Society was to ostracize any member with the wrong connections, no

matter how lofty. It was a miracle that Lady Roundtree seemed to hold a soft spot for Miss Winfield.

But even though there was no romantic future in
store for them, he did not wish to waste what time
they did have together. Not when there was such an
obvious connection between them.

She glanced up at him with a wistful smile. "Do
you ever wish you could live in a place surrounded by
this much beauty?"

Heath was imagining it right now. He saw Miss
Winfield not as an unpolished diamond, but as a
bright red rose amid a sea of pale white dandelions
who could not appreciate her beauty because her colors were so much brighter than theirs.

"What is it like where you live?" he asked.

"Incredibly beautiful," she answered without
hesitation.

"Not the Roundtree town house," he clarified. "I
meant back home on your farm."

"So did I," she said, her tone wry.

His neck heated at the gaffe. "Tell me about it."

"Villages in the West Midlands are the opposite
of London," she said after a moment. "There are no
factories, no soot-filled sky, no beggars pleading for
alms."

Heath blinked. That was definitely not the im-
pression one hoped one's capital city would make on
a visitor.

"Back home, the air tastes clean," she continued.
"The rumble of passing carriages are few and far between. One mostly hears the call of birds. And
occasionally the bleat of sheep."

"It sounds idyllic," Heath admitted.

"You would love it." Her eyes shone. "Stepping
outside at night and seeing the sky so full of stars...

The universe seems endless and full of infinite possibility."

He tilted his head at the phrasing. "What is it you wish would be possible?"

She bit her lip. "A better life for my brother. An *easier* life for my grandparents. We are proud of our farm, but they all work so hard from dawn to well past dusk. I wish I could give them an extra hour each day, when responsibilities would melt away and all that was left to do was relax and enjoy being with nature and each other."

"It sounds like you love your family as much as I love mine," he said softly.

"They are my best friends." Miss Winfield let out a long, slow breath. "I miss them very much."

His smile faded at the yearning in her tone. "It must be horrid to be so far away from one's entire family."

"Not my entire family." Miss Winfield's eyes brightened. "Lady Roundtree is my second cousin, and I've come to love her just as much as any other."

Heath's mind stopped. "You and Lady Roundtree are cousins?"

"Afraid so." She looked up at him quizzically. "Does it matter?"

Shame heated the back of his neck. It should not matter. Miss Winfield was the same person he saw before him, no matter who her cousins were.

Yet that accident of birth gave her more of an advantage in this environment than she likely realized. Many of his peers believed the non-aristocracy beneath them. Blood relatives, however...

How many young ladies made their splash because of an earl or a viscount in the family? How many younger sons puffed out their chests with importance because they were ninth in line to a presumptive courtesy title?

"Look," Miss Winfield breathed. "It's Samson and Delilah. Note the stylistic choice of shears rather than scissors... See how the eye focuses on her? The artist has chosen to bathe the hero in darkness and the villainess in light."

Once again, Heath was impressed by Miss Winfield's uncanny insight into how each artist played with perspective and color. She rhapsodized about how different types of brushstrokes invoked movement and emotion. Nothing escaped her notice.

As they walked, Heath found himself soliciting her opinion more than espousing his own. Her eye was incredible. His sisters could tease him that he had come to respect the opinions of a client's paid companion as if Miss Winfield were a Grenville herself... And his sisters would be right.

"Are you sure you're not meant to be an artist?" he asked.

She turned the question back around on him. "This outing was your idea, and I daresay a jolly good one. Are you certain *you* are not meant to be an artist?"

He gave a self-deprecating snort. If only she knew how many hours he had dedicated in pursuit of a talent he would never possess.

"I'm hopeless at art," he admitted with a smile. "I cannot trace my hand and have it still look like a hand when I'm done."

She frowned, rather than laugh at the image. "How is that possible? You are so well educated. Your ability with languages, all the details about geography and local history as relates to these paintings..."

"There is a vast difference between 'passable'

and 'gifted.'" He gave his shoulder a light shrug. "I'm not talented at artistic pursuits. I'm gifted in exactly one arena: memorizing data."

She shook her head. "I am certain that's a shocking understatement. Your multilingual literacy alone—"

"It's true." He knew his strengths. "I am analytical. French, Latin, German? All of that is just learning the rules and then following them. Recognizing patterns in grammar, conjugation... I'm no savant. I am a monkey who has memorized a routine."

The confession tumbled from his lips before he could recall it. Unease prickled his skin. He had never expected to find himself sharing such personal details with anyone, especially Miss Winfield. Yet with her, he felt like he could be himself without judgment. He held his breath in anticipation of her response.

"It sounds like an impossibly complex routine to me." She narrowed her eyes at him, unconvinced. "You must be a very gifted monkey."

"I am a well-connected monkey," he corrected with a grin. "A *gifted* monkey could use his skill with languages to write a poem for a pretty woman."

She smiled back at him shyly. "A poem about roses and strawberries?"

"Tart and sweet." It was all he could do to withstand a sudden urge to kiss her.

"What about music?" she asked suddenly. "I saw your performance. The three of you are brilliant."

"Bryony and Camellia are indeed brilliant," he said with feeling. "I am just up to my same tricks. Memorizing scales, following notes on the page, predictable patterns of chord progression."

"It's still music," she said staunchly.

He inclined his head. "I can play it, but I cannot

create it. Not like my sisters. That's what makes them true artists and me a background accompanist."

"No." Miss Winfield lay a gentle hand on his arm. "Your analytical nature is what makes you London's premier problem-solver."

He gave her a crooked smile. "I'm not the best because I'm the only one?"

"You're the only one because nobody else can do it." Her eyes shone. "You are gifted. The details you memorize, the patterns you see that no one else can... That *is* your talent. You use it every day to help other people."

His throat grew tight, and he glanced away.

Talented. Gifted. No one had ever said those words to him before. Not his prodigy siblings, not his doting mother. Certainly not the father who had never spared the time to notice his son transforming himself into a high-performance automaton in ill-fated attempts to gain approbation.

Perhaps Heath had been searching in the wrong place.

When Miss Winfield looked at him, she didn't see a future title. He wasn't his pocketbook or his pianoforte or his Society connections. She saw him as a worthy gentleman with God-given talents that he used to help people.

Who could ask for a better reputation than that?

Heath wanted to swing her into his arms, press a kiss to her lips, shout to the world that she made him the happiest of men.

He did nothing of the sort. He would not dare.

Throughout his entire life, Heath had witnessed how shunned his sister's bosom friend Faith Digby had been simply for being born to a lower class. How opening a charity school had decimated his previously respectable sister Dahlia's social standing.

In order to keep helping people as he had been doing, Heath could not accept the same fate. Gifted or not, it was his very position within Society that allowed him to help make it better.

He could not let anything jeopardize his carefully maintained social standing.

Not even love.

Chapter 15

*H*eath stared up at the brick façade before him.

This printing house was one of
dozens of similar wretched embarrassments who mis-
took scandal columns for journalism. This particular
publisher had been losing money for years, in part due
to an inability to stand out from its competitors. Until
now.

In absence of a knocker, Heath rapped directly
on the peeling door. He had easily traced the origin of
the anonymous caricatures to this address. Soon, he
would have the name he sought.

A rat slid out from the shadowed interior when a
young boy cracked open the door.

The lad glared up at Heath. "Wot?"

"May I speak to the owner of this establishment?" Heath asked, careful to keep both his voice
and his countenance free of distaste.

"No." The lad moved to shut the door.

Heath stopped it with the toe of his boot before

the latch could fall into place. "I am willing to pay."

The lad's eyes narrowed. "How much?"

Heath lifted a shilling from his waistcoat pocket.

The lad grabbed it with dirty fingers. "Master ain't here."

Heath reached into his pocket anew and this time pulled out a sovereign.

The lad snatched the gold coin even faster than the shilling. The suspicion in his eyes gave way to confusion. "He really ain't here. I'm the apprentice, so I run the machine."

Heath retrieved another coin from his pocket, but held this one just out of grasp. "I know this house publishes the caricatures."

The lad looked longingly at the coin. "Everyone publishes caricatures. But I ain't never seen Cruickshank or Gillray, if them's who you're looking for."

"They are not," Heath said with equanimity. "I speak of the most recent phenomenon, drawn by an anonymous hand."

"Oh, those." The lad's chin jutted out with pride. "We may have published those."

Heath held the coin closer. "What is the artist's name?"

The lad stared at the coin with hunger. "I would tell you if I knowed it. The pictures come in anonymous, and that's how we print them."

Heath's ears pricked with interest, and he handed the lad his coin. "How exactly do the caricatures arrive?"

"You'd have to ask my master. I ain't allowed to touch the post." The boy made a careful fist about his new reserve of coins. "He might be interested in speaking to a rich toff. What did you say your name was?"

Heath reached into his pocket for a calling card. "Mr. Heath Grenville, at your—"

With an audible gasp, the boy slammed the door in Heath's face and engaged the lock.

Heath jumped backward in surprise, then pounded again upon the door.

His knocks went unanswered.

He slid his unneeded calling card back into his pocket and returned to his landau. It would be a simple enough matter to determine the owner of the establishment and his place of residence.

From there, a man so disreputable as to profit from such rubbish must also have a price at which he'd be willing to betray a confidence with an anonymous caricaturist. The mystery would be solved in a trice.

Heath checked his pocket watch, then directed his horses toward his parents' town house. He would have to continue on the morrow. There was no time. He had sent a note to his father earlier in the week, requesting an audience this afternoon at promptly two o'clock.

As he drove, Heath pushed the case from his mind and focused instead on far more pleasant matters. His visit to the Dulwich Picture Gallery had quickly become one of his favorite recent memories.

His daydreams about someday opening his own small gallery had taken on a new and unexpected dimension.

Now when he imagined the tour he would give during his own grand opening, he pictured Miss Winfield at his side, giving her unique perspective on each piece and associated artist.

Poppycock, of course. He would not be opening a gallery, nor would Miss Winfield be anywhere near his side.

But reality's hard truths were what made one's innermost daydreams so bittersweet.

When he pulled up to his parents' town house, a groom awaited his arrival. Excitement raced along his skin.

For once, Father truly was expecting him! Heath handed off the reins and loped up the steps to the front door.

No sooner had his boots reached the final step than the door swung open and the family butler welcomed him inside. "Good afternoon, my lord."

"Heath!" his mother exclaimed in surprise when he strode into the front parlor. "What brings you here?"

He kissed her cheek. "I've a meeting with father at two. Has he asked for me yet?"

His mother's smile wobbled, and they both darted a glance at the clock upon the mantel.

"It's early," Mother assured him with a nervous pat on his arm. "You know how Lord Grenville plans each task down to the minute. If your meeting is at two, why, he must be finishing up whatever has been scheduled before."

Heath nodded tightly.

A quarter till two was not shockingly early, but his mother was right: Father had likely penciled his chat with Heath into today's journal as an appointment from two o'clock sharp until five past two.

Still, it wouldn't hurt to send a footman up to Father's study to remind the great man of their scheduled conference.

Heath crossed over to the quill and parchment on the mantel and penned a short note with as pristine a hand as he was capable.

Father,
I am downstairs, eagerly awaiting our
conversation.
Your son,
Heath

With a murmured word to a footman, the note quickly made its way up the stairs toward the baronet's study.

"While you're here..." Mother began twisting her hands together. "You must speak to Bryony."

Heath blinked in surprise. "Bryony? Don't you mean Camellia?"

His mother let out a frustrated sigh. "You cannot understand how difficult this has been for me."

"She's a countess now," he reminded her wryly. "Your eldest daughter brought the Lord of Pleasure up to scratch."

Mother grimaced. "All three of my girls have turned their backs on their good upbringing and on Society itself."

Heath sighed. "Surely the situation is not as pitiful as that."

"It's worse," Mother insisted. "Camellia is an opera singer, Dahlia voluntarily presides in a rookery, and Bryony needs..." Mother pursed her lips. "There is no hope for Bryony. She will find some way to humiliate her family even worse than her older sisters."

"I am far from humiliated," Heath said firmly. "Camellia has found true love, and her true calling. Dahlia is saving the lives of underprivileged children who would starve in the streets were it not for her big-hearted intervention. And Bryony..."

Skeptical, Mother arched a thin brow. "And Bryony?"

Heath conceded the point. "All right, I'll talk to her."

Mother gestured toward the spiral staircase. "They're upstairs, of course."

He took the stairs in twos.

As much as he believed his mother's preemptive lack of faith in her youngest offspring both flawed and unfair, life had recently ceased to follow its prescribed, unchanging pattern. Starting with his sisters.

Dahlia's lifelong best friend had not been born to the peerage, so it had been of little surprise when she expressed her interest in employing her money and advantages toward helping the less fortunate.

Camellia, however, had struck Heath with a left hook he'd never seen coming.

She had always been his ally, the one he could rely upon to mind the family's reputation as well as her own with the same steadfast dedication as he.

Ever since the musicale, his staid, predictable sister had proven herself as unpredictable as anyone else. In the past few weeks, she had signed both a wedding contract and a performance contract at one of the most prestigious opera houses in Town.

Society was reeling just as much as their mother was.

But Heath's love and respect for his sister had never flagged. Unfortunately, neither had the wagging tongues of the gossips.

He would be much further along on his various cases for paying clients if he had not suddenly needed to devote a great deal of time and resources to ensuring neither Camellia nor his family became laughingstocks.

Anyone who dared hurt his sister would bear the full brunt of his wrath.

"Heath!" Bryony glanced up from the worn deck of playing cards she had been dealing to herself and her sisters. "Marvelous timing. We can still deal you in."

He shook his head. "I'll spectate. I've a meeting with Father in ten minutes."

Three very impressed faces swiveled to stare at him.

"How did you do that?" Dahlia asked in wonder. "I've been trying for months."

"Have you tried being the firstborn male?" Bryony asked pointedly as she riffled the remaining cards.

Dahlia tilted her head back and made an exasperated sound toward the ceiling. "Why do I keep forgetting to be born first and male?"

"Unfair," Heath protested. "I wasn't born with a silver spoon in my mouth."

Bryony put a hand up to her ear. "What's that? I can't understand you over that silver spoon in your mouth."

Even Camellia cut him a flat look. "Did Father also attempt to betroth you to an elderly stranger?"

Heath sank into a wingback chair without responding. So much for talking sense into his sisters. Their points were valid.

"You don't require an audience with Father." Bryony placed a comforting hand on Dahlia's knee. "I've consolidated my investments. As soon as I can withdraw money, I'll be in more of a position to help."

"How much do you need?" Heath asked. He had never confessed that most of his client income was automatically directed toward the school's dwindling accounts.

Dahlia gave him a tired smile. "Keep your coin. You need a dowry far more than any of us do if you're to attract the perfect bride someday."

Heath affected an aggrieved expression. "What of my charm? My chiseled countenance? The shiny wheels of my new barouche?"

"Latest news just in from London," Bryony stage-whispered. "No Society lady has ever cared a fig about the wheels of a gentleman's barouche."

"Every lady appreciates a good ride," Heath replied blandly, expecting to be showered with pillows.

Dahlia stifled a yawn. "You cannot shock us with rakish double entendres. Camellia is married now, and if you ever wondered whether her 'Lord of Pleasure' is truly world-class at perform—"

Heath leapt to his feet. "Is it two o'clock? It's nearly two o'clock. I had better stand outside Father's door so that I am within earshot when he calls for me."

The girls erupted in giggles as Heath beat a hasty retreat.

He positioned himself outside his father's study, careful not to slouch. Father was keen on positive first impressions. One's heir must never disappoint.

And, oh, how he would disappoint his father if the baronet realized Heath so much as daydreamed about an attachment with Miss Winfield!

Yet he was bewitched. The sparkle in her eye, her infectious smile... Heath could not go a single moment without her pretty face once again dominating his thoughts.

At first, he had wondered if they might suit. Then, he had feared they would. But ever since that first moment at the Dulwich Picture Gallery, there had been no hope of hiding the truth.

Number one: he and Miss Winfield suited very, very well.

Number two: it changed nothing. He still could not have her.

His chest tightened. Was he happy now? Was it better to know that their compatibility ran far deeper than a sensual longing to taste her lips?

He could not wait to see her again. That he could not court her did not signify. She would only be in London a short time longer, and Heath did not wish to miss a single opportunity to share her company. Now when he thought of Miss Winfield, all he could picture was—

A passing maid frowned to see Heath standing in the corridor.

"Pardon my impertinence, my lord." She glanced at the closed study door, then back to Heath. "Are you waiting for the baronet?"

An uneasy feeling turned in his gut. "I am."

"I don't mean to overstep, but Lord Grenville left not five minutes ago."

Heath's stomach soured. "You must be mistaken."

"I was cleaning the windows when I saw the baronet leave. The groom was waiting for him." She hesitated before adding, "I'm sorry."

Heath sucked in a fortifying breath. He did not need the family maids to feel sorry for him. He needed a father.

Once again, it seemed one could not always have what he needed.

He nodded to dismiss the maid and turned back toward his sister's sitting room in humiliation.

The groom who had taken Heath's reins at the front step had not been waiting on the heir to arrive for an appointment, but for his master to depart.

Either the baronet had never bothered to read Heath's notes requesting an audience, or Father did not care to dignify the requests with a response.

Heath held his head high, taking care to appear as stoic as ever. One day, things would change. He would simply have to become even more perfect in every way.

So perfect even his busy, important father could not fail to notice him.

Chapter 16

*N*ora was poised to enter a fancy Society ball for the second time in her life. The first time, she had been terrified of being singled out. This time, she was amused to watch from the background.

Lady Roundtree and her footmen were arguing with the hostess and *her* footmen. Was it better to carry the baroness in her wheeled chair up the exterior steps and down the interior steps into the ballroom so that she could follow the same path as the rest of the announced guests?

Or would the far more logical and easier solution of simply wheeling her round the garden path and entering through the rear terrace door humiliate them all by circumventing established norms?

It was exactly the sort of ridiculous *ton* quandary that Nora could have sketched a dozen humorous caricatures about.

She shook her head as the estate's head housekeeper joined the fray to suggest adding a special carpet from the garden through the terrace so that a wheeled entrance would have just as much importance and cachet as the traditional descent down the wide staircase.

Nora stopped listening.

London was not for her. When she went back home, she would find some other way. Be a night shift maid-of-all-work at the vicarage if she had to. She wouldn't risk her sketches hurting someone she cared about again. Not when all she had ever wished to do with her art was bring other people joy.

With an aggravated sigh, Lady Roundtree sent a frustrated look over her shoulder at Nora. "What do you think, Miss Winfield?"

Nora wasn't going to be formally announced one way or the other, and as a paid companion she didn't imagine her opinion in the matter held sway. But the baroness had asked, so there was no choice but to answer.

She cleared her throat. "I believe a baroness of your importance and stature among a community of your peers would not require the artifice of a hastily added carpet. You shall impose a grand figure just by entering from as beautiful a backdrop as this garden."

All the various maids, footmen, and others stared at her in a moment of shocked silence before turning their backs and talking over each other at once.

Nora clearly had not grasped the significance and delicacy of an invited guest entering a room containing other invited guests.

Lady Roundtree waved both gloved hands to shush everyone. "Miss Winfield is right. We are wasting unnecessary time. Wheel me through the garden."

In surprise, Nora fell into step behind the footmen. Given the lengths everyone was willing to go to
ensure each arrival at the ball received the gravitas it
deserved, she was surprised that common sense had
won out. That she had been listened to.

For the hundredth time, she wished her brother
was there to experience this upside-down looking-
glass world with her. She would have loved for him to
meet Lady Roundtree, to see the same unforgettable
sights, to share the same experiences. But Carter
would be lucky to ever leave the confines of their vil-
lage.

Without the income from the caricatures, there
would scarcely be enough money to snatch a few
hours' sleep each night. What she'd earned so far had
already been spent on her grandparents' health. This
was to be her last Society ball. The baroness was much
improved. Things would soon go starkly back to normal.

If anything would ever be "normal" again.

She wondered if she would ever stop missing Mr.
Grenville.

"Come along," Lady Roundtree barked over her
shoulder.

Nora hurried to catch up.

Because the hostess's butler could not be in two
places at once, the lady of the house stationed the un-
derbutler at the head of the stairs to manage the
growing queue. The primary butler accompanied
their entourage around the side of the house and
through the terrace door to announce their unconventional guests.

As soon as the crew was properly poised outside
the garden doors, the butler took his position just inside the threshold and bellowed, "Lady Roundtree!"

And companion, Nora added in her head.

She followed the footmen as they pushed the baroness around the refreshment table to the rear of the ballroom where all the other matrons, spinsters, and wallflowers sat and watched.

Nora took her place among them. She wondered if Mr. Grenville would be here tonight.

Butterflies fluttered in her stomach at the thought. She couldn't help it. All she could think about was what it would be like to dance with him, to feel the warmth of his strong arms, to know the taste of his kiss. If it were up to Nora... She tried to block the sensuous images from her mind.

Impossible. She could not let this go any further than stolen kisses, and yet she couldn't walk away. He meant far too much to her now.

But kisses were all it could ever be.

Her best hope for maintaining her sanity in this untenable situation was to treat every moment with him as if it were light and meaningless. Ensure neither of them took their ill-fated attraction too far.

Pretending their relationship didn't matter was the only way she would be able to keep her emotions in check when it was time to go back home.

But *oh*, how she wished country girls from sheep farms really could marry someone as wonderful as him. In a universe where her connection with Mr. Grenville would not have to be relegated to the shadows...

"Mabel, what a stunning bonnet," a passing lady said to the baroness. "And that beautiful gown. I trust your broken leg has not impeded your modiste in the slightest?"

"On the contrary." Lady Roundtree lifted her nose. "Being confined to this chair has given me more time to shop the fashion plates. I won't know what to do when the splints come off a week from Saturday."

A week from Saturday.

Nora's stomach hollowed, then her chest filled with hope. She would miss Lady Roundtree, and she could not bear the thought of never seeing Mr. Grenville again, but her family needed her now more than ever. She had to go home. Nora would probably never leave them again.

As for Mr. Grenville... Her heart ached at losing him. She might not be able to see a future between them, but nor could she bear to imagine the rest of her life without him.

"Lady Roundtree!" exclaimed another fine lady. "How is your leg?"

"Close to perfection," the baroness replied.

No one ever asked about Lord Roundtree. They took it as a matter of course that his life and his wife's would have no point in common.

No one but Nora seemed to be astonished at the countless *ton* unions in which the husband and wife were practically strangers despite years of marriage.

She dreamed of something more.

Nora deeply appreciated that her grandparents still loved each other and her. She was grateful that her few memories of her own parents were that they loved each other and their children very much. Someday, she might find a match like theirs. Back home, a loving marriage was a reasonable expectation.

She frowned. Shouldn't the same be true everywhere? Lady Roundtree deserved better than a husband who did not appreciate her. All women deserved more.

"It looks like the Duke and Duchess of Ravenwood are leading the waltz," whispered one of the wallflowers.

"Aren't they magical together?" breathed another in reply.

For as much as Nora sometimes believed she disliked everything about the *ton*, their high-flown pretensions and exaggerated self-worth and mindless consumption, she could not help but imagine what it might be like to belong. To *be* one of them. To dance with her husband in a way that others would refer to as *magical*.

The wallflowers continued to whisper.

"Tonight's invitation was a work of art, wouldn't you say?" asked one.

"Handwritten by the duchess herself," her friend replied. "I positively adore her calligraphy."

Of course it was.

If the dapper gentlemen and fine ladies seemed superior to Nora, it was for good reason. They were right to deem her unworthy. Nora wouldn't be able to read an invitation even if someone sent her one. She'd be too nervous to ever coax the letters into staying put on the page.

"I wish Mr. Grenville were here," lamented one of the wallflowers. "He's always the first to ask me to dance."

"So true," her friend said wistfully. "One's dance card never feels complete without his name on it."

Jealousy licked through Nora like wildfire. She clamped her arms over her stomach to cover its somersaults.

She wasn't the only one to recognize what a stupendous catch Mr. Grenville would be. These wallflowers where the lowliest young ladies of their station, and far above Nora's league. She looked away. Mr. Grenville was mad to waste even a moment with her, however clandestinely.

It was good she would be leaving soon. At any point, he was going to wake up and choose someone better. Someone like any other unmarried lady here.

Her pulse skittered in panic. The thought of Mr. Grenville courting the kind of girl a man of his class deserved was a punch to the solar plexus. But it wasn't news.

She was in love.

Her breath caught. Nora's topsy-turvy insides weren't garden-variety jealousy of higher class ladies, but rather a soul-consuming desperation at the thought of being without Mr. Grenville forever. Her heart wasn't just inextricably involved.

It was about to be summarily broken.

"Did you hear Mr. Grenville is on the hunt for a baroness?" whispered one of the young ladies to the others.

"I'm right here," quipped her companion. "He's found me."

"He's not here, you ninny," said another. "And if he were, I would be first in line."

Nora bit her tongue, uncertain whether to be sad or glad that he was absent from tonight's ball. She wouldn't be able to speak with him anyway, and watching him dance with a future bride would be more than she could bear.

Her heart jumped as she wondered what it might be like to peer in the looking-glass and see reflected the sort of woman Mr. Grenville *could* take as a bride.

What would Nora do, if she were a debutante like the others? Would she sit back here along the far wall, hoping to be noticed? Or would she fight for every scrap of time to whirl in Mr. Grenville's arms? Hope against hope for him to steal a kiss?

She glanced at the pretty young ladies in front of her with growing unease. Had any of them been the recipients of Mr. Grenville's romantic affection or ardent kisses? Nausea twisted her belly. She could not bear the thought of his lips on theirs. Even their mere ability to accept an invitation to dance, to waltz in his arms before Nora's very eyes, was more than she could withstand.

Yet she could not hate them for it. In their shoes, would Nora not do the same?

Listening to the innocent, animated conversations of these perfectly normal, perfectly raised, perfectly sweet wallflowers was torture. It would be churlish to dislike them just because Mr. Grenville could court them and not Nora.

It was not their fault that Mr. Grenville could only be seen with Nora publicly if there were a cover in place. Like escorting a baroness to a gallery, or taking tea with a peer. She was something to be hidden. An embarrassing deviation from his rightful path.

"Did you know he can speak four languages?" one of the wallflowers continued. "I can barely read Latin and French."

Her companion nodded. "With his love of geography and travel, I'm only surprised he stopped at four."

Nora's spine curved even smaller.

Mr. Grenville really was too good for her by every conceivable metric. He was so smart, so educated, so well-read, so respected by his peers for his knowledge and cleverness. Nora would never be able to share that with him.

No wonder aristocrats were fond of saying that peasants should not try to reach past their station.

"Why, it's Lady Roundtree!" cooed a passing

lady. "And still in splints. Are you ever so bored?"

"Terribly. Although I did procure a temporary companion." The baroness sent a kindly smile over her shoulder at Nora. "I imagine Miss Winfield cannot be bored. I rescued her from a sheep farm."

"A farm!" The young ladies tittered at such an ignominious fate. "She must be so grateful to be free from such monotony."

"And the stench of livestock," added another.

Nora's throat stung, and she swallowed the thick words she could not say. All the things she was proud of, all the things her family had built their lives around... all the sacrifices she had made to save the home of the people she loved was worthless to the *ton*, and only made her look even more ridiculous to them.

Nausea twisted in her belly. If she claimed their open disregard didn't hurt her, she was only lying to herself.

Before her stoic walls could begin to crack, Nora leapt to her feet. She faced the baroness. "May I fetch you a lemonade?"

"Ratafia." Lady Roundtree pursed her lips. "And a sponge cake."

Nora nodded and stiffly made her way toward the refreshment table.

It was flanked by a cluster of cackling dandies, the loudest of which was in the middle.

"Among pups like you, I am a stallion," he concluded to boisterous laughter. "Everyone says so. A stallion among pups!"

Nora tried not to roll her eyes. She recognized this man as Phineas Mapleton, who thought more of himself than anyone around him. The last time she'd been forced to interact with him, he had gone out of

his way to ensure Nora understood how little and insignificant she truly was.

When his group neither partook of refreshments
nor moved out of the way, she cleared her throat as
delicately as possible. "Might I slip in to fetch a refreshment?"

Mapleton's sharp gaze was immediately upon
her. "Not this one again! You still haven't learned to
speak to your betters only when spoken to?"

The others laughed.

Nora gritted her teeth and said nothing. This was
not an argument she could win.

"Of course you have the manners of a sow," he
continued, to the delight of his peers. "She was raised
on a pig farm!"

Nora did not dare correct the laughing dandies
with *sheep* farm. The distinction would only prove
more fodder for ridicule.

"It's not for me." She kept her voice low, but
composed. "Lady Roundtree is parched."

"Parched?" Mapleton echoed with a braying
laugh. "I'll say. She's more wrinkled than a raisin left
to dry in the sun. Why, we should call her Lady
*Raisin*tree!"

Nora clenched her fingers. She might have to
swallow her betters' personal attacks toward her, but
she was not going to allow some arrogant prig like this
to be ghastly to Lady Roundtree.

"A true gentleman," she enunciated clearly,
"would have just as much respect for any female who
outranks him as we peasants do."

"Ooh, was that a set-down?" Mapleton snorted
with laughter. "All I hear is the squealing of a little
country pig. Go ahead and take a trough full of sweets

back to your master, little sow. I am too fine a gentleman to waste time trying to reason with animals."

"Mapleton isn't just a stallion among pups,"
chortled one of the dandies, "but a pig-tamer, too."

"Go back to the country where you belong,"
Mapleton laughed as he shooed his well-dressed cro-
nies out of the way. "You will be wrinklier than your
mistress in no time."

The "stallion" pranced off without a care in the
world, likely to recount the tale to anyone who would
listen.

Fury raced through Nora's veins. If he wished to
mock her, so be it. But her family was off-limits.

And Lady Roundtree was family.

Chapter 17

*A*fter she'd seen the baroness settled for the night, Nora closed the door to the rear parlor Lady Roundtree had given her companion leave to consider her own, in addition to the guest chambers above stairs.

She tossed her gloves onto the single chaise longue and seated herself at the beautiful escritoire the baroness had installed to ensure Nora had a comfortable spot to draw.

Tonight, she was still fuming over that prat Phineas Mapleton's unconscionable comportment toward Lady Roundtree.

Usually, after returning to the town house from some event that made her feel tiny and insignificant, Nora unloaded her emotions into a secret sketchbook containing painstakingly rendered images far too intimate and raw to send home to her family.

She shoved that sketchbook aside. Tonight wasn't about Nora's feelings of inadequacy when surround by the *beau monde*.

Phineas Mapleton had made Lady Roundtree's eyes shimmer with tears. And he considered such reprehensible behavior a success. It was all Nora could do to refrain from dumping the lemonade bowl atop his carefully coiffed head.

At the start of the evening, Nora might have privately found humor in the discussions on how to best stage Lady Roundtree's entrance so as not to put a dent in her standing—or her sitting, as it were. But she would have never disrespected the baroness.

After Nora had been sent to fetch ratafia and sponge cakes, Mapleton had been so taken with his hilarious jests at Nora and Lady Roundtree's expense, that he had circled back for more... and eventually misjudged the distance between them.

Nora would never forget the shocked expression on the baroness's hurt face when she overheard Mapleton say it was little wonder her husband preferred the company of a pretty roundheels over wrinkled Lady Roundtree. Nora's fingernails dug into her palms.

Mapleton had terrorized London long enough.

Nora could no longer passively allow such toxic arrogance to stand. She might be a stupid country peasant from a ragtag little sheep farm, but she wasn't as powerless as bullies like him believed.

She was an artist.

Hands shaking with anger on kindhearted—still *perfectly elegant*—Lady Roundtree's behalf, Nora stabbed a plume into her inkwell and began to draw.

Was Phineas Mapleton a stallion among pups? Perhaps that was the problem.

Nora dipped the tip of a plume into the inkwell.

Men like him might think they ruled over country-born women like her and baronesses of an advanced age, but Nora's pen was about to exert dominance over Phineas Mapleton.

She adored Lady Roundtree. The baroness might have just started to consider Nora as something more than a paid companion, but Nora had come to think of her as family. This had become her second home. She would not allow a bully's ridicule to harm anyone in it.

"Stallion," she muttered beneath her breath. "Ha."

Mapleton had been trying to get people to refer to him as a stallion among pups for as long as Nora had been in Town. Tonight was the first time it had worked. At her expense. At *Lady Roundtree's* expense.

He wasn't superior to the baroness. Mapleton wasn't worthy of the title of gentleman. How high could a society be if its pillars were based on casual cruelty? How lowly would Nora be if she did not stand up for those she loved?

But her options were limited.

Causing a scene in the middle of a ballroom would only have humiliated the baroness more. Their abrupt departure, when others had tittered uncomfortably at Mapleton's remarks, had mortified Lady Roundtree enough.

Although she wished she could do more, Nora could only stand up for the baroness from the anonymity of a penny cartoon.

This would be her best yet.

Her plume sailed across the page, filling the pristine white foolscap with sure black lines. The caricature bloomed into focus.

Mapleton would finally learn that words had consequences. That her pen was sharper than his tongue.

A sennight from now, she would no longer be present to give the baroness company, to protect her from those who would mock her. This was Nora's last chance to use her limited power for good.

She finished the drawing and carefully laid it flat to dry. None of the aristocrats would recall a dandy's brief interaction with a country mouse. But every one of them had heard Mapleton repeat his pet phrase all Season long.

Now they could have an image to match.

Chapter 18

*N*ora was just finishing afternoon tea with Lady Roundtree when Mr. Grenville was shown into the parlor. He hadn't strayed from her thoughts ever since the gallery opening. To be so close to him once again...

She put down her fork and dabbed at the corners of her mouth with her serviette. Splendid timing. With her luck, if she smiled at him her teeth would be dotted with mulberry seeds.

"Heath Grenville!" Lady Roundtree smiled at him warmly. "Sit, sit. There's always room for a handsome man at a tea table."

Truer words than perhaps Mr. Grenville realized. In the weeks since Nora had come to town, she hadn't witnessed the baron take a meal with his wife even once. Nonetheless, Lady Roundtree always ensured a place was set for him.

Mr. Grenville bowed and took a seat close to the baroness. "What bother. I've just come from my club and haven't a sliver of space left for another morsel of food. Those scones do look devilishly tempting. Is that blackberry jam or mulberry?"

"Mulberry," Nora replied, hoping her lips weren't stained purple from the vast quantity she had just consumed.

With a yip, Captain Pugboat pawed at the corner of Lady Roundtree's settee.

The baroness surreptitiously lowered a piece of biscuit from her plate to the puppy. It disappeared in a trice. Lady Roundtree affected an innocent expression.

"We can see you," Nora pointed out with a grin. "Would you like me to arrange a place setting on the floor for Captain Pugboat?"

"Don't be absurd, Miss Winfield." Lady Roundtree gave an emphatic sniff. "Pugs don't eat from plates."

"Why is his collar festooned with yellow ribbons?" Mr. Grenville asked.

Lady Roundtree beamed at her pet. "Because he wanted to be a lion again today."

Mr. Grenville cast a baffled look toward Nora. "Captain Pugboat is now a lion?"

"Don't be absurd." Nora playfully echoed Lady Roundtree's words. "Captain Pugboat is *playacting*. He is still very much a puppy."

"Aha." Mr. Grenville nodded gravely. "He is a master of disguise."

Lady Roundtree let out an agonized sigh. "If only His Highness would master a few simple commands. Can you not teach him to come when called, or heel when so ordered?"

"I will," Nora promised. She cast a doubtful glance at the wiggling puppy and added, "That is, I will *try*."

The baroness yawned sleepily and nestled her head in the crook of the settee. "Rouse me when you've increased his vocabulary."

Nora peered into Lady Roundtree's empty tea-cup. Every drop was gone, including a dose of laudanum. The baroness was unlikely to wake for another hour. "Shall I have a footman escort you to your chamber?"

"I'm not sleeping," Lady Roundtree mumbled groggily. "I'm resting my eyes. I'll be waiting right here when he's ready to give his performance."

Nora lifted her brows. "Where will *I* be?"

Without opening her eyes, Lady Roundtree waved a dismissive hand. "You and Mr. Grenville will be teaching my new dog old tricks."

Nora cast an embarrassed look toward Mr. Grenville.

To her surprise, he grinned right back at her with a what-can-you-do shrug.

He pushed to his feet and whispered to Captain Pugboat, "Come on, boy. Come on. Here, boy. Here, Captain. Who's a good boy? Come-come, right this way."

"If any of that rubbish worked," Lady Roundtree said without cracking an eyelid, "I would not have asked you geniuses for assistance."

Mr. Grenville's shoulders wracked with silent laughter at the rebuke.

Nora grabbed the three-tiered silver tea tray from the table and lowered it near the floor.

Captain Pugboat immediately bounded toward her.

She held it just out of reach and backed out of the parlor toward an empty sitting room. Captain Pugboat and Mr. Grenville followed right behind the bouncing cakes, like children trailing the Pied Piper.

When she reached the other side of the empty sitting room, Nora placed the tea tray on a mantel out of the pup's reach.

She turned to Mr. Grenville. "Thus far, that's the only reliable way to lead him anywhere."

"Your kitchen must produce scads of teacakes," he said gravely.

"We don't let him have the *whole* thing," she protested.

Mr. Grenville tilted his head. "Perhaps that's the problem."

He broke off a bit of lemon cake and held it out toward Captain Pugboat.

The puppy scampered up to him with his tongue lolling out.

Mr. Grenville held the cake up higher. "Getting him to come appears to be a simple matter."

"For anyone with a teacake in their pocket," Nora agreed.

Captain Pugboat barked for the treat that had not yet fallen from Mr. Grenville's hand.

"You try," he said as he kept the cake aloft.

Nora crouched. "Here, Captain Pugboat. Here, snuggle pug. Come here, boy."

The puppy's soulful eyes remain trained on Mr. Grenville's hand.

"Not like that." He tilted his head toward the mantel. "With a treat."

Nora broke off another corner of lemon cake and turned around. "Here, Captain—"

The puppy raced to her feet and pawed at the air in an enthusiastic attempt to gobble the treat.

"That's step one." Mr. Grenville nodded approvingly.

Nora laughed in disbelief. "Captain Pugboat has no idea what we want of him."

"That's step two," Mr. Grenville amended.

Nora watched as he took a big step back.

"Captain Pugboat," he called, his voice low and coaxing.

The puppy immediately abandoned his efforts with Nora and gamboled toward the other contender.

Mr. Grenville held out his palm in a halt position. "Heel, boy. Heel. *Heel.*"

Captain Pugboat did not heel.

"Are you going to give him the cake?" Nora asked when utter failure had proven obvious.

Mr. Grenville shook his head. "His Highness will earn it when he learns it. You try."

Nora put on a singsong voice. "Snuggle pug... Here, boy."

The puppy dashed back across the carpet and leaped toward her hand.

"Heel," she said firmly. "Heel, boy. *Heel.*"

Captain Pugboat did not heel.

Nora did not give him the treat.

He whined pathetically and gave her baleful stares between desperate leaps for the treat.

She looked at Mr. Grenville. "Now what?"

"Now he knows what doesn't work." He tilted his head toward the mantel. "Put your teacake back on the tray. This time when I tell him to heel, if he doesn't listen—"

"*When* he doesn't listen," Nora corrected helpfully.

"When he fails to listen," Mr. Grenville amended, "do your best to hold him still. If he behaves, he'll earn the treat."

Nora set her bit of teacake back onto the tray,

careful not to allow any crumbs to fall to the floor. Captain Pugboat would think they were for him.

"Here, boy," Mr. Grenville called. "Come here if you want a delicious and only slightly squished lemon cake."

Captain Pugboat all but climbed up Mr. Grenville's breeches in an attempt to rescue the treat from its forbidden tower.

Mr. Grenville held up his other hand in the *Halt!* position. "Heel, boy. Heel."

Nora rushed forward and bent over Captain Pugboat to hold his wrinkly, wiggling hips in place.

He jumped up and licked her nose, which startled Nora into relaxing her hold. The puppy immediately launched himself back into the air—but this time, her face was still in the way.

His wrinkled shoulders connected with her jaw, sending her head crashing backward—right into Mr. Grenville's outstretched hand.

A blizzard of cake crumbs fluttered down from the heavens.

Nora dissolved into laughter.

Captain Pugboat dashed about the sitting room in a mad attempt to leave no crumb behind.

Undaunted, Mr. Grenville returned to the mantel to break off another piece of cake. "Second time is the charm."

As luck would have it, the second time was not the charm. Or the third, or the fifth, or the tenth. But somewhere around attempt number twenty, Captain Pugboat realized what was being asked of him and finally sat on his haunches without requiring Nora's assistance to still his hips.

"Very good!" Mr. Grenville said approvingly as he gave the puppy his treat.

Nora was proud, but skeptical. "I fear we've taught him that 'heel' means 'sit for a treat' rather than 'stop.'"

"He has to stop in order to sit," Mr. Grenville pointed out reasonably. "If Lady Roundtree wished for Captain Pugboat to heel in a nuanced manner, she should have specified the pose before falling asleep."

"Resting her eyes," Nora said firmly.

As they shared a grin, she couldn't help but wish for moments like this together every day.

He made even the mundane fun and exciting. As much as Nora warned herself to keep up her shields, Mr. Grenville was exactly the sort of easy-going, fun-loving person she would love to call a friend.

If he were a blacksmith or a dairy farmer, a girl like her might even hold out hope for an eventual courtship.

But those were not her cards.

He was a baronet, not a blacksmith. Their relationship—if indeed she could be arrogant enough to claim she shared one with him—was doomed to be both platonic and temporary.

Yet she could not tear her gaze from his. No matter how platonic and temporary these stolen moments might be, their growing bond was a thousand times more precious than anything she'd ever dreamed of having with someone like him. Even if all she could hope for were crumbs, she'd take them.

"What do you think?" she asked with a smile. "Have we earned our keep for the day?"

Mr. Grenville wiped imaginary sweat from his brow. "I believe we have tamed the lion. Is it show-time?"

She glanced over her shoulder as the sound of Lady Roundtree's snores wafted down the corridor.

"Curtain call has been delayed." Nora peered up at him. "She tends to nod off at this time of the afternoon. I'm sorry you wasted your visit."

Mr. Grenville's warm gaze melted her to her core. "I've done nothing of the sort."

Her heart pounded in her chest. "Haven't you come to speak to the baroness?"

He glanced away. "I've just come from Bond Street, where I gave up my dancing master position to another man."

Nora blinked in confusion. "You give dancing lessons on Bond Street?"

"At my sister's boarding school in St. Giles," he corrected, his voice warm with affection. "I ran into their new instructor on Bond Street."

"I see," said Nora, although she was not at all certain that she did. "And coming here is how you choose to spend your free time instead of dancing?"

He grinned. "One can dance anywhere, can you not?"

"I cannot," she whispered softly. "The only way I ever attend balls is as a servant, not a young lady with a dance card."

She thought her admission would splash a dose of much-needed reality into this beautiful, fairytale moment. Remind them both of the roles they played and the rules they were meant to follow.

Yet the air around them seemed to sizzle with a delicious tension.

"One does not need a dance card in order to dance," he said softly. "Why wait for an orchestra when we can waltz right here?"

"Here?" she stammered, her pulse racing out of control.

He lifted her fingers in his and curved his other

hand about her hip.

Nora stared up at him in wonder. She placed her palm to his shoulder.

He lowered his mouth to her ear. "Listen to the music."

She could hear nothing but the erratic pounding of her runaway heart as he led her in small, sweeping circles about the empty parlor into a plane where only the two of them existed.

Her fingers trembled in his. She rested her other hand on his shoulder tentatively, unsure if she could trust herself not to run her palm down the fine black coat sleeve to feel the ridges of the muscle beneath.

She had dreamed of a moment like this for so long. Filled an entire sketchbook with images of what it might be like in his arms. She had underestimated his power tremendously.

Yes, he could be sweet and kind and charming. But that was only part of who he was. He was also strength and passion and arrogance. He had *known* she yearned to find herself in his arms. And he had known he would not disappoint.

He executed the measured half-circles of the waltz with precise, perfect control. But the hunger in his gaze spoke of something far less restrained. A sensation that he could sweep her into another waltz or into the closest bedchamber and she would follow his lead willingly.

He would not be so rash, of course. *She* would not be so rash. This was nothing more than a Court-approved, standard waltz, not a mating ritual between two lovers close to combusting.

And yet every half-turn, every sensitive, heated inch where his hand touched her body, all of it was enough to rob her of breath and lead her directly toward temptation.

No wonder this man was a dance instructor. Nora would have begged to be admitted to his sister's school herself if it meant another opportunity to be swept away in his arms. Never had every inch of her flesh seemed so alive.

She could feel his heat through the layers of cloth separating them. If she moved her palm to his chest, would she be able to feel the beat of his heart? Her own rapid pulse must be plainly visible at the base of her neck, in the breathless sounds she tried to keep in her throat, in the way she stared up at him as if no orchestra in any ballroom could ever come close to capturing the magic between them right now.

He focused his hazel eyes on hers. "We shouldn't be dancing like this."

She held her breath. "I know."

His gaze was unreadable. "Do you want me to stop?"

She shook her head and tightened her fingers in his. "I don't want this dance ever to end."

Worse than that, she wanted *more*. More than a stolen moment, a forbidden dance. She wanted to press her mouth to his, to press her entire body to his, to show him without words how close she truly longed to be.

His eyes lowered to her parted lips. "What if the gentleman should try to kiss you?"

"I've dreamt of it," she whispered. Her heart fluttered at the shock of admitting the truth aloud. At the dizzy realization that he had shown no sign of wishing to release her from his arms. "But we cannot."

His gaze heated. "I would like to see someone try and stop us."

But he lowered his mouth to hers ever so slowly, giving her every opportunity to turn away.

Her only desire was to pull him closer.

His warm lips brushed hers, seeking, teasing, stoking a fire she had tried so hard to control. Passion engulfed her.

Nora closed her eyes and gave herself over to the moment.

This was the opposite of platonic. This was fireworks at Vauxhall, a storm crashing at sea, rainbows soaring across the heavens.

She couldn't keep him. They both knew he could not offer anything more permanent than this moment. She herself would be gone soon. Surely there could be no harm in indulging herself with a simple kiss.

His tongue touched hers. Liquid fire raced through her. He tasted as dark and sweet as mulberry jam, and just as addicting. She would never have enough. Her entire body trembled in pleasure.

Girls like her knew better than to believe in love. That was a fairy story that only happened on paper, like the secret drawings of herself on a real dance floor rather than watching from the shadows.

But this, *this*, was even better. His kiss was deeper, richer, a maelstrom of color and lights, texture and heat. He made her want things she knew she could never have. If she let herself float away on the magic of his kiss, she might start to believe she could keep him.

With the heat of their bodies cleaved together in a kiss this intimate, they were two brushstrokes blended into one, a single work of art. The thought of pulling away filled her with more dread than she could bear.

Captain Pugboat's loud barks were the only thing capable of jerking her back down from the clouds.

She lurched away from Mr. Grenville just as Lady Roundtree called groggily from the other room, "If you can't teach His Highness to heel, can you teach him to be quiet?"

Mr. Grenville wasn't looking at the puppy, but at Nora. His expression was still dangerously warm and tender. His lips less than a breath away.

"Oh dear," Nora interrupted briskly before he could say something they would both regret. "I've mussed your cravat."

He made an endearingly aghast expression. "Blast, I've no idea how to fix it. I'm hopeless at such things."

"Then you are in luck." Nora grinned up at him shyly. "I am my brother's valet."

She reached up with trembling fingers and coaxed the wrinkled linen back into sharp folds. His heart pounded against the brush of her hands, matching the quickened rhythm of her own pulse.

All she wanted to do was toss his neckcloth aside and pull his mouth back down to hers.

"There." She swallowed the lump in her throat. "Good as new."

Nora suspected that she, on the other hand, was forever ruined for any other man but him.

Chapter 19

*H*eath glanced at his reflection in the sitting room looking-glass, expecting to find the guilty eyes and flushed cheeks of a blackguard who had just been kissing lips that could never belong to him.

To his surprise, the calm, aristocratic façade in the mirror in no way betrayed the turmoil churning within him.

He didn't know what made him feel worse: that he had succumbed to the call of passion in the heat of the moment, or that his reflection didn't appear flustered about it in the least.

He turned to Miss Winfield.

She had not fared as well. Her fair cheeks were delightfully rosy, and her full lips looked plump and freshly kissed.

In short, a disaster. Anyone with eyes would easily guess what had transpired between them.

Heath could not help but think she had never looked more beautiful.

"Miss Winfield..." he began.

Captain Pugboat let out an excited yip, scrambled up Heath's right boot, and began humping his ankle without further ado.

Miss Winfield's laughing eyes met Heath's. "He now has *two* tricks."

He gave a sage nod. "Lady Roundtree will be so proud."

Shyly, Miss Winfield nibbled her lip. "Thank you for dancing with me."

"I swear that the pleasure was mine," he said firmly. She could not begin to guess just how much pleasure holding her body in his arms had stirred within him.

"And for..." She blushed and looked away.

Heath was grateful she did not complete the thought. If Miss Winfield had thanked him for being a bounder shameless enough to take a kiss without giving anything in return, Heath would never forgive himself.

It might already be too late.

He had held her, kissed her. He, a man consumed with upholding the highest standard of integrity and honesty.

Had he lost his mind? Or had he finally found his heart?

Heath ran a hand through his hair in frustration.

"Stop that," Miss Winfield chastised him, and pushed a stray lock back in place.

She was achingly tender. It all felt so perfectly right. And yet Heath knew it was wrong.

He tried to imagine bringing her home to his family.

It would never work. His mother would suffer

hysterics. His father would disown him... If the baronet noticed the commotion.

Heath was the heir. As such, he'd always known his lot was to marry for the betterment of his title, not for the sake of his heart. Love had nothing to do with it.

By definition, a baroness needed to be the sort of woman who would best complement one's family, one's home, one's status, one's title. A paragon. Content in the knowledge that he would never scandalize her, and she would never scandalize him. How could she? His future baroness would be part of his world, of his class, above reproach.

And yet all he wanted to do was lower his lips to Miss Winfield's eminently kissable mouth and lose himself once more in the welcome heat of her embrace.

Heath knew all the reasons why such an infatuation was madness.

First, he should never have tarried with a woman he could not wed. Such improper comportment was the last thing a gentleman should do. He had been taught better.

Although he was still decades away from inheriting the baronetcy, its shadow constantly loomed over him. The title was the reason he could move freely in Society, but also the reason his freedom was limited to what Society would allow.

He could not have her.

But he was not ready to give her up.

"Do you have plans tomorrow?" he asked urgently.

"The same plan as every other day," she said with a bemused expression. "Accompany Lady Roundtree whilst she is awake."

"But you will be here?" he insisted. "Do you take tea at the same time every day?"

"The baroness takes tea at the same time every day, and I accompany her," Miss Winfield said, enunciating carefully. "If you wish to speak with Lady Roundtree, I suggest you arrive an hour earlier. She will be happy to have you at the table."

"I am not asking about Lady Roundtree." He took a deep breath. "I'm asking about you. If I call tomorrow at teatime, may I request the pleasure of your company?"

The silence was deafening.

"I don't understand," she stammered.

More proof that he was a blackguard.

"Because you are a paid companion and I shall inherit a baronetcy?" he asked.

Miss Winfield nodded slowly, as if he had stated the exact reason why his words made no sense. She was right.

He didn't care.

"We are so much more than our professional capacities. I would like to get to know you, if you would be amenable." He held his breath.

"Why?" she asked, her tone mystified.

For the moment, he could promise little. But he wished he were in a position to give her everything. "Why not?"

She licked her lips. "Teatime?"

"Teatime." He did not trust himself to touch her again without stealing another kiss, so he forced himself to keep a proper distance.

He returned Miss Winfield and her wrinkly puglion to their patroness, and begged his leave after promising Lady Roundtree he would return on the morrow.

With a final lingering glance at Miss Winfield, Heath strode to his carriage and sat for a long moment with the reins in his lap. He was too on edge to head straight home, so he turned his horses toward a haven of friends and shadows.

Familiar sights and smells greeted him when he walked through the front doors of the Cloven Hoof. Raucous card games, tumbling dice, glasses of port and ale, giddy laughter mingling with groans of despair.

"Problem-fixer," said a deep, low voice to Heath's side. "Just the man I was hoping to find."

He turned to face Maxwell Gideon, a client and an old acquaintance. Max was many things: clever, crafty, dangerous. Some called him ruthless and controlling. Others called him risk-taking and arrogant.

Heath was fortunate enough to call him a friend.

"Is it the caricature?" he asked. Of course it was. It had instantly become the talk of the town.

"I do look fetching with cloven hooves." Max's eyes glinted in amusement. "I'm afraid I owe the caricaturist a debt. From the moment fashionable gentlemen read 'the road to me is paved with gold intentions,' the club has been filled nearly to capacity. 'Twas as if the *ton* viewed the caption as a personal challenge."

Heath wished he were more surprised. "Then how can I help you?"

Max motioned for them to settle around an out-of-the-way table before responding. "Business has never been better. Which leads me to an opportunity I am hoping you can arrange for me."

Heath allowed a cautious smile. "What are friends for if not to help each other? Enough fencing. Tell me what you need."

"I need all of *this*." Max's dark eyes raked in their surroundings. "Without my silent investor, the Cloven Hoof would not exist. That contract turned my dream into reality."

Heath nodded. Old news. He had consulted on that contract himself.

"Are you unhappy with the terms?" he asked. "The interest is high, but if I recall correctly, the terms enable buy-out negotiations within the next year."

"I can't wait a year." Max leaned forward, his gaze intense. "I want to buy him out right now. To-day."

"That wasn't the deal," Heath reminded him.

"Let's make a new deal," Max countered without hesitating. "I have the money."

Heath frowned. "Mayhap owning the deed has become an investment too lucrative to sell. What makes you think your partner would be amenable to alterations, when the current deal is weighted so heavily in their favor?"

"I'll make certain he cannot refuse." Max's dark eyes glittered. "We're not partners. He owns the building. I own everything inside of it. All I need is a meeting."

Heath considered, then shook his head. "Nonne-gotiable. Your silent investor has been silent for a reason. You are not the only one I've made promises to."

"I don't need him to chat. I need him to sign a reversion clause. It is past time I become full owner of this establishment." Max clenched his jaw. "I have spent every day and every night for the past three years pouring my blood and sweat into every corner of this business, and he has never once walked through the door."

Heath arched his brows. "So you've learned his identity?"

"No." Max's eyes flashed. "And I don't care. I just need him gone. Can you broker the deal or not?"

Heath gazed back at his friend. "I cannot make promises. Both of you are my clients. But if you give me the terms, I will present your offer."

Max growled in frustration. "Can we not simply meet in person? Surely by now every gentleman has seen enough high-in-the-instep lords and dandies frequent my club that he realizes it won't hurt his precious reputation to meet somewhere other than White's or Boodle's."

Max was not welcome at the "right" gentlemen's clubs. It was one of the many reasons he'd chosen to establish his own. His request to meet here, in a public location co-owned by both parties, was more than fair.

"I'll ask," Heath repeated.

Max inclined his head. "Thank you."

Heath assented and allowed his gaze to roam the club's crowded interior. Max was right. His establishment was more popular than ever. Heath should be proud to have brokered the deal that allowed the Cloven Hoof to become a reality.

Instead, Heath's temples began to pound. He didn't feel fulfilled. His life felt like it was missing something important. He had helped countless others live the lives they desired. When would it be time for Heath to do the same?

Max had followed his dream and made it work. He had gone from shadowy stranger with a questionable background to lord of a semi-reputable gambling den with an impressive clientele.

It was not the direction Heath would have chosen for himself. Nevertheless, he envied those who
could pursue their passion at all costs. Camellia and
her singing. Dahlia and her charity. Heath and his art
gallery?

A cold sweat tickled his skin. His mind overflowed with images of all the ways such a venture
could go wrong. He could not abide the thought of
people judging him for his taste, or lack thereof. Soon
enough he would have a title, a wife, an heir, a spare.
That would have to suffice.

"Grenville!" One of his friends pointed to the sea
of caricatures hanging from reams of string tacked
around the ceiling. "Have you seen the latest *Lord of
Pleasure?*"

Heath sighed. Months ago, the Earl of Wainwright might have actively earned his rakish
reputation, but now that he was married to Heath's
sister there was nothing funny about the golden-
haired earl causing a roomful of women to spontane-
ously—

His heart thudded to a stop.

That was not Lord Wainwright front and center
in the new caricature, but Heath's own sister Camellia. She was not drawn in some ballroom, but rather
on stage in a recognizable London theater. The audience full of women were not swooning at
Wainwright's legendary Grecian profile, but cooing to
each other about the hopelessly lovesick expression
on his face as he gazed up adoringly at his wife.

"He'll never live this down," another gentleman
hooted.

"I heard from three people who were actually
there," shouted another. "That is exactly how his face
looked during her entire performance!"

Heath's muscles shook in both fury and horror. His lip curled as he glared at the damning inked lines. He recognized that the "joke" in this case was the scandal of being in love with one's wife, not Camellia's career choice.

But it didn't matter. That was his *sister's face*. Who knew what the next caricature would bring? Perhaps all three of his sisters would be next to have their reputations torn asunder. How positively amusing for the caricaturist.

Heath dropped into the closest chair and hung his pounding head in his hands. He was a failure. Both as a fixer of problems and a big brother to his sweet, talented sister.

What good was he at either calling, if he could not keep Cam's likeness from being passed around Town as a penny jest?

He slammed his fist on the table before him. If he had disliked the so-called artist before, it was now hatred... and personal. He was going to put a stop to this cruelty if it was the last thing he did. The caricaturist now had a formidable enemy.

Heath no longer intended to unmask the coward. He planned to destroy him.

Chapter 20

*T*he twenty hours and forty-five minutes since Mr. Grenville had taken his leave and promised to return were the longest twenty hours and forty-five minutes of Nora's life.

She knew she should not read too much into a Society gentleman's sudden interest in taking tea with a commoner. A kiss meant nothing. The very fact of him returning for lemon cakes and not to beg for her hand proved what they both already knew. There could be no courtship.

And yet she'd been unable to sleep. Unable to concentrate. Unable to sit still on her stool even when Pepys poked her with hairpins to get her to pay attention.

It was hopeless. All Nora could think about was that kiss. He had transported her from an empty sitting room to a magical ballroom with an orchestra only the two of them could hear. And then, when he had lowered those full, warm lips and touched his mouth to hers...

"Are you drawing, or are you moon-calfing?" Lady Roundtree asked crossly.

"Er, drawing." Nora snapped her gaze to the sketch in front of her. "I was... contemplating the best shading technique?"

Lady Roundtree sniffed. "You were contemplating your upcoming tea."

Nora glanced over at her sharply, her heart pounding in alarm and embarrassment.

Lady Roundtree flapped her gloved fingers toward Nora's sketchbook. "No matter how much you like mulberry jam, young lady, there will be none for you until you finish that portrait."

Nora nearly swooned in relief.

The baroness had no idea that her insides muddled together like a paintbrush in water. She still saw Nora as a poor relation whose greatest victory was a full belly.

"Finishing touches now," she promised.

Her fingers flew across the page, but her mind was elsewhere.

Not a day went by that she didn't miss her brother and grandparents dearly, and wonder how they were getting on in her absence. Slowly, however, this opulent town house was starting to feel like a second home. Lady Roundtree and Captain Pugboat were family, too.

She penciled in the final details, and presented her artwork to Lady Roundtree with a flourish.

Today's effort was the latest in what had become a twelve-portrait series of fanciful scenes starring the baroness and Captain Pugboat. In this one, the intrepid duo was taming an actual lion.

Nora could scarcely keep a straight face.

Upon viewing the masterwork, Lady Roundtree

burst into delighted laughter. When she finally caught her breath, her eyes met Nora's and they both collapsed into another fit of giggles.

The baroness held up the portrait. "Who do you think I can convince that this really happened?"

"Anyone with any sense," Nora assured her. "Whenever Cap'n P. Boat has that many ribbons tied about his neck, he fools me into believing he's a real lion, too."

Lady Roundtree motioned for a footman to add the newest portrait to the beautiful gilded frames she had commissioned specifically for this series. In moments, this sketch would join the others on the walls of her private chamber.

"I am going to discover your artistic limits," the baroness warned her.

Nora lifted her chin in challenge. "I can devise a new adventure every day for the rest of our lives, if you so desire."

The baroness harrumphed. "Next time, I want us to be harpooning a whale."

Nora snorted with laughter. "In the Thames? Or is this more of a Bath seaside holiday?"

"Pirate ship," Lady Roundtree said firmly. "Without question."

"Consider it done," Nora promised.

As she and the baroness became mutual champions more and more, Nora's fear of her double life being found out had multiplied.

She did her drawings here, under this roof, behind Lady Roundtree's back. Their names were linked. Nora had not only inadvertently brought the baroness into the shadow of scandal, but the discovery would hurt Lady Roundtree's feelings, and disappoint her deeply.

Right before she tossed Nora out on her ear.

For the tenth time that day, she wished she could give up the caricatures. But even if her family weren't in desperate need of the money, Nora was in too deep. The damage had already been done. Stopping now would not make the resulting scandal any less devastating.

But there would be no scandal.

She was very careful, both in covering her own tracks and in ensuring she only drew what Society already knew to be true.

More importantly, in a less than a sennight, it would all be over. Lady Roundtree's fractured limb was improving with every passing day. Once Nora returned home, everyone's lives would go right back to normal. Both she and the caricatures would be quickly forgotten.

A footman appeared in the open doorway. "Mr. Grenville is here for tea, madam."

A rush of excitement filled Nora at the sound of Mr. Grenville's name.

"Shall I have the repast brought to this room instead?" the footman asked.

"No, no. It's already set up the way I like it." Lady Roundtree motioned her footman toward the handles of her chair. "Take me to my favorite settee."

She and Lady Roundtree had only been installed in the parlor for a few moments when Mr. Grenville strode into the room.

Nora leapt up to curtsey. Instead, she froze in fear.

She had expected him to take her breath away, but not with a display of anger.

This was not the playful man who had helped her train a puppy with teacakes. Nor was this the rakish

gentleman who had set her heart aflutter with a decadent waltz and a stolen kiss.

This version of Mr. Grenville was darker.
Harder. More dangerous.

"What happened?" Nora stammered in alarm.
Had he somehow found out the truth?

His beautiful lips curled into a sneer. "Have you
seen the latest filth?"

She frowned. "What fil—"

"The caricaturist *dares* to draw my sister," he
snarled.

Nora's stomach bottomed.

Mr. Grenville gripped the back of a chair but did
not bring himself to sit down upon it. "I will not rest
until he is destroyed."

"B-but the drawing didn't say anything bad
about your sister," Nora blurted. "Or her husband. It's
Society who finds fault with perfectly normal mari-
tal—"

She clamped her teeth together before any more
confessions could tumble out.

Lady Roundtree winced. "I thought I burned that
one before you had a chance to see it."

Nora cleared her throat. "Er..."

"It doesn't matter." Mr. Grenville threw himself
into the rosewood chair with obvious agitation. "All of
England has seen it by now. Camellia's likeness is being used not only for mockery, but to line some
cretin's pocket."

Nora's throat clogged with shock and guilt. She
had thought she was doing a good thing. Poking fun
where it belonged, not at the innocent. She had meant
no insult to Lady Wainwright.

Belatedly, she realized even a "positive" caricature was worse than no caricature at all for a man as

fiercely protective of his family as Mr. Grenville.

Drat her pen. Nora knew exactly what it felt like to do anything within one's power to protect one's family. It was good fortune she would soon be gone. She had no doubt a man this angry would turn over every stone in London in search of the culprit.

"That's... terrible," she managed faintly. "I can only imagine how you and your sister must feel."

He threw his hands in the air in frustration. "Everyone can scrounge up some semblance of sympathy except for the black-hearted rotter behind these cruel cartoons."

Lady Roundtree's fingers fluttered in perturbation. "Do you want a teacake?"

"No," he answered flatly. "I want justice."

Nora gulped.

Captain Pugboat leaped onto her lap. Reflexively, she stroked his soft, wrinkled fur until even that made her feel like a monster. The man who had so quickly begun to fill her mind and her heart was suffering because of an action she had taken, and her only response was to stroke the puppy in her lap like a madman?

Mr. Grenville stared up at the ceiling. "Who could have done such a thing?"

Nora pushed Captain Pugboat onto the floor. She didn't deserve him.

She didn't deserve any of them.

Lady Roundtree and Mr. Grenville were in the presence of a fraud.

This was her chance to come clean to them both... Yet she couldn't do it, no matter how much she might wish she could. The consequences would be too disastrous.

If Mr. Grenville discovered the truth, the very

best she could hope for was him giving her the cut direct and never speaking to her again.

However, the most likely scenario was losing him, her cousin, her post, and the secret income all at once. Without the funds from the cartoons, she would not be able to rescue her family from poverty by helping to make their small farm self-sustaining again.

But she was done with caricatures of real people.

They weren't worth the price on her soul.

She had meant the drawings as a means of helping her family, not hurting Mr. Grenville's loved ones.

The reduced income might mean Carter's plans to make the sheep farm self-sustainable this year wouldn't happen after all. But she couldn't risk an innocent being hurt again.

Lady Roundtree set down her teacup. "Has the caricature caused her harm?"

"Worse than harm." Mr. Grenville's eyes were blank and haunted. "She's now a laughingstock."

Nausea filled Nora's stomach.

This was hell. She had never meant to hurt anyone. Not Mr. Grenville, not his sister, not even the Lord of Pleasure.

She was just the feather-witted country hick they all thought she was, trying her best to make the most of a temporary situation before being sent back home to slave to the bone beside her brother as they watched their grandparents wither and die.

There was no way for everyone to win.

"It's my fault," Mr. Grenville said brokenly. "It's my job to protect my sister."

Nora's gut twisted. It was not his fault. He was a wonderful brother. A wonderful *person*. Heat pricked her eyes at how much he was hurting. How much *she* had hurt him and his family.

She ached to comfort him, but she was powerless to ease his pain.

Worse, she couldn't even apologize for the damage she had accidentally caused.

Chapter 21

*J*t had taken a fair amount of blunt to wrangle the name of the caricaturist's third-
party agency from the owner of the print-
ing house, but Heath was finally in the office of a man
who knew the scoundrel's name.

It hadn't been easy. When Heath had finally met
with the publisher, the man had no idea from whence
the drawings came. All transactions passed through a
confidential intermediary. The printing house had no
reason to break their word.

To the publisher, digging deeper wasn't worth
the price of potentially losing their primary attraction.
Until the anonymous artist had turned London on its
ear, the printing house had been failing financially.
Now they were not. Caricatures were lucrative business.

Heath did not care. Camellia should not be part
of it.

He was going to put a stop to the caricatures
right now.

"How much?" he asked the wiry gentleman behind the boxwood desk. "My client's pockets are bottomless."

While the Roundtrees did indeed possess more money than they were likely to spend in generations, Heath's fee had already been deposited in the donation account for his sister Dahlia's school.

He was not here today as an agent of his client, the baroness, but rather as the elder brother of a sweet and caring soul, whose exaggerated features were being bandied about town in mockery. He was here for Camellia.

"I told you." Mr. Ewing gazed back at him in perfect boredom. "My clients expect complete confidentiality, which is what we provide. No sum you mention can cause me to ruin the name I've built for this agency."

Heath ground his jaw.

In his experience, there was *always* a sum at which even the most pious gentleman broke. A monetary threshold at which loyalty, propriety, and honor simply fell away in favor of the allure of gold.

Mr. Ewing, however, was proving remarkably resolute.

"I shall discover the name with or without your assistance," Heath informed him coldly. "You might as well confess, and earn a bit of coin for your trouble."

Mr. Ewing pushed away from his desk. "I've another appointment waiting, so this conversation is finished. I'm sorry you have wasted your time, Mr. Grenville. You are not welcome back."

Heath assented and rose to his feet.

He supposed he could not be surprised at the turn of events. Mr. Ewing was well aware of Heath's reputation among the *ton*, and his agency quite correctly had plenty of secrets of its own to keep.

But Heath was not so easily dissuaded.

Mr. Ewing was not the perpetrator of the caricatures. They had clearly been drawn by someone present in each moment, and a man such as this would be well out of place in Heath's circles. Which meant the caricatures had to arrive at the agency before Mr. Ewing could turn around and forward them on to the printing house.

"Good day, Mr. Ewing." Heath bowed and retrieved his coat and walking-stick. "I shan't return."

He didn't need to.

Heath need only station a quantity of key, unassuming footmen along all the likely routes. The next time a collection of carefully-bound foolscap was delivered to the agency, his men would intercept the name of the sender, if not the entire package, and deliver the intelligence to him at once.

The method might not be as fast as simply paying for information, but in the end it would prove just as effective.

He returned home only long enough to dispatch his orders to select footmen well-practiced in being both unobtrusive and resourceful, then once again summoned his carriage. He'd spent the past several days with his sister and the rest of their family. None of them had felt ready to attend any soirées where the latest *Lord of Pleasure* caricature could be a topic of conversation.

Now that he'd returned home, however, Heath recalled that the Cloven Hoof had become more than a hub for gossip. Its unrepentant patrons had strung his sister's likeness about the gambling den as if the infernal sketches were decorations for a royal parade.

Heath was going to rip them all down.

As soon as he'd handed off the reins to his carriage, he stalked up the dark path to the Cloven Hoof's front door. His muscles were still tight from the meeting with Mr. Ewing. Heath had hoped to have done with the caricaturist this very afternoon. He would have to content himself with destroying evidence.

He pushed past the doorkeeper and into the dimly lit interior. His first goal was to protect his sister. His second was to avenge her honor. One way or another, he would find the artist responsible and make him pay.

In the meantime, he would rip down every brick of this gambling den if that was what it took to rid the walls of his innocent sister's countenance.

But the walls and ceiling were empty, save for a few haphazard strings looping from one empty corner to another.

"I did it for you," came a low voice from behind Heath's shoulder.

He turned to face Maxwell Gideon, the club's owner, Heath's client, and now more than ever—a good friend.

"Thank you," he forced from his scratchy throat.

Max's black gaze didn't stray from his. "I have a sister, too."

Heath kept the surprise from his face. Although he had known Max for years, the man shrouded himself in mystery. No one had gotten close enough to know much more about him than his name, and whatever details were visible to the naked eye. To think of the dangerous, ruthless owner of an infamous gaming hell as a devoted brother who looked out for his sister...

"Then you understand," he said gruffly.

Max's dark gaze was inscrutable. "If it helps, I don't believe the jest was aimed at your sister, but rather at the gossips who find 'love' to be a meaningless pursuit."

"Perhaps," Heath said tiredly. Max had not seen his sister's shocked face at being immortalized against her will. "It doesn't matter."

"It does not matter," Max agreed. He gestured to an empty table. "May I invite you to a drink?"

Heath shook his head to the drink, but sank down at the table. He was suddenly exhausted. Perhaps it would soon be over. Perhaps he and everyone else would finally be able to move on.

"Can we talk about something other than my sister?" he asked.

Max leaned back in his chair. "Your mother still hen-picking you to find an heiress?"

The question had undoubtedly been crafted to spark a reaction. To distract Heath from his current troubles by reminding him of something as mindless as the Marriage Mart, of his mother's singleminded pursuit of her children's future weddings, of something as cold and clear and straightforward as duty.

But Heath didn't think about duty anymore when he considered the perfect woman. He thought about a young lady who was the opposite of cold or straightforward. The opposite of what his mother wanted, of what the title needed, the opposite of anything he could hope to have.

Yet whenever he closed his eyes... all he could picture was Miss Winfield.

"My mother cares about blood, not money," Heath said with a sigh. "As long as the young lady comes from the right stock, Mother won't complain."

Max's gaze was shrewd. "But would you?"

Heath did not respond. His previous thoughts must have already given him away.

He could not help it. The slightest word made him think of Miss Winfield. A snippet of melody, a work of art, a flash of red. She was part of him now. Everywhere he looked, everywhere he went, he imagined her by his side. And now that they had kissed, Heath feared he had lost far more than his good sense. He was in danger of losing his heart.

"Ah." Max lifted his brows. "So there is a girl."

"A woman," Heath corrected. But could she really become a future baroness?

Before he could consider the notion more deeply, his family must first be willing to accept her.

Even if Heath was willing to forgo the good regard of the rest of Society, he was not so callous as to risk ruining his unwed sisters' reputations. They deserved to find happiness just as much as anyone.

But his siblings weren't his only family. Mother would not be easy to convince. And if Father emerged from his study long enough to forbid the match...

Heath bit back a groan.

Max's lips twitched. "My advice?"

"Pray tell." Heath held out a palm and gestured for him to continue.

Max rose from the table, but lowered his mouth to Heath's ear before walking away. "Don't bollocks it up."

A startled laugh escaped Heath's throat.

Quite sage advice, indeed. Once he figured out the right path, he would be certain to follow it.

A shaft of sunlight streamed into the shadowy interior of the club. Heath glanced over in time to see Phineas Mapleton enter the Cloven Hoof.

Apparently, so did the rest of the patrons.

Loud neighing came from the Faro tables. Impressive braying came from the whist players. A wild whinny pierced the air from the Loo players in the back.

Heath sent a passing barmaid a startled expression.

"Haven't seen it?" With a laugh, she tossed a piece of foolscap onto his table. "It just came out a few hours ago. They're stringing them up now."

"But, lo!" called a chorus of drunken voices. "'Tis a stallion among pups!"

Mapleton's pet phrase? Heath had never believed the insufferable dandy would manage to make it catch on. Something must have happened. He picked up the parchment.

The latest caricature was a viciously brilliant work of art.

A white picket fence divided the comic in two panels. To the left were three beautiful maidens, frolicking in a meadow of flowers with a dozen adorable puppies. One of the young ladies cuddled a puppy to her bosom, another nuzzled her nose against the pup's face, and the third pressed a kiss between a pair of floppy ears.

The other half of the panel featured the rear view of a spindly centaur standing in an ankle-high swamp of his own muck. The legs and back were that of a horse, but the florid waistcoat and piqued expression belonged to none other than Phineas Mapleton.

The caption read: "Stallion among pups... or horse's arse?"

No wonder it had become an instant classic.

"Stop braying!" Mapleton shrieked. "Donkeys are not stallions!"

All of the neighs and whinnies immediate

changed to donkey-like brays.

As much as Heath despised the caricaturist, he couldn't bring himself to crumple up the paper. Mapleton had tried to talk him into an extortion scheme to blackmail their friends. Now he would know what it felt like to have his own words and deeds become fodder for mockery.

The caricaturist still must be stopped, of course. Although the anonymous cartoons never named names, every member of the *ton* would know exactly who and what the comical contrast referred to.

Heath pushed to his feet. Before he could reach the door, a red-faced Phineas Mapleton blocked his path.

Mapleton waved a pound note before Heath's nose. "Represent me!"

"I'm not a barrister," Heath replied in irritation, trying to dodge the bill flapping in his face.

Mapleton shoved the note inside Heath's coat pocket. "Now you possess it. It's done. You represent me."

Heath tightened his jaw. This was not what he meant when he had let it be known that any person who could scrounge up so much as a ha'penny was more than worthy enough to be his client. Heath preferred free will on both sides. But this was neither the time nor the place to get into a public argument with the dandy who was currently the talk of the town.

He cast Mapleton a flat stare. "What is it you expect me to do?"

"Find him." Mapleton waved a copy of the cartoon in Heath's face. "*Stop* him. I'll pay you as much as you need. Do you want me to donate a hundred pounds to that stupid charity right now?"

"Two hundred," Heath said automatically.

Under other circumstances, Phineas Mapleton would be the last person Heath would have accepted as a client. But he was already working toward the same goal. If saying yes meant a few more meals for hungry orphans, Heath couldn't turn even a horse's arse away.

"Done." Mapleton crumpled up the caricature and dropped it into the closest mug of ale. "It will arrive by morning."

Heath lifted his hand. "Then, if you'll excuse me?"

Mapleton stepped aside, glaring at dozens of rowdy gamblers who had already forgotten him and returned to their dice and cards.

Heath pushed out of the dark club and back into the sunlight. He was done playing games. Not just with the caricaturist, but with his own life, too.

Chapter 22

*H*eath had only been awake for an hour and a half, but already the following morning was off-kilter.

His breakfast table had seemed empty. His town house, too quiet. And though he had the most talented valet in all of London creating a masterwork of intricate folds with his cravat, Heath could not help but wish those were Miss Winfield's hands upon his chest.

Ever since their kiss, he could not glimpse a linen neckcloth without remembering how it felt to have her arrange his after he had tasted her lips. His heart lightened. He no longer required hearing the strains of music to be moved to dance. He just needed to have Miss Winfield in his arms.

Heath's eyes widened. That was indeed the crux of the matter. He *needed* to have her in his arms.

He was in love.

The floor seemed to tilt about him at the realization. He had known they were more than compatible, suspected their trajectory would not end with a single kiss, but he had not realized his future was already predetermined. *Love.* So what was he meant to do about it?

His blood quickened. Make room, of course. Not just in his heart, but in every aspect of his life.

Heath dismissed his valet and glanced about his dressing chamber, mentally rearranging items and furniture to accommodate the addition of a wife. His heart sang at the thought of her pert red curls brightening up his bachelor quarters.

With luck, soon there might be no room in the armoire for Heath's shirts and waistcoats because it would be overflowing with pastel pink gowns instead.

His chest thumped.

He wasn't just imagining her as his wife. He was realizing how *happy* it would make him. The two of them, together. Not in secret. Not musicless dances and stolen kisses. A marriage full of passion and art and waltzes that led to... even more passion. Not in brief snatches, but for the rest of their lives.

Don't bollocks it up, Maxwell Gideon had said. Wise words from a wise man. Heath would have to do this right.

In this, at least, there was a path one could follow. Miss Winfield was far from the expected sort of attachment, but that did not mean Heath could not proceed as he'd always imagined.

Before one spoke of one's feelings to a lady one hoped to someday court, the first step was to secure permission to do so. Under normal circumstances, the girl's father would be the one to address. In this case, Heath would be forced to ask permission from the closest thing Miss Winfield had in town to an official guardian.

Once permission to formally court her was secured, Heath would take her to meet his family. If his parents and siblings did not oppose the match, he would be free to express his feelings to Miss Winfield.

That permission would undoubtedly be the biggest hurdle.

He sent a carefully worded letter off to his sister with the instruction that his footman was to wait for an immediate reply.

Heath did not wish to tip his hand. Lady Roundtree liked him, but she was also unpredictable. And even if she granted his petition, he would still need to convince Miss Winfield to present herself at the Grenville home to be inspected and judged.

He did not wish to put her through anything distasteful. On the other hand, Miss Winfield felt the same passion for her family as Heath felt toward his. He had no doubt she would sacrifice anything if it would aid her grandparents. Just like he would have to do if his own family feared irreparable harm from such an unprecedented alliance. Miss Winfield would go away, and they would never again meet.

But Heath suspected the resulting hole in his heart would be with him the rest of his life.

As soon as his footman returned, Heath dashed out of his town house to his carriage and made haste to call upon Lady Roundtree.

When he was shown into the front parlor, the baroness was alone. He squared his shoulders. Unusual or not, this would have to work.

"Mr. Grenville!" Lady Roundtree flapped her hands at him in excitement. "What an unexpected delight! I'm afraid I just sent Miss Winfield to change from her morning gown to her afternoon gown, so she won't be able available to join us for nigh half an hour.

Have you come to discuss the case?"

Heath took the wingback chair closest to the baroness's settee, and leaned forward. "I've come to discuss Miss Winfield."

"I see." Lady Roundtree's blue eyes grew crafty. "I wondered how long it would take."

Heath blinked. "Pardon?"

She waved a hand. "Go on, go on. What have I to do with the matter?"

Heath cleared his throat. "I should properly be directing this inquiry to Miss Winfield's grandfather."

"And I hope you make the trek." Lady Roundtree lifted a cup of tea. "They don't get many visitors."

"Better than that: I intend to bring them here." Heath had already thought it over. "Any family of Miss Winfield's must also be family of mine. They will want for nothing."

Lady Roundtree glanced up from her tea. "How fortuitous. I could use a new bonnet."

"Pardon?" Heath said, then forged ahead when the baroness motioned for him to keep talking. "I am formally requesting permission to court Miss Winfield."

"You are asking me to be a paid employee's guardian *and* duenna?" Lady Roundtree glared down her nose at him.

He stared back. "I..."

"I accept." She refilled her cup. "But since I am chair-bound, we will have to divide the duties. I will be Winfield's guardian and Captain Pugboat can be her companion."

Heath wondered if the baroness had been drinking whiskey with her tea. "That is to say, you give your formal permission? At least until I can speak with her grandfather?"

"Congratulations," Lady Roundtree spooned sugar into her cup. "You have both made an excellent match."

"Miss Winfield hasn't agreed to anything yet," Heath reminded her. "Now that I have permission, I must only wait for the perfect moment to ask for her hand."

Lady Roundtree arched her brows. "Is that all?"

Very well, it was not *all*. It was just one step toward the right path. Heath ran a hand through his hair.

Before he and Miss Winfield could pursue a courtship, he would need to take her—and her chairbound chaperone—to meet his family. Trepidation crawled down his neck.

Heath's jaw tightened. Meeting Miss Winfield would either convince his family of their compatibility... or prove once and for all that love would never be more important than one's duty.

He straightened. "Do you have plans for the afternoon?"

"I'll cancel them." Lady Roundtree put down her teacup. "What do you have in mind?"

A yip and the patter of tiny paws sounded from the corridor.

Captain Pugboat sailed into the parlor, his wrinkled belly sliding on the freshly waxed floor. In a trice, he collided with the center carpet. Rather than right himself, he rolled with his paws toward the ceiling and twisted his spine merrily from side to side as if scratching his back on the baroness's Axminster carpet had been his plan all along.

Miss Winfield entered the room at a more sedate pace. Her eyes lit up at the sight of Heath.

His heart skipped. He hoped she could not detect

his inner battle on his face.

"Ring for our coats and bonnets," Lady Round-tree said.

Miss Winfield blinked. "Where are we going?"

The baroness sent raised eyebrows toward Heath.

He bowed to Miss Winfield in greeting. "To call upon my family, if you would be so kind."

"Of course," she said hesitantly.

Splendid. After Heath had sent a private word to his youngest sister warning of their possible arrival, Bryony's immediate reply had insisted she and the others cared far more for his happiness than any incidental damage to the family's reputation.

That was all well and good, but Heath's sisters did not rule the Grenville household. He had no wish to hurt Mother. And he could not disappoint Father.

When they arrived at the Grenville town house, all three sisters loomed over the butler's shoulder. Even Camellia, who no longer lived at home, must have rushed across Mayfair in her husband's fastest conveyance so as not to miss the moment.

"Where's Mother?" Heath whispered to his siblings.

"In the parlor preparing tea for Lady Round-tree."

"I love tea." The baroness brightened. "Wheel me in."

Heath shooed his sisters out of the way to make room for Miss Winfield and the entourage of footmen required to lift Lady Roundtree's wheeled chair up the steps and into the house.

"I had meant to perform introductions in a parlor like civilized people rather than crowded about the front stoop like heathens," he began with a darkling glance at his sisters.

They smiled back at him angelically.

"But since we are all here," he continued, "Hoydens, it is my distinct privilege and absolute pleasure to present Miss Eleanora Winfield. Miss Winfield, it is my dubious honor to introduce you to the three most mule-headed, intelligent, and embarrassingly nosy sisters a brother could ever have." He gestured at each in turn, starting with Camellia. "Lady Wainwright, Miss Dahlia Grenville, and Miss Bryony Grenville."

Miss Winfield dipped an immediate curtsey as her cheeks flushed rosy pink. "How do you do?"

"What is better, a waltz or a minuet?" Dahlia fired back in lieu of reply.

Clearly discombobulated, Miss Winfield stammered, "Waltz?"

"Ratafia or sherry?" Bryony demanded.

Miss Winfield shot a bewildered glance over her shoulder at Heath before answering, "Sherry?"

Camellia stepped forward. "Cream first or jam first?"

"Jam," Miss Winfield replied emphatically.

"You're in." Camellia looped her arm through Miss Winfield's, and led her toward the rear sitting room. "We've made a place for you at our gaming table. Do you know how to count cards?"

Heath stepped into their path. "Now that Miss Winfield has been properly vetted, might she at least meet our parents before you abscond with her?"

A flicker of sympathy flashed across Camellia's eyes.

Heath had his answer.

Father did not deem the occasion important enough to attend.

No matter. Heath ignored the twist in his heart.

Father might bear the title, but Mother was the one who ran the family.

Heath offered his arm to Miss Winfield. Perhaps this was a boon. He would not have to worry about what Father thought of Heath being the next Grenville to break societal rules, after all. The baronet was unlikely to take notice.

The five of them piled in behind Lady Roundtree and her footmen and streamed into the parlor.

When Mother greeted Lady Roundtree like the old friends they were, and spared not a glance toward Miss Winfield, Heath realized his sisters must not have informed their mother of the true purpose of today's visit.

Perhaps that was a boon as well. He would introduce Miss Winfield to his mother, then give the extended family some space to get to know each other before causing an uproar with an official announcement.

"Mother, I would like to present Miss Eleanora Winfield. Miss Winfield, this is my mother, Lady Grenville."

Miss Winfield executed a perfect curtsey.

Mother flashed a preoccupied smile and returned her focus to her conversation with Lady Roundtree.

"Now can we steal her away?" Bryony stage-whispered. "Mother won't stop talking about hair ribbons for at least another hour."

Heath offered his elbow to Miss Winfield before his sisters could deprive him of the privilege.

"Have you ever tossed half a deck of playing cards in someone's face?" he asked politely.

"Just my brother's," she replied with a startled laugh. "But only because we didn't have a whole deck."

"She's perfect!" Dahlia exclaimed and gave a little twirl in excitement.

They ushered her into the sibling sitting room.

"Heath invented the game," Bryony confided. "But we made it better."

Within moments of taking her seat at the gaming table, Miss Winfield was parrying words with the others and hiccupping with laughter as if she had been part of the family forever.

Heath's pulse skipped. His future bride wouldn't have to try to fit in—she already did. The afternoon quickly flew by.

"Guess what I have," Camellia called in singsong.

"Not spades," Dahlia groaned as cards fluttered about her head.

"I'm out." Heath tossed his cards face down and leaned back in his chair to spend the rest of the round watching Miss Winfield's animated expressions.

He had always believed it impossible to ever find a "perfect" woman. He couldn't have been more wrong. Miss Winfield had been right in front of him all this time.

"Ha!" Bryony exclaimed as she scooped up a pile of hairpins they'd been using to wager. "Father would be so proud."

"And Mother would disown all of us," Camellia said with a laugh.

Heath winced at the reminder. His mother would only be the first in a long line of aristocrats who would be shocked to discover he'd "taken up with a commoner." Not all of them would be pleasant or conceal their disdain. Until he inherited the title, Heath would not even be able to use that to protect Miss Winfield from vitriol. Their opinions would be harsh.

But Heath was not interested in marrying the *beau monde*. He wished to wed Miss Winfield.

If he, his family, and Miss Winfield could present a united front...

Then it wouldn't matter what anyone else thought.

Chapter 23

*N*ora could not recall the last time she'd had so much unbridled fun. Heath and his siblings had her in tears of laughter.

That she constantly confused the sixes with the nines did not matter. The object of the game seemed less about winning and more about tossing cards in one's opponent's face when they failed to match suit.

It was exactly the sort of game one might expect bored siblings to invent some drizzly afternoon when it was too wet to go outside. Indeed, the cards seemed more likely to be in the air than to be in any person's possession.

Nora loved that the Grenvilles had never stopped playing it in favor of more grown-up games like Whist or Casino. This was no true competition, but rather an excuse for family to spend time with each other.

"Are you going to the balloon launch next month?" Camellia asked her siblings.

Dahlia shook her head. "Faith and Chris are going, which leaves me on boarding school duty." She turned to Bryony. "Care to come play your violin for a few hours?"

"I've an engagement, but I'll make it up to you," Bryony promised. "New bonnets for all the girls."

Dahlia's eyes shone. "That will be a wonderful treat."

Nora's astonished gaze bounced between them as they conversed. How wonderful it must have been to grow up a Grenville! So much love, so much wealth, so many siblings. Their home seemed like heaven.

As the eldest—and beleaguered sole male—Heath could have adopted an authoritarian attitude toward his younger sisters, or ignored them completely. Instead the clan quite obviously were the best of friends.

"How goes the new dancing instructor?" he inquired.

Dahlia brightened anew. "Do you miss your post? One can always make room in the schedule for more dancing."

Nora sighed at the obvious love they shared.

Of course Mr. Grenville would be amazing with his family. When wasn't he splendid? She would not have fallen in love with the man if he were not.

Reality crept in from the shadows. As much as she would enjoy laughing around this table with them forever, the Grenvilles were not her family. This was not her home. She did not truly belong.

Their stories proved it.

"I despise soirées," Bryony groaned. "Please don't make me go."

"You love soirées," Dahlia corrected. "You hate being forced to submit to five hours of hot tongs before Mother concedes defeat to your inability to hold a ringlet."

"Nora's curls are the perfect compromise," Camellia put in. "Neither stick-straight nor sausage curls."

"We can't all be as gorgeous as Nora," Bryony grumbled. "Perhaps she could go in my place."

"Or just teach you how to arrange your hair," Dahlia said dryly, with a wink in Nora's direction.

Her lungs froze. Since coming to London, Mr. Grenville had been the first non-relative to respect her as a person, and thus far the only person to treat her as if she were an equal.

Until today. Now there were three more people acting as though Nora were one of them.

She could scarcely believe her turn of fortune.

Her fingers shook as she clumsily shuffled the cards and set them back in the middle of the table. When the top half slid to the side, she quickly righted it.

No one mocked her. No one even noticed; the Grenvilles were too busy teasing one another.

"Do *not* go to that masquerade," Camellia told Bryony emphatically. "Look what happened to me."

"Or *do*." Dahlia gave Bryony a conspiratorial grin. "Look what happened to Camellia."

"Nora would never attend such a party," Camellia scolded her sisters.

"Nora may have attended so many that she's become bored with scandalous masquerades altogether," Dahlia countered.

"What's this?" Nora's mouth dropped open in mock outrage. "When did I get dragged into your nonsense?"

"When you walked in the front door," Bryony replied, eyes twinkling.

Dahlia offered Nora a commiserating pat on the

shoulder. "It's what we do."

"You'll get used to it," Camellia added with a laugh. "It's not like we ever change."

"You ought to consider changing," Mr. Grenville grumbled. "How's a gentleman to uphold his sterling reputation with you three miscreants in the family?"

"Upholding reputations is your job, not ours," Bryony pointed out with an innocent flutter of lashes. "My job is to make you work for it."

"Mine, too," said Dahlia with a grin.

"Mine, too," Camellia agreed. "Now can we get back to the game?"

Mr. Grenville burst out laughing. "I think I won ten minutes ago."

"Didn't see it, so it didn't happen." Bryony lifted the top half of the newly shuffled deck and began to deal. "Double your wagers, ladies."

Camellia widened her eyes. "Why, Miss Bryony Grenville. Ladies don't wager."

"That's right," Mr. Grenville said sternly.

Dahlia tossed a gold sovereign onto the table. "I'll wager Heath loses."

Bryony's grin widened as she tossed an extra coin to the table. "I'll wager Miss Winfield is the only one who walks out of this room a winner."

Nora couldn't agree more. She already felt richer.

"I'm afraid my reticule hasn't any coin." She cast a sideways glance at Mr. Grenville. "I wager Mr. Grenville's cravat."

"You cannot wager a fellow gambler's cravat," he protested.

"And you can't call him Mr. Grenville," Bryony a put in with a laugh. "He's Heath, I'm Bryony, this is Dahlia, and that's Camellia."

Nora's cheeks flushed with pleasure at the unexpected honor of first-naming them so quickly. "And I'm Eleanora, but friends call me Nora."

"You consider it friendly to wager an innocent bystander's cravat?" Mr. Grenville—er, Heath—said with faux hurt.

"You don't know how to tie them anyway," she replied sweetly, to the delight of his siblings.

The next quarter hour passed in a blur of flying cards, sibling rivalry, and tears of laughter on all sides. Being with the Grenvilles was just like being at home with her own family. Nora gazed at them in contentment. Her brother Carter would fit in perfectly with a crowd like this.

The Grenvilles were utterly mad and rowdy and fun and breathtakingly genuine without airs of any sort. For the first time in weeks, Nora was among a group of people with whom she felt like she could finally be herself.

Almost herself.

Her happiness faltered. She would have to remain the Nora she presented to the world, rather than the artist she was in private. The Grenvilles were the last people she could confess her secret identity to, particularly since all of them were sworn enemies of the caricaturist.

Yet she yearned to belong more than anything. She wished she could have moments like this, a tribe like this, a life like *this*. Her stomach churned. She hated that she could not tell them the truth and still be welcome at the table.

"What do you think?" asked Dahlia as the latest storm of playing cards rained down about them. "Should we do it?"

"Absolutely." Camellia beamed at Nora. "It's

time."

Nora's heart skipped. "Time for what?"

"Time to make it official," Heath said gruffly. "No escaping now."

Her pulse thrummed. "Make what official?"

Dahlia climbed up on her chair and affected a regal stance. "Miss Eleanora Winfield, known to her friends and family—"

"And us," whispered Bryony.

"She's getting there," Camellia hissed back.

"—and *us* as Nora," Dahlia continued from high atop her makeshift throne. "I now pronounce you—"

Camellia and Bryony quickly gathered the loose cards from the table top.

"—an honorary Grenville!" Dahlia finished with a crescendo.

Bryony and Camellia baptized Nora with a deluge of fluttering cards. "An honorary Grenville!"

The garbled sound in Nora's throat was somewhere between a laugh and a sob. Her pulse pounded in her ears. She turned wide eyes toward Heath in question.

He lifted her hand to his lips and pressed a warm kiss to the back of her fingers. "You've been sworn in. Like it or not, you're one of us now."

The backs of Nora's eyes stung. She stared back at all of them speechlessly.

"Don't think you're special," Bryony teased. "You're the fourth."

Nora felt *incredibly* special. She gave a wobbly smile. Nothing could lessen this moment. "Who was first?"

"Faith Digby," Heath answered. "Dahlia's partner in crime."

"In charity," Dahlia corrected him. "Faith has

been my bosom friend since we were small. Now we run a boarding school together."

"Very Grenville of her," Camellia agreed.

Nora could only imagine. "And the second?"

"Simon Spaulding," everyone but Dahlia answered in a singsong voice.

Though she didn't speak a word, the bright red of her cheeks spoke volumes.

"Oh, and Lord Wainwright, of course," Bryony said. "Everyone needs a Lord of Pleasure in the family."

Camellia's cheeks pinkened in mortification.

Nora suddenly wanted to sink through the floor.

"Thus, it was past time for my turn." Heath gazed at her warmly. "Welcome to the family, Nora."

Her breaths were shallow as she forced herself to smile back.

"I hope we haven't frightened her off," Dahlia whispered to Bryony.

"I won't allow you to." Heath lifted Nora's fingers to his lips for a second kiss. "I am hoping to make her presence permanent."

Her heart stopped. Heath hadn't been planning on making her an offer to become his mistress. He wanted her to be his *wife*.

A bolt of longing sharp enough to scald shot through her at the idea. Courted. By *him*. Her heart ached.

There was nothing she wanted more than to be Heath's wife, to be part of this wonderful madcap family, to live happily ever after.

But she would lose him if she were honest with them. Lose all of them, all of *this*.

Nor could she wed him with such a secret hiding

between them. He would never forgive such a betrayal. She would never forgive *herself* if she hurt any
of them more than she already had.

Her skin prickled with cold sweat. It took all the
courage she had to ruin a moment so perfect, but she
forced herself to speak. "I think..."

A footman strode into the room. "Lady Grenville
requests the honor of her children's company."

"Mother," Camellia gasped. "I forgot all about
tea."

"I've never in my life forgotten tea," Bryony said
with feeling.

Heath leapt to his feet and offered his elbow to
Nora. "Come, meet my mother in truth this time."

Nora swallowed her protest. She had no choice
but to take the arm of the man she loved and allow
him to lead her to a mother she would never have.
This was not the moment to make an uncomfortable
scene for Heath. They could speak later, in private.

If such were even necessary.

More likely, Lady Grenville would put paid at
once to the fantasy of her husband's heir courting a
sheep maiden from the West Midlands.

Nora's heavy stomach churned at the idea of losing them all. She'd somehow fallen in love with
Heath's entire family in the space of an afternoon.

No wonder he would do anything in his power to
protect them. Particularly from people like her.

Even if she had not involved his sister in one of
her caricatures, a courtship with Nora would ruin
more than Heath's social standing. It would ruin his
career. The name he had so painstakingly built for
himself was as the man who kept the *ton* scandal-free.

She couldn't ruin that for him.

"Is Father downstairs?" Heath asked one of the

footmen in a low voice.

The footman shook his head. "No, my lord."

Heath's jaw tightened.

"It's nothing to do with you," Bryony whispered in Nora's ear. "Father is never around."

Heath stopped in his tracks and turn to face Nora.

She stared up at him in alarm.

"What my sister said is true." He lifted Nora's hands to his chest. "But it won't happen to us. I want you to know that I am not a mercenary suitor in search of some cold alliance. I'm looking for a partner in all senses, now and forever. With you, I've found everything I'm looking for."

"That's... extremely romantic," Dahlia whispered.

Bryony nodded, wide-eyed. "I don't think we should be witnessing this part."

Nora could not speak over the pounding of her heart.

"What part?" came a curious voice.

Nora's pulse skipped.

They had stopped just outside the threshold to the front parlor, and its inhabitants had witnessed everything.

"Mother," Heath said, releasing Nora's hand with obvious reluctance. "I was just saying that I hope to see much more of Miss Winfield."

He didn't say *marriage*. He didn't even say *possible courtship*. Yet the unspoken implication hung heavy in the suddenly thick air.

Lady Grenville blanched in obvious shock.

Good, Nora told her twisting stomach. This flight of imagination was about to come crashing down.

Heath led her and his entourage of sisters further into the room.

"You wish to court Lady Roundtree's employee?" Lady Grenville asked in baffled horror, when at last she managed to speak.

Lady Roundtree's voice boomed from the settee. "Miss Eleanora Winfield is my cousin."

A palpable wave of surprise coursed through the room.

Nora was perhaps the most shocked among them. She had known the baroness had developed some level of affection for her, but had not expected public acknowledgment. Lady Roundtree must truly consider Nora family now.

Dahlia stared at her. "The two of you are cousins?"

Nora nodded jerkily, not trusting her voice.

"I just said so." Lady Roundtree pulled out her quizzing glass. "Don't tell me you need an ear horn already."

Everyone's gazes turned to the matriarch of the family.

After a long moment, Lady Grenville gave a delicate sniff. "I cannot imagine why you are all looking at me. My arms are open. It is Miss Winfield who must decide if she wishes to accept Heath's hand."

Open arms. An audible gasp strangled in Nora's throat. Lady Grenville would make no objection?

"That settles it," Bryony whispered to Nora. "'Honorary' is only temporary."

Nora's heart leaped—and almost immediately sank. She could easily imagine spending a happy life with a family like the Grenvilles. But she already had a family of her own.

Would Heath demand she choose between

them?

Chapter 24

*A*fter returning to Lady Roundtree's town house, Nora helped the footmen settle the baroness upon a comfortable settee in the front parlor, then turned to face Heath.

His family was marvelous. *He* was marvelous. Her head swam at the thought of being his wife.

Now that Nora's days of drawing Society caricatures were relegated to her past where they belonged, perhaps her future was finally open. She hated that she could not confess what she had done to save her family, but there was no sense causing trouble over something he had no need to know.

She supposed helping one's family by any means necessary was not a worse secret than others brought to their marriages. If she wedded a rake, she certainly would not enquire names and dates of the countless women he'd bedded before her, and doubted even minimal information would be likely to be volunteered. A marriage was not about looking backward toward each other's pasts, but rather forging a new future together.

That was the primary hurdle they would need to work out before their attachment could go further. Forging a future... *where*? What of Nora's family? What of Heath's? If one of them would be required to give up everything, she had no doubt the duty would fall upon her shoulders. He was the baronet. She was the sheep maiden.

But she could not help but wish for a happy ever after.

"Stay," she said impulsively, then turned to the baroness. "If it's all right with Lady Roundtree."

"He's your suitor." The baroness motioned for her tea set. "I wouldn't shoo him out."

Heath bowed. "Only a fool would turn down an opportunity to spend an evening with two beautiful women."

"Keep your voice down." Lady Roundtree added her evening dose of laudanum to a china teacup. "I might rest my eyes for a few moments."

Nora glanced at Heath, then back to the baroness. "Shouldn't you keep an eye on me?"

"Captain Pugboat is your duenna," Lady Roundtree mumbled without opening her eyes. "And common sense, if you have any. I'm right here in the same room."

Nora's cheeks heated at the implication and she quickly turned back toward Heath. "Your family is a joy. I can see why you love each other."

"They were just as taken with you," he said with a satisfied smile. "You even set a record as the quickest honorary Grenville in history."

Nora couldn't wait to make all of them honorary Winfields in return.

"I'm sorry your father disappointed you," she said softly.

A muscle twitched at Heath's temple. "Bryony was right: Father is never present. Any disappointment is my own fault for failing to set my expectations correctly. What is your family like?"

"Wonderful," she admitted. "My grandparents have too many age and health issues now to be much help with the crops or the sheep anymore, but they love us just as much as they love that farm. If there was anything at all they could do for us, I know they wouldn't hesitate."

"Us?" Heath repeated with a frown. His face cleared. "That's right, you have a brother."

She nodded. "Carter is a full year younger, but he might as well be my twin. We've been inseparable for as long as I can remember. That is, until I was sent here." A sudden stab of nostalgia gripped her heart. "It's been so hard without them."

Worry filled his hazel eyes. "Wouldn't you... Do you not want to live in London?"

Her stomach bottomed. Here it was. The moment he would realize they couldn't suit.

"I can't leave them to fend for themselves," she said simply. "Carter is doing his best to make the farm self-sustaining again, but—"

"Nora, I have money." Heath took her hands, his gaze sheepish. "It's considered a vulgar subject to talk about, but this is important for you to hear. Even before the banns are read, I will ensure your family wants for nothing. None of you will ever have to worry about the farm again. We can send funds, servants, a lifetime supply of ostrich feathers for your grandmother's bonnet, anything they need."

"They need *me*," Nora said, her voice scratchy

with the pain of disappointing him. Of disappointing herself. She had known this couldn't work. "I know you need to be in London. Your clients are here; your family is here. But *my* family is back home. I can't spend my life here with you if it means giving them up, too."

A sudden snore rent the parlor. The baroness had fallen asleep.

Heath lifted Noras hands to his chest. "I would never ask you to give up your family. You're right that mine is here in London, but they're here because of the Season. Most peers and their families come to Town only whilst Parliament is in session, and then return to their country estates."

Nora frowned. "Where is your country estate?"

"In the West Midlands," he said, his eyes shining. "With you."

Her reply was barely audible. "The West Midlands?"

"We'll build a home wherever you like. Right next to your grandparents, if you prefer. We'll spend the Season here in London and the rest of the year near your family."

Hope gripped Nora's chest. Was it really possible? Might they find a compromise where everyone could win?

Or was this wishful thinking? Pretty words he could promise now, before he inherited the title and became as distant as his own father? She would have to tread lightly if she wished to discover the truth.

"Does the baronetcy take up much of your time?" she asked.

Heath's brow furrowed. "I don't have it yet."

"But..." She pulled her hands back to her lap in confusion. "Oughtn't you to learn the ropes? Isn't there some sort of..."

"Baronetcy apprenticeship?" Heath asked dryly. "That was Eton and Oxford. My father has a large cabinet of trusted advisors. Every year in our annual meetings, they assure me of a smooth transition in the future."

Annual meetings to discuss the inevitable event of a parent's death made inheriting a title sound positively ghoulish. Nora wished she hadn't needed to broach the subject. "In the meanwhile, I'm glad you found a career that fulfills you."

"A what?" His mouth curved and he affected a haughty accent. "No gentleman in line to a title would be caught dead anywhere near a *career*."

Her neck heated. "I didn't mean any offense."

"You were absolutely correct. Scandal-fixing *is* my career." He lifted a shoulder. "Mayhap I wouldn't be so sensitive about it if I had chosen the path that fulfilled me."

Lady Roundtree let out another snore and turned her face toward the settee.

Nora lowered her voice. "You don't enjoy being a scandal-fixer?"

"I do it to help people who need it." His gaze grew distant. "It is not how I'd prefer to spend my time."

She leaned forward, intrigued. "What would you rather do?"

"I..." Heath cast a glance toward the baroness snoring softly on the other side of the room. "Perhaps this isn't the right moment for confessions."

Nora bit her lip. He was right. They would not be able to have the heart-to-heart they desperately needed if the baroness could wake up at any moment and overhear everything.

She rose to her feet. "Come with me."

Heath looked at her quizzically but pushed to his feet without question.

She led him past the room where they had trained Captain Pugboat to the tiny parlor she used as her drawing nook. It was close enough to the front parlor to hear the baroness if she should happen to call, and not so far away as to reach the guest chambers.

The tiny parlor was too small to hold more than the single chaise, so Nora seated herself on the end with the armrest and motioned for Heath to join her.

"Is this your hideaway?" he asked as he settled by her side.

It had been her sanctuary for eight short weeks. The idea of moving into her own house... Nay, of having not one but *two* homes of her own, with the farm no longer a worry...

"Yes." She tilted her face toward his. "But first, you were telling me there was something you'd rather be doing with your life. I'd love to know what that is."

He leaned his wide shoulders back against the wallpaper. "Don't laugh."

"Never." She loved him too much to treat his ideas with disrespect. "Trust me."

After a moment, he nodded. "An art gallery."

"You want to buy one?" she asked when he didn't elaborate.

"I want to run one." His eyes brightened. "I want it to be mine."

She leaned forward. "Your art?"

"My vision." His voice sounded far away. "I want to discover the artists, select the right works, and determine the best way to display them. I want to have seasonal themes and host traveling exhibitions and introduce all manner of art to people who would not otherwise have known where to look for it. I want to provide modern artists a venue like the Dulwich Picture Gallery has given to the masters."

"It sounds marvelous," Nora said, and meant it. "You have thought about this a lot."

"Since I was small," he admitted.

She didn't understand. "Then why don't you do it? Is it the money?"

He laughed humorlessly. "I wish all I lacked was money. We have plenty of that. What I cannot have is an association to a trade."

"You can purchase unlimited quantities of art for your home, but not for a gallery?" Nora said in disbelief.

"I can own a thousand galleries," he said, his expression defeated. "I just can't run them. That's work. Something other people do. I would have to pay someone else to perform the job I want for myself."

Nora frowned. "Two of your sisters work."

"And have lost all ties with Polite Society," he returned with a frustrated sigh. "Besides all the other reasons why a man in my position would have no wish to lose my social standing, I also would hope to make my peers the primary market. They have the free time and the heavy purses to dedicate to it."

"It would be a gallery for rich people?" she asked slowly.

His gaze snapped to hers. "You don't approve."

"It seems like there are plenty of places for the rich. White's, Boodle's, Almack's," she admitted. "But if your goal is to share art with as many people as possible, then being a 'Vauxhall' is better than being an 'Almack's.' Your gallery would attract both sectors and triple the potential exposure for the artists."

The corner of his mouth curved up. "Perhaps you

should promote the gallery, and I shall concern myself with procuring its specimens."

"I hope you do it," she said, hoping he could see the sincerity in her eyes. "I think you'd be perfect at it."

He slid his hand into her hair and cupped her cheek. "Do you know what I think is perfect?"

Heart pounding, she shook her head.

"I'll show you." Without another word, he lowered his mouth to hers.

His lips were familiar now. She'd dreamed of them every night. And yet his kiss moved through her like lightning streaking across a thunderstorm. Bright, powerful, electrifying. Each brush of his mouth, each lick of his tongue, sent shockwaves of pure desire through her core.

There was no need for discussion. Nora could no longer deny that she belonged to him in every way that mattered.

His kisses drugged her like wine. She laced her fingers behind his neck and pressed her body into his. There was nothing between them but a few layers of cloth, yet she did not feel close enough. She wanted more.

As if reading the direction of her thoughts, he shifted her onto his lap. The movement broke their kiss. Before she could complain, his parted lips grazed her aching nipple through the sprigged muslin of her gown. She gasped at the sensation.

When he lifted his head, she slid her fingers in his hair to stop him.

"Do it again," she begged.

He gave a wicked smile. "I'll do it even better."

His warm, strong hands traced her curves over her hips and up her waist to the ribbon just beneath her bodice. With a few deft tugs to loosen the laces at her spine, the puffed sleeves of her gown tumbled down her shoulders.

Cool air sent shivers of anticipation down her skin. Nothing covered her breasts now but the thin linen of her chemise, billowing above her stays.

Her breath caught as he gently lowered the bodice and allowed her breasts to spill free. This time when his lips grazed her nipples, nothing was left between them. She gripped his hair tighter. When he opened his mouth to suckle her breast, pleasure and longing jolted through her.

This was what she wanted. This, and something more. A growing restlessness stirred within her. An ache that only he could fill.

"We should stop," he murmured against her breast.

She had no interest in letting go. Soon the banns would be read, and they would be husband and wife. They didn't need to hide their true feelings any longer. She could finally let herself admit how much he meant to her. Show him that she was his.

She touched his cheek. "I don't want to stop."

"Neither do I," he admitted raggedly.

In relief, she arched her back to offer him her breasts once more.

As he teased her bosom with his mouth and tongue, her heart pounded in anticipation. He carefully, deliberately, ever so slowly lifted the hem of her gown. It slid up her ankle, up her calf, up her thigh, giving her every opportunity to halt him before they went too far.

Still, he lifted his mouth from her breast to ask, "Do you want—"

"*Yes*," she begged, and gasped as his finger entered her.

The twin sensations of his tongue laving her stiff nipples as his fingers played between her thighs pushed her over the edge into weightless bliss. Her breath was choppy, her mind empty of everything but him as her muscles spasmed against his fingers.

When at last he pulled his hand away, her body longed for him to fill her once more. But this time, with no substitutes for the real man before her. She was his completely, and she wanted him to take her.

She lowered her hand to the flat plane of his stomach and released one of the buttons of his fall. His shaft sprang free to greet her fingers, hot and hard and ready.

He grabbed her wrist before she could do more than stroke him. "Are you certain?"

She slid from his lap in order to undo the other side of his fall, then swung her leg round to straddle him. "I've never been more certain about anything in my life."

"Me either," he whispered.

Inch by inch, she lowered herself onto his shaft until he completely filled her. He took her breasts in his hands, touching, suckling, making the sting of pain disappear into a renewed whirlwind of desire.

Slowly, she rocked against him, picking up speed and rhythm until they were both gasping for air as he gripped her hips and brought them both over the peak and sent them soaring into the heavens together. When she collapsed against him, she could still feel the occasional pulse of pleasure, as if her body was not quite ready to let his go.

"Marry me," he murmured into her neck. "Say you will."

She lowered her head to kiss him. "There's nothing I want more."

"*Wife.*" He held her as if they would never have to part again.

She rested her cheek against his hair and held on tight. "*Husband.*"

This was more than love. He was everything she had ever wanted. A part of her soul.

Chapter 25

*H*eath might or might not be the most fortunate man alive, but he was certainly the happiest. He smiled to himself as he slowed his landau in front of his town house. Soon, he would not be returning to an empty home, but one filled with love and laughter. In the future when he came home, it would be to *Nora*.

Three weeks of banns seemed like an eternity.

Before his groom could arrive to take the reins, the door to the town house burst open and one of Heath's footmen raced down the walkway to the carriage.

"Got a name," Larkin said as he fumbled for something deep in his pocket.

Heath's head was still so full of Nora's kisses and smiles and heated touch that at first the words did not make sense.

"A name?" he queried, trying to look like he was paying attention.

"The caricaturist." Larkin dug in a different

pocket. "Or at least his emissary."

The caricaturist.

Heath's mind cleared at once and all his senses immediately focused on his footman. "Don't tell me you found the name and *lost* it."

"Win-something," Larkin muttered as he abandoned his coat pockets in favor of his waistcoat pocket. "Winston? Winslow? Winfield?"

Winfield.

All the air emptied from Heath's lungs.

No. It was a coincidence. Nora would have nothing to do with such a terrible thing.

"Here it is!" Larkin squinted at a scrap of parchment. "The sketches arrive to the intermediary courtesy of a Mr. Carter Winfield of the West Midlands."

Mr. Carter Winfield of the West Midlands. It was not a coincidence.

It was a conspiracy.

"This Winfield fellow isn't the actual artist," Larkin continued. "He never divulged the name, but one of the letters I glimpsed mentioned a 'she.' If you wish to send me to the West Midlands, I'm certain I can ferret out who 'she' is."

Ice filled Heath's veins.

He reached for the parchment. "No, Larkin. Such a mission won't be necessary."

Heath already knew who the culprit was.

Someone connected enough to be present at Society gatherings. Someone inconspicuous enough to fade into the background. Someone cruel enough to use the secrets she witnessed to line her pockets.

Someone who had made love to him not an hour earlier as if she had nothing at all to hide.

He stared blindly at the letters printed on the

page. His head was already too full of words. Winfield. West Midlands. *Nora.*

There could be no mistaking that his intended bride was the villain he had sworn to capture. Nora was not the sweet country innocent she presented herself to be. She was Heath's sworn nemesis. The *ton*'s worst enemy.

And she'd accepted his marriage proposal knowing exactly who and what she was.

He crumpled the parchment in his trembling fist.

She had lied to him. He had believed her because he wanted to believe her. Because he'd needed to believe *in* her. Because he loved her.

Or rather, loved the façade she'd used as her disguise.

He almost couldn't think over the roaring in his ears.

The woman he'd just made love to was the self-righteous, anonymous coward who had been mocking Heath and his peers all Season.

The woman he'd just made love to was the arrogant caricaturist who thought nothing of exploiting the likenesses of Heath's own family for her personal profit.

The woman he'd just made love to was a complete stranger.

Vibrating with disappointment and rage, he lifted his reins and turned his landau toward the Roundtree town house to confront his erstwhile bride.

He wouldn't trust a word from Nora's deceitful lips ever again. She had already shown her true colors. His body shook with anger. There would be no more lies.

It was time to unmask the caricaturist.

Chapter 26

*L*ady Roundtree was resting upstairs in her bedchamber when the butler strode into Nora's sitting room. The normally orderly interior had just been turned topsy-turvy by none other than his esteemed highness, Captain Pugboat, who had determined that *sharing* teacakes was for lesser pups right before he'd taken off in a flurry of wrinkled fur and cake crumbs.

"Mr. Grenville to see you, miss."

Nora's besotted heart grew giddy. "To see me? Not Lady Roundtree?"

"You, miss."

"Please, show him in." She should not be so surprised. He had proposed to her, after all.

It was perhaps unusual to pay a second call so soon after the first, but she could not bring herself to care about adhering to such protocols. Not only was Heath Nora's future husband—he was also her first gentleman caller. He was here for *her*.

It took all her self-control not to fly into his arms the moment he entered the disordered drawing room.

"Such wonderful timing!" she said with a laugh. "I was trying to teach new tricks to—"

"I don't care." Heath's countenance was dark and angry. Those were not storm clouds brewing in his eyes, but entire battles being waged. And all of it was focused on her.

Nora's smile died on her lips.

The wacky story about Captain Pugboat frolicking on the tea tray amongst the lemon cakes no longer seemed very funny.

"What is it?" she stammered. But of course, she already knew. There could only be one answer.

"*You.*" He stared at her as if she were a specimen to dissect, a moth in a butterfly collection, something to be pinned through with a sharp needle and never looked at again. "I had no idea I was in the presence of such a popular artist."

She swallowed hard. The ruse was over. And so, it seemed, was her chance at a happy ever after.

He would never forgive her for this.

"I thought about telling you," she said hoarsely.

His flat gaze was sharp enough to cut ice. "Did you?"

She didn't blame him for not believing her.

He would probably never believe anything she said again.

"I stopped," she whispered. "I'm not drawing anymore."

His eyes flashed. "You *started.*"

She had no reply.

Hurt mixed with anger on his face. He filled his lungs as if forcing himself to remain calm.

"Why did you do it?" His voice was detached, disinterested, emotionless. Like a judge about to pass sentence.

She doubted he would like her defense. "At first, my drawings were just for myself and my family. I would sketch whatever happened that day, and send them back home in the post."

His lip curled. "So they could mock us from afar?"

"No."

So they would know how it was going. She had learned to draw because she couldn't write.

But that wasn't why she had kept making caricatures.

"C-Carter sent one of the sketches to a publisher on a lark," she began hesitantly.

A bark of laughter came from Heath's throat. "You blame your brother for your drawings?"

"I do not. When the publisher offered more money for a single drawing than I could earn in a fortnight as a companion, I could not afford to stop. My grandparents could not afford for me to stop. Our farm could not afford for me to stop. So much was riding on my ability to scrape us out of our hole. The few sheep we still owned—"

"You lied to me." His hazel eyes were furious. "While I dreamt of building a future together, you did your best to keep me in the dark."

He was not listening. Nora's fingers curled into fists. "I would think, as a secret-keeper, you of all people would understand the reason for lies of omission."

"Of course I understand the need to keep certain details from the public. You were exploiting the public's secrets for profit, and keeping your private self secret from me. *That's* why I'm angry." His gaze was deeply hurt. "These magical eight weeks have been a complete misrepresentation of who you are. Who I thought I was falling in love with. Who I thought I was going to marry. You're not that person at all."

He was right.

She had good reasons for every minute of her actions, but his heart did not deserve to be treated shabbily. Not by her. Not by anyone. She might not have had a choice, but that didn't make her any less a monster. He had loved her.

And now he didn't.

"I'm sorry," she said brokenly.

His laugh was hollow and bitter. "You're not sorry. You climbed on top of me on that settee knowing full well how I would feel once I learned the truth. Was it all some trick to bring a future baronet up to scratch? You played your hand well." He gestured at the chaise in disgust. "The deed is done."

Nora sucked in a shuddering breath. She could not let him think that the moment they had shared was all part of a grand manipulation to line her pockets. She loved him too much.

"It's not too late for you," she said, her voice hoarse. "Our private moments can remain a secret. No one is better at keeping them than you."

"No, I believe you win that award," he said, his voice icy and his gaze empty.

She winced. Although they could not save their relationship, she could do him this courtesy. "I cannot be ruined if there is no scandal. No one will know we made love."

His eyes beseeched her with equal parts hope and pain. "Did we make love if I don't even know who you are?"

"You do know who I really am," she burst out,

and took a halting step toward him. "I love you. Your happiness matters more than my own. Your place in Society is critical. Your career is important to so many. I've never thought I was good enough for you. There is no trap. You can walk away. You are under no obligation to me at all."

He stared at her in stony silence, a man at war with his honor and her betrayal.

She had known learning the truth would mean losing him forever. Curse those bloody caricatures. If she could have known from the start she would one day meet him and fall in love...

But she hadn't. And here they were.

Soon, she would go back home where she belonged.

His world was not meant for her. She'd had no call to believe the future they'd painted was any more substantial than a dream. But not like this. Her heart twisted. She hadn't meant to ruin Heath's faith in her so irrevocably. She certainly hadn't meant to trap him into wedding someone he despised.

She'd meant it when she'd said he was under no obligation toward her. Losing Heath would carve a void in her soul that she could never fill.

But no matter how ardently Nora loved him, if being anywhere near her caused him pain, she would walk away and never look back.

Chapter 27

*H*eath stared at the woman he loved and thought he knew.

He had suffered through his parents' estranged marriage, witnessed a hundred loveless unions by peers in search of money or power. He'd expected to marry for duty, but a secret part of him had hoped for something more.

He'd yearned to believe that something as simple and pure and honest as true love could exist for someone like him.

But there was nothing simple about his relationship with Nora. He had known from the start that she did not fit Society's definition of a perfect bride. Her lack of status, of a title, of money, of connections... the very fact that for someone of her humble origins, taking employment as a companion was a step *up* rather than down.

All those impediments were things he had slowly come to realize he could look past. He did not need a bride's dowry or connections. More importantly,

Nora's lack of status was due to happenstance, rather than any fault of her own. In the face of true love, such details had become irrelevant. He could not discard her for circumstances beyond her control.

The caricatures, however... She done them on *purpose*.

Perhaps she'd begun them out of a sense of duty to her own family, long before she'd met Heath, but she had consciously chosen to continue down that path. She'd gone so far as to immortalize his innocent sister. And all but lie to his face by allowing him to fall in love without the courtesy of knowing the truth.

Heart heavy, he turned to face the woman he had intended to spend the rest of his life with.

Nora was pale and trembling; her face puffy, her eyes bloodshot. She looked heartsick and miserable.

Good. So was he.

But here they were.

He rubbed his hands over his face in sudden exhaustion. The words needed to come out. "Just because I love you doesn't mean I can forgive you for lying to me. For letting me make love to a version of you that doesn't exist."

"I know," she whispered, her voice cracking. "I accept that. I deserve your rage."

Her admission did not make him feel better.

He let out a breath. "Then why did you do it?"

She closed her eyes. "I told you. For my family."

He shook his head. "I understand poverty. I meant why use your obvious talent to hurt and mock the beau monde? Do you hate us so much?"

"*Do* you understand poverty?" she countered, her over-bright gaze haunted. "How often have you fallen asleep mucking out a stall or a chimney and startled awake a scant hour later to start the day all over again? How many times have you and your siblings been forced to butcher your last source of income in order to feed your starving bellies? How long has it been since you first realized that if you didn't do something desperate to change the future, none of you would live long enough to see it?"

He stared at her, trying to process her words. These were not hypothetical situations suffered by hypothetical indigents. These were real memories Nora had been forced to live through. The woman he loved.

Nora's voice shook. "You're right. We *are* different. You accept money to sweep scandals under the carpet. I accepted money to bring them to light. But that gossip already existed. I made certain my sketches weren't news to anyone."

"You went out of your way to make peers of the realm look ridiculous to the rest of the population," he stammered reflexively as his brain scrambled to catch up to his heart. He'd been so angry for so long. But the self-righteous argument no longer made sense given the context she'd just given him. Perhaps it had never made sense.

"Commoners daren't find humor in their betters, you mean?" Nora's eyes were glassy, her face pale. "Of course that's what the high and mighty want. And I know why. Making the *ton* appear even more perfect than they actually are makes all of us who are nothing feel even more worthless and inconsequential."

His lungs caught. The naked pain of her words twisted his heart.

All these years, he had thought he was taking the right actions. He still believed helping others was always the right thing. For the first time, he was forced to face the possibility that his selection of who in particular deserved his help had been far from unbiased.

Heath helped the *beau monde* because he knew them. He was a member of their community. He was surrounded by them every day of his life.

He helped his sister's charity because it belonged to his sister. He loved her. He'd known her ever since her first breath.

He didn't consciously believe that individuals outside of his class were unimportant, as his actions had made Nora feel.

It was worse than that. He simply hadn't thought about those people at all. The *ton's* outcry against her irreverent caricatures was because they exposed the *beau monde*'s ugly side to those beneath them. How much hubris did that outrage portray?

Worse yet was Heath's belated realization that his plan to pay any price to unmask the caricaturist afforded him no greater moral high ground than Nora having sketched the drawings in the first place.

He had accepted money from a client whose stated goal had been to humiliate the caricaturist by being the first to spread gossip of his true identity.

It had not seemed hypocritical at the time. But he could not remain willfully blind to the obvious.

"I didn't mean to hurt your family," she said again, her voice small and miserable. "I was trying to save mine. I'm sorry I caused you pain."

He took a deep breath. It was time to speak the truth. "So am I."

She frowned up at him in confusion.

Heath tried to find words to express the turmoil within.

Nora had followed the wrong path and tried to make it right. She had chosen returning to poverty over continuing lucrative caricatures. *That* was the true character of the woman he loved.

She was willing to spend the rest of her days slaving on a sheep farm because she was willing to sacrifice her own happiness for those she loved.

Had he not prided himself on doing the same? What was love, if not the ability to understand and empathize with someone else's perspective?

He stepped forward and took her hands in his.

"We're both flawed," he began. Understatement at its finest. "Only by helping each other be better can we hope for a future together."

Her blue eyes were wide with emotion. "What are you saying?"

What she needed to hear.

The truth.

"I forgive you for choices you made out of financial desperation." He gripped her hands tighter. "I am still hurt and angry that you trusted me with your body, but not your truth." He let out a breath. "But you were not wrong about how I would react to the news. I hope you can forgive me for that."

Her hands trembled in his. "You... forgive me?"

"I love you," he said simply. "If we can work through this, we can work through anything life can send us. From this moment forward, we are a team."

Tears shimmered in her eyes. "I love you so much more than words can say. There's nothing I want more than to face the world and the rest of our lives together."

"We'll be unstoppable." He cupped her damp cheeks with his hands and kissed her until they were both gasping for air.

A sudden frown creased her brow. "What about your clients?"

His stomach twisted.

She was right. It wasn't just Nora he must worry

about. Not one, but two paying clients were waiting for him to bring the caricaturist to light. Heath had taken their money and given his word.

"It's all right." Nora took a step back, her smile wobbling as if she had just surmised the direction of his thoughts. "I shan't ask you to break your word as a gentleman."

Heath's temples pounded.

One's word as a gentleman was inviolate. Yet he could not be all things to all people. He had given his word to paying aristocratic clients. But he had also pledged a vow to Nora by asking her to be his wife. By taking her innocence.

No matter which path he chose, Heath would have to break his word to someone in order to keep it for someone else. He could not protect his clients' interests and protect Nora.

He pulled her back into his arms.

"I choose you," he said hoarsely. "I choose *us*."

She buried her face in his cravat and shuddered against his chest. "But how can you?"

"I don't know," he admitted. There was bound to be scandal.

She lifted her head to gaze up at him. "Did you promise to reveal my name or to make the caricaturist stop?"

Hope flickered within him.

"I promised a name to Lady Roundtree," he said slowly.

Nora's face crumpled. "Lady Roundtree?"

"It's all right." He lifted her chin with his knuckle. "She loves you. She will forgive you."

Nora's eyes shimmered. "She's the only one who will have to know?"

"Yes. As for Mapleton, I only promised that I

would make the caricaturist stop."

She reared back in his arms. "You took *Phineas Mapleton* as a client?"

"I was planning to unmask the caricaturist anyway," Heath pointed out. "His money went straight to my sister's charity."

"That man is a scourge." She swallowed as if repressing a bad memory. "The things he said... How everyone laughed..."

Mapleton was indeed a scourge. "As I recall, I glimpsed a caricature you might have drawn of him."

She sighed. "You're right. His behavior does not excuse mine."

He tucked a stray tendril behind her ear. "Are you disappointed your career as a caricaturist is over?"

She shook her head in embarrassment. "There are so many other things I would prefer to be drawing."

"Why don't you?" he asked.

Nora shrugged. "Who would wish to see high fashions designed by a country bumpkin?"

"I suppose it *could* be convenient if you happened to marry a man who owns a gallery," he offered slowly.

She hesitated. "About getting married..."

Had she changed her mind? His heart thudded. "Are you saying you've no wish for me to be your husband?"

"I'm saying you won't wish for me to be your wife." She bit her lip. "The caricatures weren't my worst secret."

He stepped backward in disbelief and trepidation. "What else did you do?"

"It's what I cannot do," she burst out. Her face

filled with agony. "I can draw, but I cannot read. Not easily, that is. The letters just dance and blur... I would be an embarrassment by your side."

Relief washed over him.

"I'm not hiring you to be my temporary companion, daft woman." He grabbed her shoulders so that she would meet his eyes. "I am asking you to be my wife."

"Even if my brain doesn't work like it should?" she asked doubtfully.

"I fell in love with your mind exactly how it is." He dropped to one knee. "Will you let me prove it by taking my hand in marriage?"

"Yes." She melted into his embrace with a choking laugh. "*Yes.*"

Chapter 28

Four months later

From the familiar safety and anonymity of a ballroom's rear shadows, Nora stared out at the busy dance floor before her. She had not been able to shake a bewildered sense of unreality. Nonetheless, the proof was right before her eyes:

This cozy soirée was for *her*.

She had been married for less than two months, and already her wildest dreams had been exceeded. Her life was perfect. *Heath* was perfect. And the dozen people who had responded so enthusiastically to a dinner invitation in her new home—

"There you are, my love!" Heath pulled her from the shadows and swung her to the dance floor beneath a crystal chandelier. His voice was teasing. "No wall-flowering allowed when you're the belle of the ball."

It stole her breath to whirl amongst what had become a small, but treasured circle of friends. Lord and

Lady Wainwright, Dahlia and Simon Spaulding, Bryony Grenville and her latest lovesick suitor. Nora
made a mental note to prod her about it later.

Even the row reserved for Society dames was
filled with friendly faces. Lady Grenville, of course.
Lady Roundtree, whose kindness and loyalty had
never wavered. Even Lady Pettibone, who might
breathe fire at others but had chosen to give Nora her
blessing.

Far more important than the rulers of the *haut
ton* was the elderly couple seated in the very same row
as the important ladies.

Nora's grandparents had made their first jour-
ney in order to attend the wedding. They'd had such
fun in Town that talking them into a second visit had
been no hardship. Grandmother and Grandfather had
been delighted to learn that Nora and Heath would
build a country home near the farm and come for long
visits every single year.

Lady Roundtree had even agreed to allow Captain Pugboat to accompany Nora on such trips. A
romp amongst rolling green hills was the perfect holiday for any growing pup.

As far as Nora's brother...

Carter was paying far more attention to the refreshment table than the other guests, but that was
entirely her fault. She'd had the kitchen stock the buf-
fet with her family's favorite treats and a few new ones
she'd been certain would prove irresistible.

"Is this really happening?" she asked her husband as he swept her into her favorite waltz. "Can one
person truly be this lucky?"

His eyes shone with love. "*Two* people can."

He was right.

The rest of their lives would be filled with beauty.

Epilogue

*D*espite the eager queue stretching around the block, Heath could not help shifting his weight in nervousness.

Today was the grand opening of his gallery. It had taken months to select just the right pieces and arrange them in just the right order. At least, he hoped he'd achieved the magic he wished to convey.

He had put Nora's work in the north salon, exciting canvases from a young Welsh painter in the east salon, stunning sculptures from a Scottish talent in the west salon, and a breathtaking sequence by a Cornwall-based artist in the south salon.

He hoped the steady river of patrons found as much joy in the carefully chosen selection as Heath had experienced whilst discovering it.

Nora squeezed his hand as the next dozen patrons streamed through the door. "Already a success, I see. I knew it would be."

"Of course you did. You engineered it," he told her fondly.

His wife could move mountains with her pen.

Three days earlier, an anonymous caricature had appeared in all the newspapers. In it, everyone who was anyone was standing outside the Grenville Gallery of Art, which bore only a sign reading SOON in the front window. Among the spectators, every sketched lapel bore a different flower. The queue tumbled over itself like a basket of kittens as they tried to peer inside the mysterious window.

The caption beneath had read simply, "Limited engagement."

Her stratagem had worked brilliantly.

Not only had everyone who glimpsed the caricature been compelled to be the first to know just what was so interesting on the other side of that door, wild speculation had only fueled the chatter. What was in the gallery? Was wearing a flower the key to being permitted inside?

More than half of today's crowd had pinned fresh blooms to their person in case the accoutrement was a requirement for entry or privileged status.

"I still can't believe you invented a fashion," he whispered to Nora.

She grinned back at him. "That's my job."

Pride coursed through him as he squeezed her to his side.

Over the past few months, Nora had quickly become the most sought-after designer of fashion plates in the city. Tailors and modistes paid any price to have her sketch their creations, and Ackerman's was trying desperately to convince her to sign a contract exclusive to them.

The north gallery salon was stocked with her latest designs, some of which had never before been presented to the public. Other pieces had already been glimpsed upon the frame of such personages as the Duchess of Ravenwood.

They were a splendid team. Nora had already been marvelous when he married her, but together they were so much more than either could be alone. Her art would help his gallery succeed, and his gallery would help artists spread their reach.

He tried to stay to the shadows in order to allow the art to speak for itself.

Many familiar faces peppered the crowd. Maxwell Gideon, Lord Hawkridge, the Fairfaxes, Lord and Lady North-Barrows. It seemed everyone Heath had ever met and a whole host of new acquaintances had come to the grand opening.

"Are you happy?" Nora whispered up to him.

Happy? It was all Heath could do not to pump his fist in the sky and bellow a victory shout.

He whispered back, "I have never been more contented."

Joy and mischief sparkled in her eyes. "Then you're going to have to try harder."

He frowned. "What are you—"

She pointed toward the door. His family was just entering the gallery.

Camellia and her husband, Dahlia and hers, Bryony. Their mother. And beside her...

His heart leaped in shock. "My *father* is here?"

Nora squeezed his hand.

Heath stared in disbelief and hope.

His father had received the invitation. He had *come*.

When their eyes met through the crowd, the baronet nodded his head gruffly and pointed to his lapel. A pink rose bloomed from his breast pocket. Heath's breath caught.

Father had not been forced to attend the grand opening. He had chosen to show his support of the gallery and his pride in his son.

Heath's head spun.

"You did this?" he whispered to his wife.

She pressed her palm to his cheek and gestured at the gallery. "*You* did this, my love."

"*We* did this." He swept her into his arms in elation.

"Stop that," she giggled. "You'll cause a scandal."

"Let them talk," Heath said, and lowered his head for a kiss.

Acknowledgments

As always, I could not have written this book without the invaluable support of my critique partner and editor. Huge thanks go out to Erica Monroe and Shavonne Clarke. You are the best!

Lastly, I want to thank the *Historical Romance Book Club* facebook group and my fabulous street team. Your enthusiasm makes the romance happen. I thought of you as I wrote this story.

Thank you so much!

Thank You for Reading

I hope you enjoyed this story!

Sign up at http://ridley.vip
for members-only freebies
and special deals for 99 cents!

**Did you know there are more
books in this series?**

This romance is part of
the *Rogues to Riches*
regency-set historical series.

In order, the *Rogues to Riches* books are:

Lord of Chance
Lord of Pleasure
Lord of Night
Lord of Temptation
Lord of Secrets
Lord of Vice

Join the *Rogues to Riches* Facebook group for giveaways and exclusive content:
http://facebook.com/groups/RoguesToRiches

In order, the *Dukes of War* books are:

The Viscount's Christmas Temptation
The Earl's Defiant Wallflower
The Captain's Bluestocking Mistress
The Major's Faux Fiancée
The Brigadier's Runaway Bride
The Pirate's Tempting Stowaway
The Duke's Accidental Wife

Join the *Dukes of War* Facebook group for giveaways and exclusive content:
http://facebook.com/groups/DukesOfWar

About the Author

Erica Ridley is a *New York Times* and *USA Today* bestselling author of historical romance novels.

In the *Rogues to Riches* historical romance series, Cinderella stories aren't just for princesses... Sigh-worthy Regency rogues sweep strong-willed young ladies into whirlwind rags-to-riches romance with rollicking adventure.

The popular *Dukes of War* series features roguish peers and dashing war heroes who return from battle only to be thrust into the splendor and madness of Regency England.

When not reading or writing romances, Erica can be found riding camels in Africa, zip-lining through rainforests in Central America, or getting hopelessly lost in the middle of Budapest.

For more information, visit EricaRidley.com.